Once Upon a
COWBOY'S HEART

Sarah Da Silva

Cover by Melody Jeffries

Formatting by True North Press Design

Paperback ISBN - 979-8-218-76655-9

Dedication

"Just so, I tell you, there will be more joy in heaven over one sinner who repents than over ninety-nine righteous persons who need no repentance."
Luke 15:7

This book is dedicated to my Good Shepherd.
The one who left the 99 to find me.
If you found me, I know you can do the same for the person reading this.

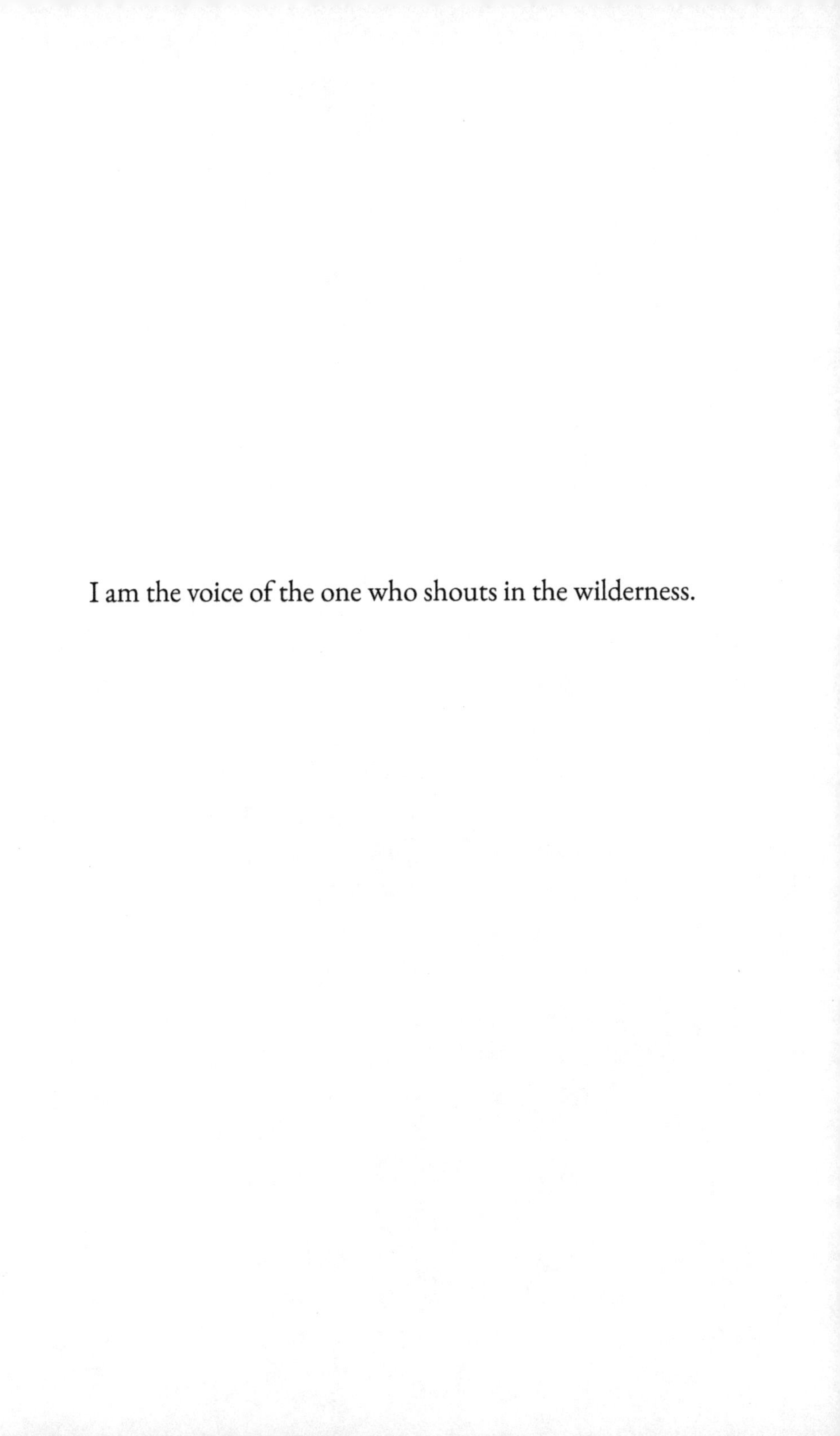

I am the voice of the one who shouts in the wilderness.

This book isn't perfect. In fact, it's far from it. It definitely has grammar mistakes and probably other minor mistakes, but never once was that the purpose.
This book isn't supposed to be perfect.
This book is to reach that one person that needs hope.
A person who is in desperate need of direction.
Someone who needs hope, love, and joy back in their life.
Someone who needs to find their way back to God despite all the things they have been through.
I wrote the book for you.
It might not be a best seller, but if you read it and are impacted, then I have done my job well.
I did my part. So now, let God speak to you through this book.
And remember: The pain and suffering you're in must be exposed (and not hidden) so that God can heal you.
He wants to heal you so you can spread the goodness of God to other captivated souls.

Hello readers!! I am thrilled that you have picked up my book. This is a closed door romance book that deals with real world situations and difficult topics, to make you feel seen and to bring more light into those topics.

Deals/mentions about:

- Abusive relationship(s)
- Neglectful parents
- Sick Family Members
- Addiction to Alcohol & Painkillers
- Bar Scene(s)

So I hope you enjoy this book that I have poured hours of love and dedication into. This story is very special to me and I hope in some way, shape, or form, you feel seen and loved. That you aren't alone in the difficult seasons of life.

My books will always be closed-door, so you can swoon away with no worry that there will be unwanted stuff inside.

As the author, I hope you find hope, love and joy inside these pages. I hope you feel the Love of Jesus and that you see him at the end of the tunnel.

Well, I won't hold you any longer. Grab your favorite drink and snack, a fuzzy blanket and prepare yourself for a very emotional swoony ride!!!

Jesus loves you and so do I!

Happy reading!

Praise for Once Upon a Cowboy's Heart

"There is something beautiful in reading someone's journey to faith. Something so real. It is one of the many ways we see the grace and mercy that God can have in our lives when we let Him heal us. The purest form of love that accepts us in all our brokenness. But instead of seeing us as damaged, He puts us back together, makes us new, and brings us home. Reading Amelia's journey to faith is a perfect example of that. Sarah Da Silva has done a wonderful job in writing a story that embodies an unexpected journey of faith, self-discovery, and rekindling of a flame that never extinguished! You will enjoy this book so much!"

—Annie (@narnianbooklore)

Once Upon a COWBOY'S HEART

Amelia
Prologue

10 Years Before

Flowers and rainbows were polar opposite from the life I lived. Happiness appeared to be impossible. And all my life I supposed riches were the one thing to fulfill someone. Yet, I felt more broken and lost because of it. My family was scattered and broken like the rocks in the sea.

In it all, Mathias was my one thing to keep me afloat. The one person who made sure I didn't drown in my lake of tears. His shoulders were the only ones I leaned against when my sadness was overbearing.

His brown eyes glistened in the dead of the night. "Amelia, did you even hear me talking to you?"

Mathias shook my shoulders. His face illuminated with humor, a smirk on his perfect face. My mind danced among the stars, words went through one ear and out the other. "Of course I was listening to you." I pressed my lips together to suppress the laughter.

His arms crossed over his chest, an eyebrow raised to the sky, "Then tell me what I just said."

I smirked; *I am going to take full advantage of this moment.*

"You were just saying how wonderful I am and that you couldn't live without me." I responded with my hands above my head, shaped into the form of a halo.

His laughter enveloped me. Space, time, and all understanding froze for a single moment. His laugh sounded like ocean waves crashing against the shore on a hot summer day. It trailed across my skin, happiness rooting deep into my heart. My body instantly froze, and my brown eyes were glued on him.

Saving this sound for later.

His laugh, a sound which brought me comfort. The trees, flowers, and birds were blessed with such an intoxicating sound. This was the perfect way to spend a grueling day.

It was a late afternoon in Love Creek, Tennessee. Life had soaked every ounce of strength out of me and all I needed was to escape. So when Mathias saw me walking towards our secret spot, he rushed to follow me. We were tucked away from any prying ears. Surrounded by nature's perfection. Every moment gave me another reason to keep trying.

"That is absolutely true, but that is not at all what I was saying." His laughter was no longer a booming sound. It was as gentle and soft as he was.

How I love him, I admitted silently.

I would only ever admit those words to myself. He knew everything about me, inside and out, ugly and pretty, but that was the one thing I would never let him know. Those precious, yet terrifying words threatened to slip multiple times, each time I caught them before they could cause any damage.

"What did you say?" I questioned.

Mathias Anderson was one of those types of guys who's voice stood out from a crowd. Whatever word that came out of his lips demanded attention. He existed to help others, always excluding what he wanted.

A peaceful sigh left his lips. "Where do you think we will be in ten or so years?" His voice softened.

Of all his questions, this was the one question that constantly stumped me. It left my mind in tangles because my tomorrow seemed to be a lifetime away. Life was hard enough now, did I really need to be anxious over something that I had no clue about?

Where will I be? What will I be doing? Will I finally become the person I want to be?

"Where do you think we will be? I mean we are just 16 years old. We have our whole life ahead of us." I avoided the question, my uncertainty was the only thing I was sure of.

He talked ab0ut his future with so much certainty. His life was already planned out before him. A loving family that supported him. He never rejected or rebelled when his parents asked something. He was a faithful son, and I was a prodigal daughter who never found her home.

"I think we will be working in our dream jobs." Mathias responded to his own question.

His leg tucked underneath him. "I will take over our family's farm, and you will be the most famous painter this world has ever seen." His eyes were as big as the moon, filled with excitement and joy. A smile he only blessed a few people with.

"Your art," he continued with passion and fire in his lungs. "You, Amelia, your art will outshine all painting this world has ever seen."

He reached for my hand, our fingers perfectly intertwined together. His thumb brushed back and forth against my numb skin.

"We will be best friends and nothing in this world will separate us. Cause you're mine, Sunshine."

I gave him a wobbly smile and tear-filled eyes. *No one ever calls me that except him. No one ever sees worth in me like he does.*

His kindness was worth more than the riches my parents could ever give me. His attention was worth more than the stuff I would ever have.

His caramel brown eyes focused on me. They made me feel noticed and supported. A constant reminder that he didn't see me as a mistake.

"You're mine, Cowboy." There was no more faith in me, but I believed every word. He was mine and despite anything that was going to happen, our paths would always cross.

Amelia
Chapter 1

The crisp fall air in the big city had been a soothing medication for my haunting headache. My hair kept pulling against my scalp; my clothes looked like they were found in a dumpster. It stuck to my skin; the stench made my nose hair burn. A mix of spirits and liquor spilled all over, making me crawl in my own skin.

Eyes as red as tomatoes and mascara that complimented the dark bags underneath my swollen eyes.

I hadn't bothered to get ready but instead was drinking a much needed iced coffee. Most people were appalled at me drinking iced coffee in the fall, but I never asked for their opinion.

The moment I woke up, I took a high dose of my medication to soothe the headache. It didn't.

I need to buy more.

Last night was a blur: loud music, people, and alcohol. Nothing was crisp and clean in my mind, instead it was a sore memory. Puzzle pieces I didn't have the energy to put together. All I remember was that I was at a club and woke up on my sofa. Lily probably took me home when I knocked myself out.

My phone rang in the distance, and I knew it had to be Lily checking up on me. My mind was already preparing for her long, boring speech.

"Hi." My throat scratched every time I spoke. It felt like a hundred cats trying to claw their way out.

"Hello, hungover princess." A hint of sarcasm in her voice. She wasn't proud of me; her voice always gave away her emotions.

I couldn't make anyone proud.

It was already an engraved truth in me; no matter what I did and how I did it, no one would ever be proud of me. It was a painful lie that turned into my reality.

"My head hurts so bad." My hand rested on my forehead, trying to rub the pain away. I prayed the liquor from last night wouldn't last long.

She chuckled lightly. "No wonder. You were crazy last night." She huffed at the end, which I knew meant it was worse than I originally thought.

My peace depends on liquid in a cup.

A small groan left my swollen lips. "How bad was it?"

She let out a long sigh. "It was pretty bad this time. You took your pills and went out to drink right after your lunatic boyfriend hit you."

She never had the courage to say it out loud, but I knew what she was talking about. I always went out drinking to forget two things: life and my boyfriend. She told me countless times that I needed to break up with him, but I never listened.

I extended my feet and leaned them against the small table in front of the couch. The autumn air intertwined itself with my lungs. Sun beams seeped through the windows.

My thoughts were interrupted by Lily on the phone. Her voice broke the silence. "You need to find help Amelia. It's really getting out of hand."

Deep down inside, I knew she was right, but how could I stop? How could I stop doing something I taught myself to cope with? I taught my body to desire pills every time a shock of pain went through my body. My body needed a drink after every fight.

How can I stop drinking when it gives me an immediate sense of peace?

"I know what you're thinking. You really have to stop, Amelia! You're killing yourself, and sooner or later, I won't be able to save you anymore." Her voice filled with despair. She acted like she could hear my every thought. Lily always cared the best for me; all she wanted was for me to succeed. In all of this, Lily was the only one who remained by my side.

Everyone told me to stop drinking for my own sake. Their words replayed in my mind like a song. I couldn't and wouldn't stop drinking. I wasn't going to let go of the one thing that made me feel something.

"I know, Lily. Thank you once again."

I could sense her sad smile through the screen. We both knew that I wasn't going to listen. It was going to go in one ear and out the other. "You're welcome, but please find help."

I hummed to her petition, knowing full well I couldn't make such a promise. It has been over three years that I dug myself into this endless pit. *I have no strength to dig myself out now.*

She hung up after I explained in detail what I planned to do today. Nothing. Just rest and nothing more. Lily took it upon herself to care for me, to be there when I needed someone. Sometimes I felt like she was doing too much, but at least someone cared about me.

THE LINGERING SCENT OF LEMON AND LINEN infused my house. Even days after, the cleaning lady always made sure everything was perfect. Everything placed in its designated spots. *It won't last more than three days.*

After consuming my iced coffee, I strolled into my small cozy kitchen. I wasn't the greatest cook, but I knew how to not die. No one knew how to cook eggs, bacon, and french toast better than me. It wasn't a comfort food, but it was fast enough to make.

After my last bite, I reached over for the pill bottle. The bottle was almost empty after only two days.

Headed toward the door, I grabbed my car keys and jacket. The crisp fall air enveloped me. The weather was way too warm for late August, but Tennessee weather could be unpredictable sometimes.

The leaves changed from the brightest summer green to a deep red and yellow color. The sidewalk was covered with fall leaves, which left a magical touch. I wasn't outside as much as I used to be.

The big city was awake before dawn and went to sleep after midnight. People rushing to get to work or homes. Beeping sounds filled the streets. There was no silence in the city, but I had gotten used to it.

In front of my house, there was a huge apple tree. Its

leaves were piled around the roots, protecting itself from the cold. Last night, Lily had parked my car beneath the tree, providing shade and protection.

The car had been a birthday gift from my parents. My 26th birthday was like the rest: a happy birthday and a gift worth thousands.

Can't believe I am turning twenty-seven this year.

Once I pulled out of my neighborhood, my car stopped playing music. I glanced at the fourteen inch screen to see my mother calling me.

I knew this was coming.

I wanted to ignore it so badly, but if I didn't pick up the phone she would call the police.

Brace yourself, Amelia.

"Hey, Mom." My strained voice broke the tension-filled silence in the car.

The silence before the war.

"Amelia Smith Johnson, what happened yesterday?" Her voice filled with disappointment, anger, and frustration.

Wow, not even a hello. This is what we've come to.

"I don't know, Mother, why don't you tell me?" I rolled my eyes. My hands gripped the steering wheel tighter. I honestly didn't care what she had to say because it was always the same thing.

She was far past disappointment. "Pray tell me, why did I receive a call from Lily at three in the morning that my daughter passed out at the bar? With pain medicine and a bottle of tequila?" Her voice screeched. Her high-pitched tones immediately damaged my ear drums.

I really shouldn't have picked up the phone.

I released a curse under my breath because my dear friend couldn't keep her mouth shut around my mother. It wasn't necessarily Lily's fault that my mother watched me like a hawk. She had eyes and ears everywhere. She knew anything I did or said in a heartbeat.

I hate mother intuition.

"Watch your language," she warned.

"Sorry ma-" I took an unsteady breath. The problem I always stumbled across was that she never believed me. I could never confide in her, yet she wants to know everything about me.

She treats me like one of her employees and not her daughter.

I didn't feel an ounce of regret because after a few hours I remembered how I ended up there. My boyfriend, Brandon, came home angry and wanted pleasure. I didn't want it and protested against it, but he yelled, cussed, and slapped me across the face. It wasn't always this abusive but things had changed.

Now I live with a constant bruise somewhere on my body and a ringing in my head.

Where has my life ended up?

Where have I ended up?

I don't know what I ever saw in him. What attracted me? I guess it was because he was the only person who would pet my ego and give me compliments that I lacked from my own family. I learned the hard way that outer appearances were nothing compared to actions.

My mother tried to soften her voice, but you could still tell that she was aggravated. "I forgive you, but I will only give you one more chance, Amelia. You have to control yourself. If you fail again, there will be consequences."

I had mixed feelings about her consequences because I knew both sides to them. She cared about public appearances, about perfect faces for her famous marketing company. One bad move could cause her horrific press. I was careful most of the time. I slipped into bars when it was dark and slipped out before anyone realized.

On the other hand, my parents probably never told anyone about me. Deep down inside I knew they were ashamed of me. My bad habits weren't up to their standards. She hung up the phone; the music slowly started to fill the void. My thoughts were already at a million miles per hour.

Not even a goodbye or an I love you.

I don't remember the last time that she said she loved me. My mom always hated everything I did, it never lived to her expectations. And my dad didn't care; he didn't care about anything other than his company.

I've always been in one toxic relationship after another. One heartbreak after another. So I taught myself how to drown the thoughts and pain away. My mom thought it only was an addiction, but it was my resort.

My only resort.

I was in a small accident a few years ago and had to have surgery for a broken leg and internal damage. They gave me Fentanyl to control the pain, but instead of only taking it while in pain, I continued. It gave me a calming sensation. I have lived off Fentanyl for three years now. Thousands of dollars have been spent on medication; *at least it wasn't my money.* The world would spin when I didn't take it. The doctors were in disbelief that I suffered with pain.

Lies.

I didn't suffer from physical pain anymore; it was emotional.

A FEW SHORT HOURS LATER, I ARRIVED HOME. NEW bottles of whiskey and Fentanyl would be the strength I needed to conquer this week.

"This should do the trick," I muttered to myself.

I downed more pills than I usually took and drank the booze that had been on the countertop for the last three days. Instantly my body relaxed at the impact of the alcohol.

You're not supposed to mix medicine and alcohol together, but I never went to the hospital because of it. Mixing both kept me sane and partially happy.

Why would I stop something that was working?

A loud banging at the door tugged me from my thoughts. My stomach instantly went cold, already knowing who it was. My heart pounded a thousand miles per hour as I prepared myself for the worst.

His grating voice yelled from the other side of the door. "Open the door, Amelia."

When I didn't answer, he released a string of curse words. I peeped into the little hole in the door and saw his angered face. He looked like he was about to kill someone. He might even kill me tonight.

Maybe that wouldn't be so bad.

My hands trembled as my fingers wrapped around the metal handle to unlock the door. Once the door was unlocked, he pushed himself in and slammed the door behind him.

He glanced back at me. *Something was different about him.* His eyes held a secret. The last few weeks, Brandon had become more aggressive and secretive.

Brandon walked straight into the kitchen, placed a bottle of wine on the table. Sometimes I wondered who was worse; which one of us needed the alcohol more.

It had only been a few minutes since I took the medicine, but the moment he stepped foot in the house, I felt worse than before.

What is happening to me?

"What happened yesterday?" he grunted, cursing under his breath when the wine spilled on his shirt.

He never asked to see how I was. It was always for his benefit. He was like my mother in many ways, always wanting to control my life and decisions.

"Why would you like to know?" I hissed back. His grip on the drinking glass visibly tightened.

"Amelia, why do you have to be so difficult? I love you. I do everything for you. Why is it that when I ask you simple things, you overreact?" Brandon rolled his eyes. He always tried to act like I was the one in the wrong.

I leaned my hips on the countertop of the kitchen island. My arms were crossed against my chest. *I will not fall for this again.*

"You know it's funny how you say that you do everything for me, but I can't recall a single time you did something for me." I fiddled with the seam of my shirt. "All I know is that the bar has become my best friend. It's better than having to deal with you everyday." I snapped back at him.

Apparently, today I am feeling feisty.

Brandon slammed the empty drinking glass onto the countertop. He used the back of his hand to wipe his wet mouth. "Maybe if you did what I asked, which isn't much, I wouldn't be like this." He strolled closer to me as he ran his fingers through his hair. I swore I saw lipstick smears on his lips and cheeks.

My stomach hurled and turned at the sight of that. *Maybe I wore red lipstick without knowing?*

"All you have to do is listen and obey. Do what I want and we are both happy."

He strolled past me and plopped himself onto the sofa. Leaning his head back on the head rest, his haunting voice finally silenced.

Why don't I just break up with him?

As days passed, that was going to be a greater possibility. Brandon gestured for me to sit beside him, his hand patting the space beside him.

With an unsteady breath in my lungs, I treaded over and sat beside him. I sat a few inches away, making sure there was enough space between the both of us.

His hand grazed my arm, giving me an unsettling sensation. He leaned in closer and I instantly smelled it.

Did I put perfume on today?

"Give me a kiss," he whispered against my skin. His breath against my skin made me want to throw up. His sexual words slurred together.

His stubble brushed against my neck, and my body froze at the touch.

"Not now," I gulped, trying to keep myself from throwing up.

His hand gripped my arm, and a small yelp left my lips. He pulled me closer to him, forcing my gaze to meet his. Brandon never looked at me correctly; his eyes were always focused on something else.

I need to leave.

With a harsh movement, he pulled me flesh against him.

His body leaned closer to mine, leaving me completely locked in his embrace. His hands gripped my waist; his nails dug deep into my skin.

Minutes passed by. All Brandon did was turn around and fall asleep. I couldn't shake off his disgusting touch. His imprints on my body made my mind uneasy and stomach ill.

I stared at the bottle of liquor on the counter like it was my last saving grace. There was nothing else that I could do to forget the hole I dug myself into.

You got yourself into this mess, get yourself out.

AMELIA
CHAPTER 2

I didn't feel like myself all morning. I woke up with the pill container in one hand and an emptied bottle of wine. My mind couldn't remember what had happened last night. Faint flashes passed through my mind.

After I took a long steamy shower, I put on a comfortable sweatshirt and sweatpants, leaving me with a slight feeling of comfort. The downstairs lights were on; the TV was playing, but there was no one downstairs.

Brandon wasn't in sight, and I let go of the breath that I had been holding in without knowing. Walking closer to the connected kitchen, there was a blue sticky note stuck to the stainless steel fridge.

Good morning, babe

I had to go to work, but will come home in time for dinner. The whiskey is in the cabinet; save some for me.

Brandon.

His handwriting was awful, like that of a child, and the thought of him coming back left me disgusted. No one could read Brandon's handwriting except me.

Why don't I break up with him?

That idea occurred to me several times a day. It was tempting to break up with him, but I wouldn't know what to do afterwards.

I brewed a cup of straight black coffee to help me stay awake. Nights filled with torment and lack of rest, it's been so long since I had a peaceful night of sleep. A night where my body wasn't in fight-or-flight mode.

Tennessee was where I always called my home. Even if I didn't always live in the city. From sunrise to sunset, there was no break in the city. Enough noise that allowed you to stop thinking.

My parents and I moved here when they both got a job offer they couldn't refuse: a once in a lifetime opportunity they wanted. Their business slowly grew into an empire. Every week they said they had one last goal to reach, and then we would go on a vacation together.

Hours became days, days became weeks, and weeks turned into months. They created another business and skyrocketed like never before.

I never had to lift a finger. Everything I could ever want would only be a snap away. Their money replaced the attention my parents no longer gave me.

My life was filled with stuff, yet it lacked peace, joy, and what I most longed for: love.

I blinked several times, looking into a bare fridge. A small groan left my lips. *Great, now I had to leave the house.*

THE TREES AROUND ME SWAYED IN THE BREEZE AS I strolled down the pavement. It was as if I had stepped into a priceless painting. Just reminding myself of the painter that I once adored.

Sadness filled my heart knowing that I could never paint since it wasn't considered a proper job. The precious feeling of being lost in the paint strokes. My fingers covered with acrylic paint, the paintbrush against the rough canvas. It was all a distant feeling that my soul deeply missed.

I blinked away the blurring tears to admire the couples that walked around me. Twinkle lights on the trees, illuminating the path. The fresh smell of butter croissants and freshly fried donuts flowed from the small bakeries.

I froze in front of the cutest Paris-themed cafe, debating if I should buy myself a treat. My stomach grumbled the closer I got.

Stop eating sweets; you are going to get fatter.

Instantly, I turned in the opposite direction. Brandon constantly complained about my weight even though I wasn't overweight. His comments were the only thing that stopped me from carb happiness.

When I arrived back home, the market bags slid down my arms and onto the floor. My legs were tender from the long walk.

"I am just going to put away the dairy and take a nap," I whispered into the silence.

A loud banging on the door ripped me away from my deep slumber. I blinked several times as I rushed to open the door. My blurry vision encountered a grinning Lily.

"Hey, hangover princess, I thought I would come and check up on you. Maybe cook you something," Lily announced as she scurried inside.

In her hands were bags filled with fruits and vegetables. Lily knew how bad I was at grocery shopping because I never bought anything healthy.

She pulled out several bags of different vegetables. "What's wrong? I don't even have to look at your face to know there is something wrong."

I nodded towards the blue sticky note Brandon left. Her eyebrows knitted together as she quickly glanced over it. Her gaze went from the note to me and back to the note.

"What do you think he wants to talk about?" she questioned. Her attention went back to the grocery bags.

I leaned my hip against the counter and gazed at the note. "I hope it's to break up 'cause I can't deal with this anymore."

She agreed. "Why don't you make the first move?"

She knew how many times I threatened to leave him but never actually did. *It was easier said than done.*

I did nothing but laugh. "Good joke."

Her face went still, her hands placed on her hips. "No, I am serious. Why don't you break up with him? If we both know that he doesn't treat you how he should, just leave."

"I really would like to stay alive and would like to keep my face intact," I mumbled in response, completely avoiding her gaze.

She slowly shook her head, knowing that she wouldn't be able to change my mind.

I needed to decide myself.

"Changing the subject, I was alone at home and wanted

to spend time with someone, so I invited myself over." She shrugged her shoulders with the biggest smile and began cooking dinner.

We only knew each other for about five years, but it was like we knew each other longer. Lily didn't have to ask to use anything in my kitchen. She had extended the same offer, but I rarely went to her house.

"No problem." I plopped myself onto the barstool.

Time flew by so fast as we talked, I hadn't noticed she had already finished dinner and was making a sweet treat for me. Our friendship rule was sweets before salty.

"You know the way into my heart. Thank you!" I gushed over the colorful plate. I drooled over the crepes. They were filled with strawberries and Nutella.

We sat at the dinner table; conversation continued to flow between us. Talking to Lily was effortless, easy like breathing.

Before she left, she gave me the biggest hug. She reminded me that I could face my fears, and that it wasn't impossible to leave this toxic relationship.

My fear was Brandon.

Only a few hours later, Brandon arrived. Without saying a word or looking at my face, he went directly to the shower.

He hurried down the stairs, not taking a glance at the food on the stove or the leftover crepes. His health wasn't much better than mine. Brandon would prefer leftovers from a restaurant then a freshly cooked meal.

I fumbled onto my feet. Fiddling with my hands, cracking every tense bone. "I need to talk to you," I announced, adjusting myself to face him.

We both sat at the dinner table. His hand stroked my thigh; a chill feeling followed his touch.

I took an unsteady breath in and blurted it out. "I want to break up."

His fork dropped on the plate. He slowly turned his head. "Why?"

I forced myself to look him in the eyes, and this time I knew I wasn't dreaming. Faint red lipstick covered his face.

"I do-don't love you anymore." My voice cracked several times. My mind went completely blank as I tried to find the right words.

He leaned his head back against the wooden chair. He drew his hand away from my leg and crossed his hands. His legs bounced in a constant motion underneath the table.

"Finally. I knew this was going to happen one day or another. I was just waiting." He took a deep gulp of his whiskey. Without looking at me, he stood up and walked away.

"Wait, what?" Taken aback by the words he spoke. He said them as if they meant nothing.

He placed the plate in the sink. "Amelia, I never loved you. I never cared about you; you were simply a distraction for me. And then you stopped doing the things I asked you to do right away, and I found pleasure in another woman." He said those words like they meant nothing.

He paced around the room, not knowing the shock his words brought. The knife in my soul dug deeper. I didn't want his words to hurt, but they did. Never in a million years would I have expected him to do this. I never knew that it was going to get this far. My feelings and heart didn't matter; I was just a toy to him.

I abruptly stood up. The chair scraped against the floor. "What?!" I demanded an answer.

"I met this girl at my workplace and we hooked up. She wanted me, unlike you."

My hands turned into fists. Anger radiated through my body, bones shaking at the emotional impact. "How long?"

He shrugged once again as if it meant nothing to him. "Two weeks ago."

I released a string of curse words out loud and screamed at him with the little strength I had. "I suffered two extra weeks because of you!"

My legs trembled at his confession. My broken nails dug deep into my light bronze skin.

My eyes burned with hatred for this man. As I looked deep into his evil eyes, I wondered how I could ever love a man like him. A million years wouldn't be enough time to understand him and his wretched ways. He was a double-faced man, a sweetheart to others but to me a devil in disguise.

"You bastard! You are such a-" I yelled at him.

There was very little willpower in me not to throw something in his face. I wanted to slap him and see him regret everything he did and said to me, but I wouldn't waste my breath on him. He was as stubborn as a mule.

He stopped in his tracks. He raised his hand to hit me. "Don't you call me a bastard!"

"Well, at least I didn't hook up with another guy while I was dating you even though I didn't love you!" I hissed those words at him, not caring if they hurt him. "I should have broken up with you earlier. You're just another piece of junk that walked into my life, and I took it, thinking it was gold."

He slapped me across the face. A tingling, burning sensation burned in my cheeks.

"You should put your foot where your mouth is, or it's going to get you in a lot of trouble!"

Brandon instantly slapped the other cheek, but this time it slightly hit my eye. Tears mixed with anger stirred inside of me, leaving me in a pile of emotions.

"Pack up your stuff and leave now," I snarled at him with a step back so he would miss if he tried to hit me again.

He sneered foul words. His footsteps echoed throughout the house. The bang of the door made the house tremble at the impact. The anxiety pounded uncontrollably in my heart. My fear erupted like a waking volcano.

Even if we never belonged together, I didn't wish betrayal on my worst enemy. It felt like a part of your soul was leaving. Maybe I was just convenient and unworthy of love.

Was there going to be an end to this endless pit?

Several moments passed before Brandon rushed down the stairs again. His suitcases kept hitting the walls and staircase with loud *thuds*.

He froze in front of me. His eyes were fierce with hatred and anger. His hand rose to slap me again, but my body instantly took a step back.

"I hope you fail in life, Amelia. I hope you rot and die alone." Before he slammed the door, he whipped his head around. "I hope you'll recognize that you will never be worth anything. That you aren't worthy of love."

Even moments after he left, I couldn't move. An icy dread and heaviness fell over my soul. It was like I was having an out-of-body experience.

Maybe I am dreaming.

Minutes quickly turned into an hour. I rubbed my sore cheeks. "I need a drink."

In my mind, heaven and hell collided, and it was a constant war. My brain couldn't think or process anything; it was a humbled mess of mixed emotions.

Unsteadily, I strolled to my room to get ready to lose myself. I didn't want anyone to find me, no one to ramble in my head about my bad choices, so I tossed my phone onto my bed.

No one would bother me, and if I ended up dead after tonight, no one would bother.

What was I made for?

I DOWNED A HANDFUL OF PAINKILLERS BEFORE entering the bar. Maybe today I could forget my problems. The security guard didn't even ask for my ID anymore. He knew me by name and greeted me with the biggest smile.

This specific bar always overflowed with hundreds of people who wanted to forget about their outside lives. The air was thick with alcohol, sweat, and drugs. Bags thrown across the ground, waiting for someone to trip and fall. Random people who made out in the middle of nowhere. Uncoordinated men who tried to dance with two drinks in hand.

Disco lights were the only things that illuminated the space. The darkness made me feel welcome and at home. No one knew who I was here; there were no expectations on my shoulders.

I quickly sat on the only empty barstool in front of the display of alcohol. The bartender smiled and asked what I wanted to drink. I needed something to kick the daylights out of me. Something to knock me out dead. "Strongest you got and make it a double."

He nodded and strolled away. His face was familiar to me, which wouldn't be a good thing to some. As I waited for my drink, my mind roamed miles away.

I was to blame for this mess; it was inevitable for my heart to get broken. My heartbreak wasn't anyone's fault but my own.

The bartender slid the drink across to me. With a swift motion, I downed the whole glass.

Nothing.

There was no reaction, so I asked for another, and another, and another. I wouldn't allow myself to stop until my feelings were drowned, thoughts dead, and consciousness gone. I wouldn't stop until I couldn't feel myself.

The bar spun rapidly. *Finally,* completely boozed on alcohol, I swayed to the dance floor.

Today I am going to let myself lose it.

My legs couldn't keep themselves up, so I leaned on a random guy who stood beside me. The guy's facial expressions were unrecognizable, but instantly he went with it. His body swayed with mine; our bodies danced to the fast tempo. A sly hand wrapped around my waist, gripping my flesh against his skin. His other hand gripped a cup filled with beer.

"What is a pretty lady like you doing here?" His lips were pressed against my ear. I yelped at the way he gripped me.

"I am here to lose myself." my drunk voice admitted.

The man had a sly smirk on his face. My head throbbed with the loud music. My body felt exhausted from the constant swaying, but before I could push myself away, he leaned in for a kiss.

I placed both hands firmly against his chest, pushing him away. That man was so drunk that he didn't care. He shrugged and turned around to find his next victim.

Bodies multiplied; the world spun with each step I took. A constant ringing sound in my ears. My nose hairs burned with the sweat that ran down my forehead.

The darkness flooded my vision. My body was instantly desperate to grasp onto something. Voices of catcalling men around me who brushed their hands against my exposed arm. My mind insane with the hundreds of conversations.

The heart inside my sore chest pounded uncontrollably. A raspy, ragged breath clawed its way into my lungs. Somehow I felt like a fish out of water. I felt completely powerless and disconnected from any sense of reality.

What in the blazes was happening to me?

A knife dug even deeper into my heart. The air heavy and thick.

I was born for this.

I was made for this.

This is who I am, and I need to learn to accept it.

A failure, a disaster, and a disappointment to all.

The man beside me challenged me to a contest. He confidently declared that the loser had to pay for the other person's drink. Pride filled his dark eyes.

Despite the agony my soul was in, I accepted his prideful request. This wannabe must have been new because he didn't have a clue who I was or what I was capable of.

I downed twice as many shots as he did. *This is nothing.* He looked at me like an alien; his gaze traveled up and down my body in disbelief. When he paid the debt, he stormed off and yelled bitter curse words into the darkness.

I guess there is a positive side to this.

My heart had almost reached its breaking point. I was so close to feeling nothing.

I swayed around on the barstool, looking at the baffled bartender. "I am impressed. No one has beaten that man since the beginning of the night."

I smirked at the praise. "Give me another one."

"No, ma'am, you're way past your limit for the night." He slowly backed away with both hands up in surrender.

My hands clenched, nails dug deep into palms. I struggled to keep my mouth shut and not lash out at him, but then a brilliant idea popped into my mind.

Desperately, I looked around me and found a man with his back turned to his full cup of whiskey. Before my mind processed anything, I downed the whole cup in a breath.

I fumbled to find my purse, unable to see anything in the darkness. Once I felt the strap of my leather purse,

I threw it over my shoulder and swayed at the weight. My footsteps looked like a boat being tossed in the raging sea.

The mini-skirt around my waist shrank with each passing second. Heels that dug into my swollen red feet.

A knife-like pain pierced my gaze with every blink.

I gazed all around the room, desperate to find a way out. I was so lost in that mess; I knew I would pass out in the middle of the dark bar.

Yet, right before I lost all hope, I saw him. Even from a distance, I could tell that they were his eyes in the pitiful darkness. Those round, fiery brown eyes. He stood just before the open door and was looking directly at me.

Why is he here?

He spawned out of thin air, and just by glancing at him, my heart pounded even faster.

I swayed, no longer able to keep my balance. He was taller and stronger. Despite the blurriness in my vision, I was more than sure it was my childhood best friend.

Why is he here?

I took an unsteady step forward. My voice raspy and dead, I whispered quietly, "Mathias?"

Before I could hear any response, my body came into painful contact with the floor.

AMELIA
CHAPTER 3

Mathias. Mathias. Mathias

His name constantly rang in my head. Those eyes were the only thing that kept coming into my memory.

But why him? After all these years, why now?

It had been about ten years since I last saw him. It's been an eternity since those beautiful chestnut eyes looked at me.

But why was he there?

Ten years ago, I left and he didn't come chasing me. I never expected him to because his whole life was rooted in Love Creek. After several moments, I realized I had drunk half a bottle of Cabernet wine.

Flashbacks from last night flashed through my mind. After I passed out on the floor, someone called the ambulance. They took me to the nearest hospital and kept me there until I was sober. The thirty minute drive back home was painful. My head pounded furiously with each speed bump I went over. The aftermath of the fall left my body in complete misery.

Suddenly, I felt a small vibration against my right leg.

LILY

Hey hangover princess! How are you doing?

ME

I broke up with a cheating ex, drank half a bottle of wine before noon, and I think I saw my childhood best friend outside a bar yesterday.

LILY

WHAT?

My fingers rested on top of the digital keyboard, unable to think of how to answer.

What would I write? How would I write it? How would I tell her what happened yesterday without saying I went to the hospital?

I didn't want to tell her and give her another reason to be disappointed in me. Lily wore her heart on her sleeve and she did everything for me.

Yesterday would be too much.

So I decided to leave her on read. My brain instantly went back to the rabbit hole of thoughts.

It felt like all the worst yet best things happened to me in less than a month. My emotions were worse than before. I thought that letting go of an abusive ex would heal me but it didn't. It just left a bigger hole to be filled, it made me feel alone. I thought drowning myself would heal me but it turned me into a worse person. Every place I went to find a solution, everything that I thought was right, it set me back even more.

Besides, I was a ghost. No one saw or cared about me.

No one knew who I went through or the thoughts that ran through my mind.

My parents didn't care about anything or anyone besides their public image. Everything to them was appearances and money.

I wanted to be loved but was I deserving of that?

Several moments later, loud banging came from my front door. At first I thought it was Lily desperate to know what happened. Except it wasn't. It was an angry mother and father.

I rub the nape of my neck as I slowly unlocked the door. They pushed past me and into my living room. Not a care in the world to ask how I was or how my day was.

My mom had her arms crossed over her chest. Her cheeks were a bright pink color. Her eyes raged with fury and disappointment.

As usual my dad was on his phone, not even bothering to look at me in my face.

She screamed cuss words in the center of my living room. "You're such a failure, Amelia Johnson. I have been patient and I have loved you."

I couldn't help but laugh at such a lie.

"Loved me? How have you loved me when all you do is complain about everything I do?"

Every bone was instantly tensed. The strength in my arms faded from how strong I gripped onto the edge of a chair.

Why should I even call her Mother? How can I call someone such a loving title if they never are there for me?

She spun around, pointing at everything in the house. Selfish show-off pride on her face as she pointed to each item she paid for. "Look at everything you have Amelia, is this not enough for you? Do you need me to buy more for you to be happy?"

The way she said that made my heart twist in agony because she didn't understand. My mother would never understand that love wasn't an object. It took me over ten years to realize that.

"Stuff doesn't bring happiness! This never made me happy. This all was just to postpone and ignore the fact of something you guys never gave me: love."

She took a step back, hand pressed against her chest. Her mouth opened and closed several times. Words failed her. Silence was the only thing that spoke for the both of us.

Father was in the corner on his phone. Once in a while he would look up and listen into the conversation. Most of his adult life, his eyes were always glued onto that small device. The world spun around him, and sometimes I wondered if he was even alive.

"You're disinherited," she whispered to herself. She paced back and forth in my living room. Her head nodded as she talked to herself.

Those words slightly affected me but not to the level I thought they would. Never in my life did I feel worthy or wanting of her inheritance. I saw the way it damaged their relationship, and I wanted no part in it.

She looked at me once again. Fury mixed with hatred in her eyes. "I raised you to be extraordinary! We made this company, working our butts off to give you a life, and yet you're such a disappointment." Her tone slowly increased. Her bag now was tossed onto the floor, her hands waved constantly in the air. "You fail to change and you humiliate me with how sloppy you are. I honestly need to have a talk with the Big Man Upstairs about why He gave a worthless daughter to me, out of all people!"

My mother didn't know how to keep her emotions in check. Her attitude and body language was a complete mirror to how broken her heart was. Her stomps across the floor sounded like a child who hadn't gotten a lollipop.

She wanted a perfect child. A child that society loved and was flawless in every way. She wanted a child that she didn't have to give much attention to. Maybe what she really needed was a pet.

With each yell, my ears burned. Each word she spoke was simply a slap across the face. Her attitude was fuel to the raging fire.

When I finally lost it, I began yelling the words that were pent up as well. "You wanna know why I am such a disappointment? You wanna know why I am a failure in your eyes? It's because of you! You're the reason!" Those words even perked my father's attention. The both of them had their eyes glued on me and listening carefully to every word.

"You want to know why I don't live up to your standards? It's because I was abused. I was yelled at. I was prescribed drugs, and it became an addiction. This all happened because you thought I needed 'fixing.' I am not one of your marketing jobs, Mom. I can't be fixed." I took a step closer to her and dropped my voice. My raspy words barely were above a whisper. "You try to fix things, but, believe me, every time you try to make me feel better, you only make things worse. I never had a mom or dad. I have neglectful guardians that caused more damage than addiction could ever do."

All the strength and bravery I had in that moment instantly faded away once I stopped talking. The urgency to speak about what I had pent up all these years finally burst. The dam broke and there was no holding it back. I told them the raw emotions and feelings that I was forced to deal with.

"You don't raise your tone to me, missy!" She spoke sharply. Her finger was so close to my face, trying to get in all my business.

"You're not my mom and I don't want to be yours. You took everything from me, everything! The one true person I cared and loved, you ripped me away from."

Mathias.

Once again that name and those eyes flashed across my memory.

She took a steady stride closer. Her lips in a tight line as she sneered, "I did it for your own blasted good."

I pushed her finger away from my face and took a step back. "He saw me; you never did. You don't know the definition of good. All you think about is yourself. All you care about is money and appearances."

"That stupid Mathias. He was nothing. He was just a dumb boy that you spent your worthless time with," she hissed loudly. I knew what she was trying to do. My mother was trying to get underneath my skin and make me say things that I know I will regret.

My eyes burned with unshed tears. The lids of my eyes were unbearable to keep open. The knuckles on either of my hands were white as snow.

She is wrong. Mathias Anderson has been the only good thing that has ever happened in my life.

She grabbed her purse and keys off the floor. Aggressively she put on her designer fur coat and glanced back at me. "I have no regrets in life except one. The only regret I have in life is you. My biggest sloppy regret is you." She slammed the door behind her. Awkwardly me and my father just looked at each other before he shrugged his shoulders and walked away.

Everything will be okay.
Hopefully, I will be okay.

IT HAD BEEN A FEW HOURS SINCE MY PARENTS stormed out the house. Those hours gave me enough time to cry, to scream, look into the void, and pace around the house.

Quickly, I began packing my belongings. With each piece of clothing that I folded, was a hundred tears shed. With each reminder of my ex and parents was another scream yelled. Unable to contain it anymore, I allowed myself to cry the biggest and sloppiest meltdown ever.

Ding. My phone vibrated from across the almost empty room.

FATHER

Your mother wants you to leave the house by this weekend.

Without thought, I threw my phone across the room and continued to sob. My body was so tired from everything that had happened that it didn't know what to think. My heart ached in ways that I didn't know were possible. And in between emotional cries, my belongings were packed and I had nowhere to go.

I quickly grabbed my slightly cracked phone and texted

Lily. My eyes couldn't stop leaking so the letters on the scream were blurring into one.

ME

Can I crash at your place?

LILY

Sure. I am at work right now but I will be back home shortly. What's wrong?

I didn't want to worry her over text because how could I explain everything that happened in a small text message. How could I explain that my parents bluntly admitted to my face that I was their biggest mistake.

ME

Nothing, I will arrive there in about 35 minutes.

I slowly paced around the house to remember everything that had happened within those four walls. Every cry, party, laugh, and things that weren't even worthy to pass through my mind again. I was letting it all go. Somehow the good memories were staying and the bad ones were going with me.

I slowly locked the front door. Complete fear overtook my body. Before I walked away, I slid the keys underneath the door mat. Walking away was the most painful thing because the future scared me a whole lot more.

When I slid inside the car, another dam was broken.

Every heartbreak. Every painful word. Every drunk moment I had gone through. All the abuse I had to endure. Every knife that passed through my heart. Everything that was pent up for years was released in a matter of seconds. I felt like I was choking on frigid ocean water.

I ARRIVED AT LILY'S HOUSE THIRTY-FIVE MINUTES later and before my knuckles touched the door, the door swung open. He wore a working belt with clothes completely covered with filth. Jeremiah had the biggest smile on his face, but when he glanced at my puffy, red face his smile faded. Without a word, he enveloped me into a hug.

I didn't really know Jeremiah, but somehow he was like a long lost brother to me.

"Hey Amelia," he announced. Without me asking, he began taking the bags from my hands and placing them beside the staircase.

"Hey, Jer." My voice cracked.

Jeremiah was Lily's husband. He was a golden retriever and was the best person to be around. He knew how to make someone feel seen, heard, and cared for.

He walked into the kitchen and began washing his paint covered hands. "Talk to me."

He gestured for me to sit on the nearest chair. Quickly, Jeremiah opened the fridge and grabbed a glass of water.

I gave him the most sarcastic laugh I could manage. "You already know everything because Lily says everything. What do I need to explain?" A whisper would be louder than the way I talked to him. My voice was almost gone. A thousand cats tried to claw their way out, each swallow was another wave of pain.

He shifted in his seat and crossed his arms. "Why were you kicked out of your place?" I didn't tell him that I was kicked out but by the amount of bags I had on me, one might assume.

I shrugged like I didn't care, but in reality it was all beginning to set inside my mind. "Crazy manipulative mother."

He chuckled quietly and said nothing.

I FOLLOWED AFTER JEREMIAH INTO A PARTIALLY remodeled room. "Lily has been asking for me to redo this room, and as a belated birthday gift, I am finally doing it." He chuckled with both hands on his hips like he was superman.

I gave him a dramatic eye roll. "Her birthday was in March and now it's September."

He scrunched his nose and stuck out his tongue.

"You're such a child." I shook my head in disbelief at his childlike attitude. Jeremiah knew when to be funny and serious, but I wondered if he had ever really grown up.

He grinned fully knowing that his plan was working. If Jeremiah couldn't help me with my problems, he was going to try to make me smile.

He had painted the walls a pastel pink color. It definitely had Lily's face written all over it. And if I knew the both of them, then they probably went back and forth several times on the color. Yet Jeremiah wasn't the type of person to get mad or worked up about something not going his way.

I leaned against the bright white door frame. Slowly I looked at all the details and admired all the furniture. Even if plastic wrap covered all the furniture, I knew it was going to look so cute at the end.

He looked up at me from where he was painting. "Well,

you can stay as long as you would like. I am not home most of the time due to work, but my home is your home."

"If I had a house, I would say the same thing."

He looked at me to make sure it was okay to laugh and then burst out laughing. And just for a split second, I forgot about everything that just happened.

LILY HAD GOTTEN BACK HOME A FEW HOURS AGO and Jeremiah was already deep in sleep. From downstairs, you could hear his deep snores.

We both had stayed up the majority of the night with a cup of emotional wine. When I finished telling her what happened, her face was pale. Lily's eyes were wide open, they glistened with unshed tears. She was in complete disbelief.

"Darn it, Amelia. That must have been horrible. How is the anxiety? How are you emotionally?"

I exhaled and took a long sip. Words didn't feel grand or big enough to describe and explain the confusing feelings inside my chest. She raised her eyebrows and instantly knew what that sign meant.

I took a deep breath in and glanced at her. "The meds aren't working like I want them to. Anxiety feels like hell and I feel lost. Also, I have lost everything that I had in less than a span of a week."

She rubbed her hand against my leg which was crossed on her fuzzy cream colored couch. The warmth of a smile warmed my broken heart. "We will get through this, together."

She squeezed my hand and finally said good nights. I plopped myself onto the bed in her guestroom. My brain was so exhausted that it didn't have the energy to think anymore.

The lavender essential oils I used in my hair relaxed all the tense bones within me. The silky pj's against my skin made me feel a bit more peaceful. The fuzzy socks - which wasn't going to last the entire night - felt like a giant hug around my swollen feet.

Pain? Used to it.

Tears? Wasted.

Hope? Lost.

I looked across the window at the moon. It was a full moon. Its light shined without ceasing.

I want to be like that but is it possible?

Is there hope for me?

I'm beginning to think that I needed someone who loved me despite all my flaws.

Amelia
Chapter 4

The lively sounds of doors closing and echoing footsteps woke me up from my deep slumber. An aromatic scent that filled the house - cinnamon, coffee, and bacon - made my stomach growl with hunger.

Quickly, I changed clothes and brushed my teeth. My stomach rumbled when I turned the corner and saw a table filled with breakfast. Happiness and the hint of cinnamon filled the air and made my sore heart happy.

Lily had her back towards me. She added fall themed creamer into both our cups of coffee. Lily had the cutest collection of mugs, always switching them out for each holiday and season.

"Good morning." Her voice radiated with happiness and joy.

"You're an angel," I whispered. The aromatic coffee faintly blew against my face.

Pumpkin and coffee was the best autumn combination known to man.

"Thank you," I responded before I took a long sip of coffee.

Both of our plates overflowed with French toast, eggs, and bacon. Just by a glance, I was already full.

You're fat; stop eating so much.

Brandon's voice was a nagging fly in my ear. His comments wouldn't leave me alone, and they seemed to follow me everywhere I went. Even if I tried to fight against those tormenting thoughts, I always gave in. I couldn't even remember the last time I ate a full plate of food.

Chatting with Lily was as easy as breathing. There were no barriers, and we could talk about the most random things without worrying about what the other person was going to think.

She knew the unhealthy relationship I had with food, that I wouldn't eat as much as I needed to, but she never judged. Lily knew the mental struggle I had found myself in, so she never pushed those buttons. She knew how sensitive it was and didn't want to talk about it unless I was ready.

"So Jer went to work, but later tonight, he is going to bring a friend over to watch some TV and eat BBQ," she announced between the bites of her food.

I barely nibbled on anything and she was already almost finished. I swallowed the hot coffee. "I feel like there is an 'and' coming."

She grinned, "He is really cute. You might already know him but he is such a gentleman."

"Oh, really, just a reminder that I just left a toxic relationship. So I am not dating, not for a long time."

Her smirk was covered by the brim of her cup. "You will meet him tonight if you like it or not. And I never said you should date him." She giggled like a schoolgirl when she found out someone had a crush.

She is hiding something.

One thing about Lily was that she wasn't hard to read. She wore her heart on her sleeve and always expressed what she felt.

"Sure, but you ain't tricking anybody." I gave her a side eye before I threw away most of my food.

IT WAS ALREADY LATE AFTERNOON. A LIGHT golden glow kissed all the trees and buildings. The birds slowly stopped chirping as they flew to their nests. Trees and flowers no longer danced in the wind.

Jeremiah and his friends hadn't arrived yet, so it was just Lily and me. We were preparing everything for our dinner and then a relaxing night to come.

"I forgot to buy something!" Lily screeched from the kitchen. Her voice would have shattered the glasses at her high pitched scream.

Instantly, I had my wallet in one hand and my jacket in the other. "Send me a text message for what you need."

BEFORE I EVEN STEPPED FOOT INSIDE THE HOUSE, Lily began taking the brown paper bags out of my hand. Lily was desperate to finish dinner before the guys got here. All you could see was Lily dashing from one side of the kitchen to the other side. The meat had already been seasoned and prepared for Jeremiah to cook.

When she realized she hadn't said thank you, she whipped around and flashed me a big smile. "Thank you so much, Amelia."

The air in the house quickly shifted from cinnamon to cumin and peppers. Different spices swirled in the air as Lily cooked. Lily said she needed a little bit of help, so I stayed on dish duty.

I couldn't help but smile at how different we were as I tied my hair up into a bun. She was the complete opposite of me. She was passionate and determined. Once she put her mind to something, it was impossible to stop her. Unlike me. My decisions have always been swayed by anyone surrounding me. I couldn't decide anything for myself.

Her phone blasted music through the kitchen; the glasses trembled at the bass of the music. Thank the heavens we both had the same taste in music.

Whisks as our microphones, we sang our hearts away. She was covered with food, and I was covered with soap and water but we didn't care. All we cared about was to sing and dance like no one was watching.

I knew dinner was going to take longer because of our very professional concert but I wouldn't have it any other way. When our strengths died out, we noticed our bright magenta cheeks.

"You remember when you were at the bar and you told me you saw your childhood best friend?" Her question broke the comfortable silence. Lily's lips were in a big smile. Her hair pointed in all different directions.

"Yes. Despite all the doubt and questions I have, I know I saw him." I answered.

For the first time in hours, I hadn't thought about him. Yet with the mention of his name, his eyes and factual features came back to memory. Just the mention of him brought along so many feelings.

Feelings are so confusing.

"I honestly want to know more, if you don't mind me asking," she whispered, unsure if I would be okay to open up that part of my story.

I don't know if I was mentally prepared to open that part of my history. If anyone else had asked then I would have said no, but Lily has never left me. She has been with me through the bad and ugly, and I knew I could trust her with this part of my life.

I huffed out a small nervous laugh. I had never regretted any of our history. He was joyful. He brought so much happiness and love into my life. I missed that more than anything. I needed it more than I realized and maybe I was just too stubborn to realize it.

"He was amazing. He was the definition of joy." Memories flashed across my mind of all the moments we had together. "I remember the way his eyes would crease when he was laughing or the way his dimples would appear when he would give a big smile. Those smiles were my favorite. He told me once that he saved them just for me. We were inseparable until-"

My words were silenced because that gloomy night came back in full force. The fully packed car, the way my parents yelled at him and his family. My parents cursed them for turning me into a lunatic when in reality his family were the ones who had shown me what it meant to be loved.

My mother pulled me by my ear to leave. And that day I knew my heart would never be the same. I was leaving the only people who made me feel loved and seen. My heart shattered in a thousand pieces when my mother ripped the necklace around my neck and threw it onto the floor. It was a promise and reminder from Mathias and it was so beautiful.

The necklace was a small sun with golden and gem details. He said that I was his sunshine. *Whatever it may be - the world, fear, or time - nothing will ever keep me from you. I will always wait, Sunshine.*

His brown eyes instantly shattered when the necklace broke into a million pieces. When he lifted his gaze, our eyes instantly connected. The connection we had was far greater than anything. There were no words for how he made me feel.

I was ripped away from the one person who saw me. Who made me feel important.

I cleared my throat with a sudden urge to cry. "I cared about him more than I cared about myself. We promised to one another that if we didn't get married by twenty-three, we would marry each other."

A promise that every girl and guy best friend made to each other. A promise that had passed its expiration date and there was no going back.

It's been ten years. Ten years since I have been able to hear his laugh, see his smile and instantly melt with one of his gazes.

A warm, fuzzy feeling filled my heart. "You should have seen the way he lit up when I agreed to it. You would think he had won the lottery with the look in his eyes."

Lily was a hopeless romantic. Her eyes glistened as she listened to my sappy life. She mumbled quietly even though no one could hear us, "Were you in love?"

Her eyes were filled with awe, and her lips were set in a small smile. I knew she was holding herself back from crying at the story.

"We were young and naïve, but the answer to your question is yes, yes I was. What we had was different from anything I ever experienced, but it's too late now."

She smiled as she gazed at me with a warm expression. "I feel like you have told me his name before, but I can't quite remember it."

A lump formed in my throat. "Mathias Anderson." All the tension and fear instantly melted in my body with just saying his name out-loud. *I can't believe I am saying all this out-loud.* "He was my everything; he was the only one who truly knew me. He is only a memory now, but I now hold on to it like it's my last breath." Tears pooled in my eyes. It almost seemed cinematic the way the tears ran down my face slowly. "I messed up Lily, he didn't deserve it. I could have done something. Even after all these years, I remember him. Every detail of his beautiful soul, but he probably doesn't remember me."

I finally exhaled the breath I had held back. My heart pounded faster just by talking about him. Yet it wasn't until that moment that a thought flashed through my mind. *What if he forgot who I was?*

That single thought hurt me in ways I couldn't even explain. The harsh reality struck me like lightning.

What if he moved on and acted like I never existed?

Lily and I sat there in silence, gazing at the burning candle and flowers in the center of the table. There wasn't anything I could possibly say to describe even a fraction of this feeling.

A few minutes passed by and footsteps filled the silence. Their boots fell to the floor with a light *thud.*

I shrugged my shoulders to avoid another downpour of tears. "Mathias Anderson deserves someone better than me and I wouldn't be surprised if he has already moved-"

"Amelia Jones, I have never forgotten you for a single moment." A deep unmistakable voice spoke behind me.

AMELIA
CHAPTER 5

"And I never will."

My body completely froze at the sound of his voice. Even after so much time, his voice was recognizable from miles away.

I slowly spun around in the barstool, my gaze still focused on Lily. She had the biggest smirk on her face like all the pieces of her plan were falling into place.

Instantly it clicked. She knew who Mathias was and didn't have the audacity to tell me.

I didn't know if I wanted to hug or yell at Lily.

I finally turned around, our eyes immediately locked with one another. Again, those big brown caramel eyes. They were completely and absolutely perfect to me.

It took me several seconds to make sure I wasn't dreaming. Discreetly, I pinched myself to make sure this was real because if it wasn't, then I didn't want to wake up.

After ten years, Mathias Anderson had grown into a full grown adult.

Of course he did. That's called life and time.

Nevertheless, he grew multiple feet and now he had a beard, but he still looked like my childhood best friend.

Gosh, those dimples. Those dimples had power over me. They did unspeakable things.

"Mathias, is it really you?" I whispered.

"Somebody pinch me," I pleaded.

"Ouch!" I whipped my head around to see Lily who was struggling not to laugh. "You said to pinch you."

When I turned back around, Mathias had a smirk on his face.

"Tell me something only my Mathias would know." *Then I would know that I wasn't dreaming.*

I can't believe I said, "*My Mathias.*" I might as well dig myself a hole because in 30 seconds, I already managed to embarrass myself.

You can't say he is yours after all this time. He can be married for heaven's sake.

He gave a low laugh and took a small step forward. "When we were young, I would give you a wild flower each time I saw you and you would collect them." He smiled. "You painted a picture of each one. You refused to throw them away even after they died, saying that they were forever memories. I never knew why. It was weird and a bit strange but it was something you loved to do and I loved seeing you happy."

My breath hitched at that memory. That seemed to be a lifetime ago. That memory wasn't fresh in my mind but as he retold it to me, I remembered it.

The way he would always pick a wildflower from his mother's garden or from our secret place. He never picked the same one and sometimes he didn't pick the prettiest one.

"Sometimes the flower with a missing petal has the greatest potential."

It really was Mathias.

No one knew that I kept those flowers. It was just our little secret.

"We were best friends and we were in it together, nothing ever separated us. We would run off to the woods, play games, and we would share our darkest secrets." He slightly frowned. "And even after you left and they took you from me, I would wait at our spot in hopes that you would come back."

I tried so hard to blink back the tears because it felt like that happened just yesterday. The pain and scars were so fresh; they still hurt every time that I breathed.

With each sentence, he took a small step closer. My eyes released a slow steady stream of tears. The tears cooled my hot burning cheeks. "I didn't have a choice."

My heart hammered in my chest. My stomach fluttered uncontrollably.

"I know you didn't but they never could rip you away from my heart. They never took away the memories I had with you. You always have been with me."

He took his hands out of his pockets and fiddled with the drawstring of his brown hoodie. It had a sunset and a galloping horse in the center, with the cursive words around it, *"Let me always admire the sunrise and sunset. Let me admire the small part that I have of you."*

I opened and closed my mouth several times, trying to find the correct words but there were none. After several minutes of silence, I finally managed to say three little words. "It's really you."

His forehead formed a small crease line. He opened his

mouth several times like he wanted to ask me something but before he could, someone else broke the silence.

"Barbeque is ready." Lily hollered from the backyard.

We stood there for a second longer. Our eyes connected and said things that words couldn't explain. There was a certain level of familiarity between us, like a part of our soul was revived. He took one last glance at me before walking in Lily and Jeremiah's direction.

DINNER WAS BRIGHT, FUN, AND FULFILLING IN ALL the senses. There wasn't a moment of silence between us.

Jeremiah made the worst possible jokes but it was impossible not to laugh. Every few moments, I would steal a glance at Mathias. I still couldn't believe he was here. My mind tried to wrap around the fact that he was sitting right in front of me. Mathias Anderson sat right in front of me and his eyes were glued on mine.

He is actually here? What is he doing here? Why? How?

My heart pounded rapidly the more I tried to find the answers to those questions. I fiddled with my hands underneath the table to keep myself from biting my nails. However, when the anxiety was too much to bear, I excused myself from the table.

I quickly rushed to the bathroom and locked the door behind me. The woman I saw in the mirror looked more pale than a ghost. *I might pass out.* I splashed cold water onto my face.

What is happening?

For a second, I thought that I was hallucinating. Maybe I

drank too much or took too many drugs because nothing felt normal.

After I calmed myself down, I downed a handful of painkillers and headed downstairs. The stairs slightly creaked with each step I took.

When I turned the corner, Mathias was leaning against the kitchen countertop. His eyes were glued on mine like he had been waiting for me.

I slowed my steps, cautious. He had two wine glasses in his hands and slowly extended one to me. I took it from his hand, careful to not brush my fingers against his.

Jeremiah and Lily weren't in sight and I knew they were trying to play matchmaker. When I glanced at the dinner table, everything had already been put away.

I might have taken longer than I actually thought.

I gazed back at the oven clock. *It's been thirty minutes.*

"I can't believe I am with my Amelia Jones. My inner child is so happy right now." He shook his head with the biggest grin on his face like he couldn't believe it either.

I didn't respond because I couldn't trust myself to say something that wasn't going to embarrass me. Slowly, I strolled around him in the direction of the backyard.

Lily's backyard was beautiful and breathtaking. Small twinkle lights were strung back and forth on wooden poles. It gave the space a magical feeling. The dark sky allowed the stars to shine brightly.

The sky is the greatest art masterpiece.

Mathias sat on the white garden chair beside me. His long legs extended in front of him as he leaned his head back with his eyes closed. Mathias looked so relaxed and centered, not a care in the world. It gave me a moment to look at him, to soak every beautiful part of him.

His strong jawline underneath his small beard. The way his face relaxed even more with each deep breath he took. His slightly crazy hair like that he had run his fingers through a hundred times.

Was it weird for me to think he was handsome after ten years of not seeing him?

"Take a picture, it will last longer," Mathias whispered into the darkness. He slightly opened his eyes to take a peak at my horrified expression.

I shoved his shoulder slightly and laughed. "I wasn't staring. Stop being so self absorbed, Mathias."

When he stopped laughing, he focused those eyes on me. I never could comprehend how his eyes were the portals into his soul. The way I could tell everything he felt just by a glance at them. *Was that just me or could anyone else do that?*

"And you still haven't changed a bit. Still the bubbly and beautiful Amelia that I once knew," he responded. He lifted the glass to his lips and took a small sip, his eyes focused on the sky.

Even after all these years, he still has a fascination with the sky.

I knew that he had told me the reason why once but I already forgot. His explanation was a vague memory.

I turned slightly, my leg crossed underneath me. He sensed that my eyes were focused on him, so instantly he turned his head in my direction.

We didn't say anything because we were never people who felt forced to talk the whole time. Abruptly, I asked the first thing that came to memory. "Why are you here?"

I instantly winced at those word., They came out harsher than I had intended. All my life, I expected that when I saw him again, I was going to be whole and happy. I didn't want him to see me the way that I was.

Broken, unhealed, and hurt.

He didn't say anything for a few seconds. His face showed a mix of emotions. "Well, I didn't expect that to be your first question after ten years, but I wouldn't expect anything less of you."

He took a steady breath in and gave me a lop-sided grin. "I never really left Love Creek. I am always at the farm helping my parents or spending time with Jeremiah." He looked away before he asked, "Why are you here?"

"It's nothing." Suddenly I was uncomfortable with the question.

I wasn't going to open up with him so early on. Neither was I going to explain the reason I now lived at Lily's house. I knew that if I explained everything that happened, he was going to blame himself. He was that type of person that always put the weight of the world on his shoulders.

I focused my gaze on the cup of wine, trying to focus on anything except him. I blinked hard to try to blink away the burning sensation. Memories flashed in front of me like a movie. My breath went rapid and shallow.

Gosh, I shouldn't be this happy and scared to see Mathias.

I slightly jumped out of my own skin when I felt his hand brush against my knee. "Are you ok?"

His voice was filled with worry. His eyebrows scrunched together at the sudden emotional change.

I shook my head and stood up to give space between me and the man who made me into a crazy mess of feelings.

Mathias still had the same effect on me.

"I am fine, just tired. Stressful week but it was nice to see you again. Goodnight."

I walked back inside before he could say or ask anything.

Great save, Amelia. He totally won't think there is something wrong with you now

That's me.

Too broken, too lost. And too weird to admit anything to anyone.

I quietly slipped myself into my room and gently closed the door behind me, not wanting to wake anyone up. I leaned against the door in complete silence. A few moments passed before I could hear the backdoor slide closed. Sounds flooded from the kitchen. He turned the sink on for several moments before he walked out the front door. Like the gentleman he was, he closed it quietly to not awaken anyone.

I let out a breath of air that I didn't know I was holding.

In one month, I had left a toxic relationship with a man who cheated on me. On top of that, I had the biggest fight with my parents. And if that wasn't enough for my heart, I finally met Mathias again. The man that I loved so much, so long ago.

Amelia
Chapter 6

Lily and I had planned to go shopping over the weekend. The holidays were almost here, and Lily barely had any time to do anything besides work.

Today would probably be her last break for the next few weeks. So we took advantage and went to all our favorite shops in town.

We had taken a lunch break earlier on so that we wouldn't have to stop later. My stomach almost turned inside out. I wanted to eat the hamburger with the most calories but an inner voice stopped me.

You're too fat.

You need to get skinny, or no one will love you.

Instead, I picked a salad, and in all honesty, I didn't want it. I didn't want a salad that had no chicken, no dressing, or anything interesting. It made me feel like a rabbit. The waiter even gave me a strange look when I basically ordered a bowl of only lettuce.

"I don't know how to feel about my best friend going behind my back and inviting my childhood best friend over." My feelings have been all over the place since the day I broke up with my ex. Nothing seemed clear anymore. And having Mathias now in the mix made everything a lot more complex.

She looked at me, paying attention to everything that I said. She didn't interrupt me a single time, letting me speak everything that was on my mind.

When I finally stopped talking, there was silence. She looked down at her food and then back at me. I could see the gears inside her head turn, thinking about what to say.

She took a small sip of her ice-cold lemonade. "It was just a happy coincidence."

I gave her a stink eye because we both knew full well what she did. She never said that Jeremiah's friend was named, *"Mathias."*

She leaned against the chair, with a smile on her face, and asked the question that I knew she was dying to ask. "What happened after me and Jeremiah went to sleep?"

I shook my head in disbelief. If Lily could live on three things alone, it would be Jeremiah, baked goods, and romantic drama.

I sighed because there wasn't any point in trying to fake or lie about what happened. "It's like the time between us never existed. Like we have been friends all along." I shrugged my shoulders. "I acted weird at the end, and then everything went downhill from there."

I shook my head to shake off the replay of that night.

She raised her eyebrows and took a slow bite of her sandwich. Her silence pressured me to continue on. "He said something, and it triggered something in me. I might have responded harshly. Then I just left."

It was like a terrible dream. A bad dream that I wanted to delete.

Lily nodded, understanding the unspoken words. She knew that certain words and certain questions got me riled up. She tapped the top of my hand and gave me a smile of comfort. "Don't let it affect you. He doesn't know what you have gone through and how hard it is for you right now."

Then, in the blink of an eye, her sweet smile turned into a smirk. "But that doesn't mean that you don't care about him. Even if it's just a little bit."

"I care about him as a friend, but anything else is off limits. There would be too much on the line, and my heart isn't ready for that."

Of course I still cared about him, because how could I not? How could I not care about someone that I grew up with and lived with for so many years? Yes, time and space separated both of us, but it never took the fond memories between us.

"I know you feel like you can't, but take this small piece of advice. Sometimes healing comes from a person who shows you love and sees your darkest fears without you having to say anything. Just a look in your eyes and they know everything." Her eyes had softened at those words because she knew.

She has seen me in deeper and darker places than this. We haven't been friends for long, but the few years that I have known her feel like forever. And all the times I tried to push her away, she never let me.

Yes, there have been moments where we took a *"break"* from one another, but when we came back, we were stronger than ever.

In the midst of the dark times, there is always a small light. All you have to do is find enough courage to go after it.

"Thank you, Lily, for trying to make me happy, but no. It was hard enough to face him after everything, and I don't know how things will go this time around." I shook my head.

Everything seemed to be dark territory. I couldn't see anything except the next step.

Lily was the type of person who would climb mountains for me. She would risk her life and the world, and I have done nothing in return.

I guess that's genuine friendship. True friendship is when you show love to someone, not depending on feelings or anything else. Yet you love and you treat the person despite whether or not they return the act.

My mind instantly went back to Mathias. My thoughts have been consumed by him recently. Not romantically, but I kept replaying our childhood.

Our story ran deeper than the veins in our bodies. Our story made us who we are. Even though we lost our way for many years, that story, that seed never left my heart. Even if I tried to forget him, my heart would always remember.

All the times he would walk me back home even though it was in the opposite direction of where he needed to go. All the time he would invite me over to his house because he knew I needed to be fed. The times he would celebrate my birthday when my parents forgot. The countless escapes where we would talk the night away.

The flowers. Sunsets. The stars. Gifts.

Mathias and his family helped make my childhood. Even though my parents forgot to take care of me or, better yet, didn't want to take care of me, his parents were always there.

And despite all the years of trying to forget him and put everything in the past, I couldn't because it was a part of me.

The memories had made me who I was, and no drugs, no alcohol, and no broken family could ever take that away from me.

"Amelia," Lily's voice crept into my thoughts.

I blinked several times, trying to refocus my attention. Drinking and taking medication had a tendency to have that effect on someone. "What?"

"You just dozed off. You were in another dimension. Are you okay?" She looked worried. Lily's eyebrows were scrunched together. Her eyes darted all over my face, trying to find out if I was okay.

"I am fine, thanks." I whispered. My gaze dropped to the plain, boring salad in front of me.

I have lost my appetite.

My stomach turned and turned at the thought of taking another bite of this boring food. Lily gave me another long look before taking the last bite of her food. I sighed internally in relief that she didn't ask any questions because I don't know how I would have answered them.

IF I WALKED ANOTHER TEN MINUTES IN THE shopping mall, I was going to drive myself crazy. We had been in almost every single store twice. Then, when we finished at the mall, we went to other stores. My feet were throbbing, and they begged to be put up. My bones felt like spaghetti, and the shopping bags I held engraved themselves into my skin.

We had already gotten home and taken showers. I took

full advantage of the hot water to release the tension in my bones. The small bunch of lavender that was hung on the shower head made me feel like I was in paradise.

When I walked downstairs, Lily had already prepared the movie. We were watching Pride and Prejudice for the millionth time, with some popcorn, snacks and wine. Although throughout every movie we watched, we talked more than we watched.

"You know, I want to hear in detail about you and Mathias."

I shoved a handful of popcorn into my mouth. "Let's focus on Mr. Darcy flexing his hand."

She giggled. "Girl, I think we have watched this movie so many times that we dream about the hand flex scene."

Silence.

Our eyes were glued to the screen and our hearts melting at the sight of Mr. Darcy.

Why can't fictional men exist?

I asked myself because all the men that I thought were perfect turned out to be a Mr. Collins. Someone who talks about boiled potatoes and other nonsense.

"We were childhood friends; we did everything together. Every breathing second we had, we were always together." I smiled at the good times. "Then my parents' business took off, and they wanted to move to the big city." My voice trembled at the end because all the feelings and sensations instantly came back.

I took a shaky breath to finish my sentence. My past constantly turned me into a puddle of tears. "I was ripped away from him. I wish I could go back. And my parents prohibited me from ever seeing him again. They said he was a bad influence on me."

I shifted in my seat. My heart felt the heaviness of the memories once again. "I know he waited and waited hoping I would come back, but I didn't. Our childhood memories were forgotten as if they had never happened."

When I looked up, her eyes were full of compassion and love. She didn't judge or question anything else. She knew how much it took out of me to say that, how difficult it was to remind myself of those days.

"When two broken people meet each other, they have compassion for the other person's suffering. You will never find fulfillment and healing in someone. Jesus Christ is the only person who can do that. "

If Jesus Christ is real, then why hasn't he healed me yet?

MATHIAS
CHAPTER 7

"You did me dirty, Jeremiah." I grumbled back at him.

He cleared his throat over the phone and used his innocent angelic voice, "And might I ask how I did you dirty when I am always an angel."

I huffed out a laugh. "You know why."

He stayed silent for a moment. His footsteps were the only sound that assured me he hadn't turned off the call. "It's time to forgive and forget, bro."

I hate when he says that.

I know I should forgive and forget but it's easier said than done. Maybe the past had a deeper grip on me than I thought.

"It's not that easy and you know that. It's difficult to forget the past. No matter how far ahead I think I am," I quietly admitted. Even though Jeremiah annoyed me from time to time, I knew I could always open myself up and he wouldn't judge.

Jeremiah and I have been friends for a while now. A few years ago, we worked a job together and then slowly became brothers and best friends. Jeremiah and I were only starting adult life when we met.

He was the craziness to my calm.

I'm normal, and Jeremiah- well, he is a confetti popper. Even though he was the life of the party, Jeremiah knew how to be serious. Sometimes he would give me a slap of reality.

"I know that feeling." He didn't sweeten his voice anymore.

I looked up at my white ceiling and thought about Amelia for a second. When I saw her for the first time a few nights ago, my childhood-self jumped over the moon.

Yet when she pushed me away after I said something, it crushed my heart that things weren't how they used to be. We no longer were children. We were adults, and I had to accept the fact that maybe everything would not go back to how it used to be.

He broke the silence and said three words that I didn't want to hear, "She's broken, too."

I felt my grip on my phone lessen at those words. "What do you mean?"

My stomach twisted and turned at his words. I knew she had gone through something. Maybe she was fired or anything along those lines, but by the way he said it made it seem bigger and deeper.

"First, calm down." He breathed in deeply and signaled for me to do the same.

He knows me better than I know myself.

"Second, it's not my story to tell. Maybe it's a reason for you to see her again and find out for yourself." I could sense him shrugging across the phone screen.

"You really know how to keep a guy on his toes." He knew how to keep me on my toes and push me far beyond my comfort zone. I guess that was what loyal friends did with one another.

"It's my job as your best friend." Jeremiah proudly responded.

We chatted about what we were going to do for the day and turned off. Even though the conversation was finished, my mind kept thinking. He said something along the lines that he and Lily were going to watch a movie together. Those two probably watch more movies together in one month than I do in a lifetime.

I TOOK A COLD SHOWER TO AWAKEN ME FROM THE daze that I was in. The frigid water hit my shoulder like a bucket of ice; a small shutter escaped my lips. As the seconds went by, my body grew tolerant of the cold water. Although my mind was miles away.

Amelia.

That woman consumed my thoughts without even trying. The night I saw her for the first time after so many years, she smiled several times, but it wasn't a genuine smile. I knew she didn't truly smile.

Amelia's laugh would send a shiver down my spine. The way her cheeks turned a bright shade of pink or the way her nose scrunched. I haven't seen her much these past few days, but there are some things about her I will never forget.

I DASHED DOWN THE STAIRS, ALMOST LED BY THE smell of pancakes, jam, and a whole lot of love baking in the kitchen. The house smelt better than anything. It wasn't candles or essential oils; it was my momma's cooking.

She was the type of lady who would cook at any hour of the day. She would cook all day if she could. If she was mad or stressed, she would cook. If she was head over heels with my pa, she would cook. Any emotion she felt, she would cook, and it hurt no one. It was beneficial both to herself and to my stomach.

When I peeked my head into the kitchen, she giggled at something outside the window. Even from a few feet away, I saw her bright red cheeks and a big smile on her face. Her smile reached from one ear to the other, showing how content she really was.

I tiptoed behind her, surprised she didn't see me because my 6'2" body always towered over her. I was tall, and everyone could hear and see me from a great distance. When I saw what she was smiling at, a small grin crept onto my face.

My pa made a bunch of sappy love faces to her as he mowed the grass. Every time he passed by, he would send a kiss or make a funny face. However, when he saw me, he froze in place and started laughing uncontrollably.

My momma looked back in my direction, and her small frame shook with laughter. Her cheeks were bright red, and her lungs were slightly out of breath. They were more in love now than when they first got married.

Why does love change people?

"Hello, honey. Your father is a child stuck in a man's body." She giggled at her own comment.

I looked down at what she was doing and noticed the freshly picked and cut apricots on the counter. The preparations for jam making had already begun.

I gave her a gentle kiss on the cheek. We chatted for several moments before I turned around and began plating my food.

On top of the rustic table, there was a fresh pint of freshly squeezed lemonade. It looked almost fake from how perfectly the ice cubes and lemons floated on top.

"So how are you today?" Her southern voice flooded the room.

Of everyone in the family, Ma was the one who had the strongest Southern accent when she spoke. Me and Pa were in the middle; the city had seeped its roots into us. From the number of times we went there and had friends from the city, we slowly picked up a few things.

"I've had better days," I managed to say between big bites of food that I shoved into my mouth.

My eyes rolled back from the flavors that burst inside my mouth; it never got old. I don't know how she made anything and everything better, but she did. Every single time she would blow my socks off.

She looked at me with a face that silently said, *"Oh, tell me more."* The repeated movement of the knife slowed down.

"I saw Amelia again," I finally admitted. It was like a weight had been lifted off my shoulders. My momma knew everything about me. It was impossible to keep secrets from her.

The knife hit against the countertop. "Oh"

All she said was, *oh,* and I knew why. Neither of us expected to hear that name ever again. Amelia was super close to my momma. And her heart was crushed into a thousand pieces when she left.

That's another thing about her. When my momma

loved, she loved with every ounce in her body. She never loved someone halfway, and that was a blessing and a curse.

People loved her and cared about her. They always wanted to be around her and help her. My momma wore her heart on her sleeve, which was a blessing to all and a curse to herself. She loved so much that anyone and everyone could hurt her.

She turned to look at me. Her hip leaned against the countertop with her arms crossed over her chest. Her hair pointed in all directions but she was more than beautiful to me. I learned to be loved and to love because of her.

Her apron said, *I am the best chef according to my son. True, she was the best chef.*

I chuckled to myself because I remembered the day she opened that gift and loved it the moment she laid her eyes on it. She had used it every day since then, and I wondered if it was time to get her a new apron.

Her mouth opened and closed several times, choosing her next words carefully. A few seconds later, they settled into a straight line. And after what seemed like forever, she finally spoke. "And what happened?"

I sighed and leaned back on the wooden chair that my pa made for Christmas a few years ago. "Jeremiah and I were out buying some things for dinner, and then later we went to his place." That night relayed in my mind like a movie. "When I arrived, she was there too. I discovered she's best friends with Lily and has been for a while."

She looked at me for me to continue because that wasn't a satisfying answer. "She has changed, but I am really glad she's back."

She walked in my direction and sat on the seat across from me. Her caramel-honey round eyes looked deeply into mine. Every time I looked at myself in the mirror, I was grateful to have a fraction of her beauty.

I loved her eyes way more than my own. Her gaze always displayed all the love that was within her.

For a few moments, our eyes talked about things that words weren't sufficient for. Words were powerful, but emotions couldn't be contained by letters.

Her eyes said things from *"Are you ready for this?"* to *"How are you feeling?"* all the way to *"If you need anything, I am always here to help and support you."*

She squeezed my hand. "It's not your fault. You were in a hard place, remember? We needed your help, and you sacrificed everything to be with us. It isn't your fault, and it isn't her fault."

I squeezed her hand and gave a small smile. "I agree with every word that you say, momma but-"

She patted me lightly on the hand before she stood back up. "You have always been like that. You put others before yourself, and I love that about you, but you have to learn how to take care of yourself."

Her comment made me chuckle. "I learned from the best."

She smiled and pressed a gentle kiss on my forehead. After a long hug, she went back to her favorite safe place-the kitchen.

I looked down at my mostly empty plate and played around with the last few pieces.

She has always told me it was in my DNA. Helping people was my purpose, but sometimes I took it too far. Sometimes I lost sight of what I wanted and needed.

Even good things can be taken too far.

She reminded me that God created me to be a peacemaker but not for me to forget my wellbeing. I mindlessly walked to the sink to wash my plate.

Quickly, I slipped my feet into my almost dead cowboy boots.

I need to get a new pair.

Although as quickly as that thought came into my mind, it left. The key to my truck was in my right hand, and as I opened the front door of our red barn-style home, I was greeted with a dose of fall air. The orange-colored leaves danced in the sky as they slowly fell to the ground.

More leaves instantly fell as the breeze blew quicker. It was days like these that reminded me that change was a good thing. Change was a good thing, and I needed to slow down once in a while.

Before my hand touched the handle of the truck, I closed my eyes and breathed in deeply. The cool air filled my lungs and flowed through every vein in my body.

Slow, steady breaths released the tight tension from my shoulders. My heavy eyelids slowly opened. From several feet away, I could see my Pa standing in the distance. One of his hands blocked the sun. While the other hand waved to catch my attention. I waved my hand to let him know that I was coming.

Our house had many acres attached to it. Endless acres of land surrounded us, but it wasn't bare; it was filled with life. Barn animals were spread all over the land, plantation growing and producing fruit in every bare space. After all the years of hard work, it finally paid off.

My parents have lived here for many years before I was even born. This was what I grew up knowing and I wouldn't change it for anything. I have lived a fulfilled life with animals and my family surrounding me and the city could never compare to that.

This year it was different though. We were hosting the annual fall festival on our property. So we worked longer, faster, and harder to make sure everything was perfect.

Momma's orders.

When I finally reached my Pa, he greeted me the same way he has my whole life. "Hey buddy."

I faked an eye roll but had the biggest grin on my face. "I ain't eleven years old anymore, Pa."

"Right, sorry, you're a man and I am old. I guess that's how time works." A small smile spread across his lightly bronzed face.

I threw my keys onto the nearest picnic table as he explained what needed to be done. Each day there was a checklist. There wasn't a long list, but it definitely was going to keep me busy all day.

Currently, we have planted pumpkins, corn, sunflowers, and endless other crops. Each year we planted extra to sell to small businesses and friends, yet nothing compared to the harvest we had this year. Today I had to harvest all the fresh produce, clean the mess, and start on the raised beds. And surprisingly, Betsy didn't get out last night, which happened every blue moon.

I walked over to our classic red and white colored barn. White shingles, red walls, and wooden double doors. It definitely was the statement piece on our property. And to know that my parents had built it, gave it an extra touch.

I grabbed my shovel, gloves, and anything else that I might need. The old engine of my truck took a minute to start up. This truck has been through it all and it was still working strong. It was also much easier to drive the supplies across than to walk with everything by hand.

After a one-minute drive, I knelt on the ground and got to work. The dead roots didn't stand a chance against me and my shovel. Dirt went everywhere with each plant I ripped. The black trash bag beside me was instantly filled with trash to throw out.

The vegetables seemed to multiply in the basket beside me, which I wasn't going to complain about. It was rewarding and a blessing. Seeing all our hard work pay off was worth more than gold and riches.

I was deep in my thoughts, lost in the moment, that my soul jumped out of my body when Jeremiah spoke behind me.

"What are you smiling about?" Jeremiah asked.

"Darn it, Jeremiah. Why would you scare me like that?" I hissed at him. Jeremiah knew I hated when he did that, but that never stopped him.

Both of my trembling hands were placed over my heart. He grinned at yet another successful attempt at scaring me.

The definition of being a good friend isn't valued because of money or what you could give the person. True and stable friendships exist when you aren't easily offended by one another. It's also when you have to support each other in love, even when you slap the living daylights out of them.

I sat upright and brushed the dirt off my jeans. Jeremiah's cheeks were bright red from his nonstop laughter. It wasn't hard to make him look like a tomato.

"Your dad asked for some extra help, and I heard your mom's cooking afterwards, so I accepted." He rubbed his stomach as if he were already starving. "Lily and Amelia are out having girl time."

He has told me many times that Lily overworks herself and does so much for other people, but barely anything for herself. So whenever his wife treated herself, he looked like he had won the lottery.

I turned around to put the orange squash in the back of my truck. Instead of helping, Jeremiah just watched me, which always meant he wanted something.

"What do you really want, Jeremiah?" I mumbled as I walked back and forth from the truck to the wooden raised bed.

There was way more than I had originally thought. And I could only imagine how much fruit there was on the fruit trees.

I don't even need to go to the gym anymore.

"You're crushing hard, man." Jeremiah acknowledged.

I placed the last load in the back of my truck and turned around, my arms sore. My shirt was completely soaked with sweat and dirt.

I need a long, hot shower after this.

"No, I am not. She just walked back into my life."

I know better than to fall in love with a girl that I haven't forgotten about for the last 10 years.

He mimicked my stance. Jeremiah's eyebrows furrowed closely together. "I know it might take a while for you to agree with me, but it's true, Mathias. May I remind you of all those late nights?"

Endless phone calls and late nights where we would talk endlessly about my emotions. He knew me from the inside out and knew everything I have ever felt toward Amelia.

He always had a listening ear, and after every conversation he would always say, *"If it was meant to be, it will be."*

"What has Lily turned you into? You're such a romantic now." I shoved his shoulder as I walked past him.

"That's my job as your best friend. I need to prepare my speech for your wedding." He teased again.

He did not.

I turned around and gave him a deadly look. With each slow step I took closer to him, he took one back. His hands slowly lifted above his head as if he were surrendering. Right before I took another step, he dashed away.

I rushed after him, my boots stopped me from running full speed. Jeremiah would look over his shoulders every few seconds.

"You're too slow."

"Catch up, old man."

When I got close enough to him, I tackled him to the ground. He struggled to set himself free and when he went to yell, I covered his mouth with my hand. Seconds later, I bit back a yell when he pressed his teeth into my hand.

I hissed but I wouldn't give in. We were almost the same height but I had more muscles then he did which gave me the advantage.

"Dude, take that back." I declared.

We both go to the gym together but I do it more often than he does. He did it to keep his body in shape for his wife. I did it because my job demanded it.

It always worked to my advantage because I always beat him in any sport. Football, soccer and even wrestling. Jeremiah has made it his personal goal to beat me in something but that day still hasn't arrived yet.

"Never. I believe in fate and destiny." He yelled as he struggled to get out of my grasp.

"What has Lily done to you? How many romance movies have you watched?" I finally got off him because I couldn't do it anymore. We were no longer college boys who had the energy of a kid. I was old with wrinkles and an aching back.

The ripe age of 27.

"Don't ask. I lost my man card since I married that woman. And I ain't complaining." He put his hands up and surrendered and wiggled his eyebrows like a fool.

Ever since he married Lily, which was about two years ago, he changed. The old people of Love Creek always said that you change because of the people you hang out with. I never really believed that until I saw Jeremiah and Lily together. In the past, Jeremiah hated romance or anything to do with passion. Now, he always watched the latest romance movie with Lily while they had face masks on.

WE WORKED FOR A FEW HOURS UNDER THE scorching sun that shone above us. I could feel my skin already toasted and slightly burnt from the heat.

Sometime during the day, I had abandoned my t-shirt. I couldn't stand the feeling of a tight shirt that was soaked with grim and dirt as I worked.

As soon as I get inside the house, I am going to take a long shower.

We quickly put everything back right after my momma called us for dinner. We competed in everything, and putting away the gardening tools wasn't any different.

Once I parked the truck in front of the house, I turned off the engine of the truck. Jeremiah got out of the car first but was kind enough to wait for me. Before we stepped foot inside the house, Momma loudly announced, "Take off your boots before walking into my house, boys."

She popped her head into the living room and gave us a stern look. Her eyes fell to our dirty boots and then to the freshly mopped floors.

"Sheesh, and I thought that this only happened at my house." He mumbled under his breath.

"I heard that!" Momma yelled back.

I chuckled at Jeremiah's stunned reaction. My momma had the hearing of an eagle; she could hear a pin drop from miles away.

Jeremiah and I sat side by side and untied our books on the porch. My cowboy boots were holding on by a thread; *literally.*

I have used it for the past 5 years and never gotten a new one or thrown it away. I didn't like spending money on myself because I felt like it would be a waste of money, but now, it was necessary.

It might just be me overthinking, but I think I can feel the floor underneath my shoe.

"Good evening, Mrs. Anderson." Jeremiah said as he waltzed into the kitchen with the biggest grin on his face. He pressed a gentle kiss on her cheek before giving her a hug.

Quickly, I ran up the stairs and into the bathroom. My wavy hair looked like a bird's nest. My brown eyes were dull compared to the dark circles underneath.

I need a shower.

"I need to take a shower." I yelled into an empty hallway.

No one answered me, which meant they were too busy talking or had stepped outside.

Here, we had limited hot-water usage per day of hot water. It wasn't so easy to heat water and have it available whenever we wanted. So ever since we noticed that problem, we established shower and water usage.

I turned on the faucet in the shower and let myself enjoy a steamy shower today. Most of the time, I took a long cold shower to restore the sore muscles, but today I needed something to relax me. Hot showers were a present to myself. As the water trickled down my head, shoulders, and chest, I closed my eyes and let myself feel everything.

I allowed myself to feel every water droplet that ran down my body. The masculine scent of my shampoo ran down the sides of my head.

When I finally opened my eyes again, I felt like I was a whole new person. Quickly, I hurried to shut off the water and put on my clothes.

Lying in my bed right now was way more than tempting.

As I strolled down the stairs, small whispers came from the kitchen. Instantly I knew who it was.

"What are you talking about?" My eyes drifted from my parents to Jeremiah.

I knew they were talking about me, and I was partially afraid to know what.

I don't trust Jeremiah with my parents when I ain't present because I don't know what he will say. He is a very dramatic person who exaggerates everything.

"Us, oh nothing. We weren't talking about anything. We were talking about- about." My mother fumbled over her words.

She's nervous, I could tell by the way she fumbled over her words and the way she fiddled with her hands.

"Sure." I looked at the three of them once more before my stomach rumbled again, "Can we please eat?"

AMELIA
CHAPTER 8

"So what do you want me to do?" I asked her as she showed me around the cozy bakery.

It was absolutely stunning and looked like you were inside Paris. The display cases were filled with desserts that I had never heard of before but looked like mini bites of heaven. Old pink wallpaper covered the walls. Wooden tables were strategically placed around the space. Pink and floral wall decor decorated the walls.

It was perfect in every way. People sat down on the benches while they did their work. Others had lunch or coffee dates. Of all the people, one family caught my eye. They were in the back corner and were laughing at the little one, who had just eaten a donut and was covered with chocolate. My heart warmed and tingled at the sight. Something inside me shifted at that sight.

I want what they have.

Lily mentioned several times that Love & Sugar was hiring, and I finally decided to check it out. She wasn't the owner, but Lily assured me that the owner was a close friend of hers.

She said that since it was getting closer to the holidays. Each day got busier than the last. Orders were already being placed for Christmas, Thanksgiving, and birthdays. I could see in her eyes that she really wanted me to work with her, and with the amount of begging she did, I caved in.

"Haven should be here somewhere. She is the biggest sweetheart, and I know you will love her." She flashed me one of her big, bright smiles.

Lily wore a pink blouse with cream-colored pants. An apron was securely tied around her waist. Her dirty blond hair clipped away from her face.

When we had reached the end of the tour, she turned around with a clipboard in hand and continued chatting about all the minor details I needed to know. We were in the middle of the clean kitchen. It wasn't big enough to fit many people, but it was perfect for this bakery.

"The supplies will arrive later this evening. While you wait, could you knock some stuff off this list?" She extended me a small piece of paper with her neat cursive handwriting on it.

I glanced over it quickly before nodding and heading to work. I didn't really get training, but this shouldn't be too hard, right?

When I turned the corner, I finally noticed the mess that the customers had left behind. Napkins on the floor, crumbs everywhere, and juice spilt, yet no one had the courage to clean up.

Have I ever had a job? No.

Do I think I am built to work in a bakery? Not at all.

Is it similar to cooking at home? Maybe, I have yet to figure out the answer to that question.

But do I have to do it anyway? Yes.

The trash bags were twice my size, and the dishes seemed endless. There were few tasks on that list, but each seemed to take me about a decade to complete. I had been here for a few hours and spilled water, coffee, orange juice, and trash on myself.

The perfume I sprayed on earlier mixed with other smells. My stomach turned and hurled at the scent that lingered on my body.

I did not look my best. Also, I figured out that today was going to be a very long day.

As I walked past a body mirror near the bathroom, I gasped at my reflection. My hair looked as if it had been dunked in oil. I threw it up in a bun in hopes that no one would notice.

I didn't know that the first day was going to be this hard. I don't know if it's because it is my first job or because I am genuinely bad at working.

How can someone be bad at working?

Whatever the reason, Lily deserved more credit that I gave her. The fact that she does this and enjoys it blows my mind.

I heard the truck pull up from the back and rushed to tell Lily that I would be outside helping.

Totally not running away from any further cleaning.

When the doors revealed who had brought the supplies, my breath stopped. The man I have been trying so hard to forget stood before me. Mathias leaned against his truck and looked in my direction with the biggest grin on his face.

He looked at me as if I had been caught-handed. Then I remembered what I looked like.

A wet rat.

A rat that was left out in the rain — and by the grin on his face, it was funny. Probably not in a good way, which made me slightly more embarrassed.

My body started to get hot, and even though I couldn't see my cheeks, they were definitely a bright pink color.

Mathias laughed before he cleared his throat and tried to make a serious face. For the record, he failed miserably, "Tough day?"

I pretended to roll my eyes. "No, I can do this in my sleep. Super easy." I made sure I drew out those last two words to further prove my point.

He laughed once again, his hand gripped onto his shirt like his stomach hurt from how hard he laughed. His voice boomed off the walls, and it seemed to echo off the walls and trees.

When his laughter finally died down, I decided to change the subject. "Hey, do you know where Lily is? She asked me to drop these off." He pointed to the back of his truck. It was filled with crates of ingredients and new machinery for the shop.

"She's inside but asked that I help instead." My hands were stuffed into my pockets as I took small steps closer to the truck.

Endless crates of vegetables like pumpkins, corn, and other ingredients were inside wooden crates. Two pastel blue stand mixers stood beside the crates.

He nodded and then started unloading crates off the truck and handing them to me. With each crate he passed down, our hands brushed against each other for a second. A tingling sensation would erupt on my hand with every interaction.

Every moment or so, I stole glances to look at his face. Mathias's face was scrunched up, which indicated his concentration. He released a big breath after every heavy box. The boxes multiplied every time we took one down; *How many boxes were there?*

When the silence grew uncomfortable, I asked the first question that popped into my mind. "So how's your mum?" He handed me the last box before answering.

"She's better than ever, and how are your folks?" He asked.

I was glad that he was more focused on the task he was doing than on me.

I shifted, uncomfortable with that question. It's been days since I last talked to them. I didn't know how they were or what they were doing. My mom completely blocked me on everything, she truly didn't want anything to do with me.

"I wouldn't know." My eyes gazed down at my sore feet to try to avoid eye contact. I could feel his gaze steadily on me for a few seconds before he continued on.

He hummed a response and turned around to close the back of his truck before turning towards me. "Well, that's it." He used the back of his hand to wipe the sweat off his forehead. "Tell Lily that there will be more soon, and if she needs more pumpkins, they will be ripe soon."

"Sure thing." I responded, balancing on the back of my heels.

He continued to look at me, and when I looked up, our eyes instantly connected. I could finally see those brown eyes in full detail. They looked like a small painting. Full of detail and of love. Full of affection and knowledge. His eyelashes were the perfect length and framed his eyes so well. Mathias didn't have a single flaw to me; *he was an angel.*

I remembered the days and the hours I used to spend just trying to capture them in a painting. Oil paints, acrylics, yet nothing could ever capture a fraction of the beauty in them.

I've always been mesmerized by them. They looked like melting chocolate over ice cream or hot chocolate on a cold day.

His voice broke the silence and brought me back to reality. "See you soon?"

"Of course." We release a breath in unison, a small spread across our faces. His dimples and the way his eyes shone when he smiled were amazing.

He just walked into your life after ten years, and you're already memorized by him.

Talk about being desperate.

Somehow I convinced myself that I wasn't desperate. I simply recognized once again what captured my heart all those years ago. Although I don't think I could ever forget. No one forgot about the things that made you fall in love with a person, even if it was many years ago. Even if we weren't in love anymore, I would always be attracted to them.

I stayed outside until he drove off, and let the sigh that I had been choking on. My cheeks instantly heated when I reminded myself of what I looked like.

The front door of the bakery opened and closed several times. Voices of people filled the bakery, my chest instantly tightened. I didn't know how it could get any busier than it had and I definitely wasn't prepared.

I downed a few more pills and prepared myself for another bath of liquids.

WHEN LILY LOCKED THE FRONT DOOR AND TURNED the sign to say *'close'*, an instant sense of relief went over me. The only thing I looked forward to was my bath and bed.

After we checked the entire bakery, we grabbed our purses and headed towards the car. Lily tried to start a conversation, but my expired mind couldn't process anything.

"Don't worry, you'll get used to it." Lily tapped her hand on my shoulder and let out a small chuckle.

The moment my eyes looked at the fluffy bed before me, I had to restrain myself from throwing myself on it. The only thing that kept me from doing that was the grime that had dried on my body and the greasiness of my hair.

"I am going to take a quick shower." I yelled from the entrance of my room. Lily replied with a faint answer from the kitchen.

All tension released from my bones the moment the hot water touched my body. The bathroom smelled of lavender and eucalyptus from the essential oils. With each deep breath, my body relaxed even more. Every breath made me feel like I was walking on the clouds.

After much debate, I wrapped a fluffy white robe around myself. Lily was letting me borrow it until I could afford my own things. Each slow brush stroke untangled my chestnut brown hair.

I feel like spaghetti.

I waddled into the bedroom, small water droplets

dripped from my hair and onto the floor. After several seconds, a suave aroma of pizza slowly intensified in my room. My stomach grumbled at the scent. Quickly I rushed to put on some grey sweatpants and an old boy band t-shirt.

By the time I got downstairs, Jeremiah had gotten home and was kissing Lily with his arms wrapped around her waist. He whispered something in her ear that made her chuckle uncontrollably.

I wanted that.

And truly I did, but I always thought of it like gold. It was difficult and rare to find.

Maybe I found true love but my spoiled self threw it away too soon before I could see the blossoms.

Maybe Braydon was the one?

Maybe he just hurt me because I hurt him too?

I pulled myself together and cleared my throat to indicate that I was there. When they saw me, Jeremiah moved to the sink to wash his hands. His eyes constantly glued on Lily. You could see the love in his eyes and the way he was obsessed with her voice.

"Hey." Lily greeted in a cheerful tone.

"Hey." I replied as I slipped myself onto the island barstool.

"So, are you ready for pizza and game night?" Lily questioned with two cups of wine in her hands and a big bright smile that showed off all of her pearly white teeth.

She giggled like a schoolgirl, unable to keep her excitement contained. Bags of candy, bowls of popcorn, and boxes of pizza on the table. She had prepared everything in the blink of an eye; Nothing stops a woman from eating her snacks.

"I am only here for a slice of pizza and then I am gone.

My bed is calling my name." Jeremiah said before shoving a slice of pizza in his mouth.

Lily gave him a side eye. And without having to say a word, her gaze expressed everything.

"You know what, I suddenly don't feel tired anymore. Maybe we should watch a movie too!" He said with a nervous tone.

The moment he looked at me with a scared expression, I couldn't hold it back and burst out laughing.

I continued to giggle as I opened the box of plain cheese and pineapple pizza. The cheesy glory melted in my mouth and the flavors were immaculate.

Everything tastes better when you're hungry.

Pineapple on pizza is underrated. It is like a salty and sweet mixture, nothing beats it. Every bite of pizza was like a bite of heaven.

As we settled down and picked our snacks, we debated which game we were going to play. There were several board games and card games, but nothing beat UNO.

"UNO!" I yelled loudly. My last card was hidden beneath my leg. It was unfair we were playing on a glass table because as soon as I was close to victory, Jeremiah and Lily would team up against me.

They said I am very competitive and ruthless but that depends on who you ask.

Once Jeremiah placed his card, I could place mine.

Both of them signed in unison. All their cards spread on the table to count how many points each player had.

I leaned back with the biggest grin on my face, "It feels so good to win."

"You know, I let you win, Amelia." Lily said with sarcasm in her voice.

"Yeah sure, you always looked at my cards and always tried to hit me with a plus two or four. Great sportsmanship." I giggled.

Lily's head was leaning against Jeremiah's chest. His arms were wrapped around her waist, his lips pressed a gentle kiss on her forehead.

"Can you two please stop being love birds?" I pretended to be disgusted. I felt like a kid watching their parents act all loving in front of them.

They glanced at each other. A small smirk formed on their faces. "Sure. On one condition, you let me and Jeremiah set you up on a blind date."

My eyes went wide at her comment. I couldn't believe she just asked that. "Two things. One, why and two, no." I crossed my arms across my chest.

Their eyes communicated something and that made me nervous.

What were they planning?

"Ok, how about this. We play another game." Lily looked If you win, we will never be all lovey dovey in front of you again," Lily grinned. "But if I win, then you go on a mystery blind date. We will decide it by a game of your choice."

A part of me feels like it wasn't going to be a mystery blind date.

My stomach turned into a mix of emotions. Slightly nauseous from the greasy pizza and buttery popcorn. I hadn't eaten pizza in a long time, and the more I sat there, the worse I felt.

The food mixed with the emotions and left me completely paralyzed.

Why if I lost the game, then what?

Despite what my mind told me to do, I agreed. "Fine. My game of choice is Jenga."

Mathias
Chapter 9

"But why?" I narrowed my eyes at Jeremiah, who appeared at my house without any warning.

For ten minutes, he kept asking me to go on a blind date. Jeremiah is the most random person you will ever meet.

"I know this girl, and she's a good friend of mine," His eyes and smile slightly dimmed. "And she went through a nasty breakup and needs someone to brighten her life. It's only one night, and I know she's your type." He wiggled his eyebrows up and down.

I forgot to add that Jeremiah is way past hopeless romantic. Romance flows through his veins, and that's all thanks to Lily.

"Like you know what my type is." I huffed.

I shifted my hat on my head to block the blinding sun. He was losing his patience, which I loved to do. Jeremiah constantly annoyed me and this was my turn to do the same.

"Can you please agree with my awesome idea or can you just agree with my awesome idea?" He scrunched his sour face and shifted his weight to his other leg. His foot constantly tapped against the dewy grass.

"I want to know your definition of awesome." I questioned him.

Jeremiah was smart most of the time, I had to keep the guy humble. I still wonder to this day how we are best friends and I still haven't gone insane.

He tried his hardest to give me puppy dog eyes, "Could you please, for the sake of all humanity, go on this blind date for the sake of a special friend?"

I also keep forgetting to add he's very dramatic.

He was trying his hardest to do puppy dog eyes. All I wanted was to laugh. His hands were right underneath his big baby pout.

I dragged my hands down my face and accepted my defeat. He would never let this down until I said yes, "Fine, when is it?"

I knew that the only way I was going to keep him quiet was to give in. Even though Jeremiah was very annoying, he was also super persuasive.

"Tomorrow at seven," He rubbed his hands together like a mad scientist. "I will pass you the address tomorrow."

Jeremiah ran away before I could even protest.

Great, I am going on a blind date that my crazy best friend set me up on.

Where would I be without him?

I CONTINUED WORK FOR THE REST OF THE DAY. And right before the sun began to set, I hopped onto my Morgan purebred horse.

She was such a beaut, and I loved her so much. One of my oldest horses but the most special one. Her dark colors glistened in the late sunlight. Her evenly paced walk gave me a moment to relax.

The beautiful sunset in all its glory left me completely breathless. The pinks, purples, yellows, and oranges mixed in the sky, created an unmatched hue.

A perfect perfection.

It was therapy for my soul at the end of a hard day. A gift that I didn't need to pay for, but was worth more than money and riches.

After years, it finally dawned on me that I had to take care of myself as much as I did with others.

Even if it's hard and I feel like I don't deserve it, I need to try.

Nightfall soon came, and another level of beauty fell upon the earth. One star shined brighter than the other. The moon glistened in the midst of the darkness. A dark blue and purple sky complimented the celestial elements.

It was gorgeous and beautiful in every way. Nothing on this earth could compare to this. Not a single artist could compare to what God had created.

"What am I going to do, Sky?" I whispered to her as my fingers ran through her long dark brown mane.

I knew she couldn't respond, but she gave me so much company. She gave me company when I felt alone. She continued to munch the grass on the floor, unfazed by me.

My hands were underneath my head to give me the best angle to see what I adored. The sky and all its splendor constantly reminded me of two things: God and Amelia.

THE MOMENT MY BODY WAS COMPLETELY RELAXED, where there wasn't a single heavy thought in my mind or a burden on my shoulder, was when I finally put Sky back in her stable.

With small steps, I slowly strolled back to our farmhouse style ranch home. Each step gave me another reason to be grateful. The constant memories always filled me with warmth.

Our red and white barn home had been hand-built with a lot of love from family and friends. Light grey smoke poured out of the chimney. It infused the air with a burnt wood smell which I had grown to love.

Before I even stepped on the front porch, a big dose of fall overwhelmed me. The moment September arrived, we used cinnamon and cloves non-stop.

AND I KNEW MY MAMA BAKED ANOTHER FALL treat. If I knew her well enough, there were a few fall scented candles burning in the kitchen. There never was a moment that a candle wouldn't burn or a simmer pot wouldn't boil.

In my mind, I could already hear my momma's voice yelling at me, *"You better not step on my freshly mopped floor with those dirty boots."*

My parents never stayed up too late, their snores in the distance gave them away.

This house was built with love and care, but it wasn't built by professionals. Each part of the floor had a special type of creak.

My parents were dead asleep but never once did my sweet momma ever forget about me. She left my dinner plate in the microwave and a note on the counter in her delicate cursive writing.

My little stubborn mule,

You work your butt too much and don't let me spoil you. Eat this plate of food, and don't forget to take off your dirty ol boots.

I mopped the floor, I better not see dirt on the floor.

Love ya,

Momma

I chuckled because it was like I could hear her voice as I read it. A small smile on my lips, my heart warmed by the love my parents had for me.

I prayed a quick amen over the food. When I opened my eyes, my stomach grumbled. It's been hours since I last ate, and it wouldn't be long before I devoured this food.

Momma was a classic southern woman. She baked beans, rice, chicken, and green bean casserole. I was never a particular fan of casserole, but don't tell her that.

Over the years I have concluded that southern women will put more on your plate if they find out you don't like something.

"I put sweat and tears into the food and you better eat it or I will shove it in your mouth." Momma said with the biggest grin on her face.

"But momma it's not good." I grumbled underneath my breath. My fork pushed the food around.

Even if I didn't like casserole, my momma's casserole was the only one I could eat. She added something that made it different; *maybe it's motherly love.*

Simple dishes like this made me feel young again, before problems and adult life entered the conversation.

WHEN I FINISHED, I LEANED AGAINST THE WOOD chairs in the dining room and sighed.

Someone was going to have to roll me to my bed.

I gently took off my hat and grabbed the small picture I shove between two layers.

It was an old picture and you could tell by the creases in the paper and the faded color. The creases were proof of how much I love this picture. It might just be a picture to some but to me it's a piece of my heart.

I had the biggest smile on my face. My front teeth had just fallen out. Back then my family would call me an open window. I hated it but mamma told me it wasn't rude. I never believed her when she said that.

In front of me there was a small birthday cake. Carrot and pumpkin cake, maybe from ingredients we planted and grew. Momma always strived to bake everything herself. If she could make it herself, she would.

I remember that birthday like it was yesterday. She took hours to make the cake. Her face scrunched up, concentrating on writing *"Happy Birthday"* with orange frosting. It wasn't perfect but nothing could ever be better than something homemade.

I was seated on a chair. My eyes glistened with happiness with everyone surrounding me. Big smiles and grins on each face. And my best friend sat right beside me. Her eyes stayed on me, never breaking contact. She rarely smiled because it's when her parents began to forget about her.

And while they forgot about her, her smile kept me going every day.

Amelia Jones' smile kept my heart going and my mind running. Reality always tried to remind me about the moments we messed up but we were children.

We were bound to make mistakes.

Our arms were linked together. Her head rested against my shoulder, bright pink cheeks on her beautiful face. My heart warmed every time I glanced at this photo. All I wanted was to see her smile like that again.

There wasn't anything I wouldn't do to go back into the past. Go back to the good days.

I slipped the picture back into my hat. The warm water ran over my hands as I washed the plate. Every step released a shock through my body. Every muscle screamed in pain and agony.

All I wanted was sleep.

After I took a quick shower and laid in bed, all the tiredness left my body. I hated when that happened because it allowed me to overthink.

My mind raced. It ran a million miles per hour, leaving me feeling like I was all over the place. Events replayed in my mind thousands of times. I beat myself up for things I could have done better and things I couldn't control.

That night was the death of me, I reminded myself.

That night was when the old Mathias died, along with all the hope he ever had.

My heart pounded faster and faster. My stomach grew cold and unsteady. That day was crisp and clean in my mind; a night full of pain and suffering. It was the night that everything changed, that I changed. A day where someone asked me to become someone I wasn't.

My momma always told me to forgive and forget, but how can you forget something that hurt you and changed you? It didn't just mess with the surface, it messed with the roots of my soul.

It forever became a part of me.

"BUT WHY DO YOU WANT TO BREAK UP WITH ME? I have done everything you have ever asked me to do." My heart twisted with the words that came out of my mouth. "I have given you the most precious things. What more do you want from me?"

"You are so, so...." Brittany had a look of disgust.

"So what, Brit?" I scowled at her. She had a special talent to make me impatient.

"You're so religious!" She finally shouted the words I had been waiting to hear. "You save yourself for marriage. You won't get a proper job-" Brittany mumbled useless reasons as to why she didn't want me anymore.

My ears burned and my heart raced uncontrollably, "And what is a proper man's job to you?" I hissed back. *We were playing fire with fire.* "Is it where I have hundreds upon thousands for you to spend on useless junk? So that you can turn yourself into a real life Barbie and show off to your fake friends the latest designer bag you have. Is that all that really matters to you?"

Her face grew pale, her body frozen still. A horrid expression on her face. Her blue eyes burned with hatred, but not for a single moment did they look away from me.

I was sick and tired of the same hole I dug myself into because of her.

She took a slow step back. Her body shook from the icy breeze. She was crazy enough to wear a spaghetti dress in the middle of winter without a jacket.

What did I ever see in her?

Brittany's eyebrows were scrunched together, small creases formed between them. Her slim cheeks and nose were bright red. Acrylic nails formed tight fists beside her hip. She looked at me like I betrayed her. As if she didn't know who I was.

She had no right to be bitter and hurt.

She always stabbed me in the back. There wasn't an ounce of faithfulness in her bones. I was the one she ran to when she needed money or needed a distraction. And after several months of slow torture, I have had enough of her.

Deep down, I knew the real reason she wanted to break up with me. Everything she said was just the tip of the iceberg.

"I love my parents. I love the earth. I love the outside. And I am not meant for a desk job or a company job that sucks the life out of me." My voice was husky from all the screaming and the yelling.

The pounding drum within my head made it unbearable to keep my eyes open.

I stepped away from her. Leaving as much distance as possible, my arms crossed over my chest. "I know the real reason you're breaking up with me. I know why," It's harder to say it out loud than keep it within my broken heart. "You're breaking our engagement. I know you found a man that can offer you riches and gold," I took another step back. "But just know that it's not worth anything without true love. Know that you have lost me, I gave you everything I had. My love, but that wasn't enough for your stubborn and ungrateful heart. My prayers to the next guy who has to deal with you."

I walked in the opposite direction, leaving her alone in the middle of the parking lot. I let myself quietly cry inside the car. Tears slowly blurred my vision.

I don't care if people say real men can't cry. If this makes me any less than a man, then so be it.

I wasn't upset that she betrayed me. But after all this time of being hurt, backstabbed, and betrayed, it finally had caught up to me. All the pain and denial I allowed myself to live in, came with full force.

When the traffic light turned green, I rapidly blinked away the tears. Even though I didn't have Brittany by my side, a certain level of loneliness inside my soul remained.

Maybe it was because I desired to be loved, but that type of love hasn't found me just yet.

Or maybe the love I needed was beyond anything anyone on earth could ever give me.

THE NEXT MORNING I WOKE UP TO THE SMELL OF caramelized french toast and sizzling bacon. My room was practically above the kitchen, and I could hear the sizzling pops of the bacon.

My momma knew the way to my heart; *food.*

The sun began to peak over the horizon, the sunrise colors illuminated my room.

I fumbled down the stairs, trying to regain my center of balance after sleeping like a rock. My arms stretched above my head, instantly it gave me a wake up call.

"Good morning." Momma sung happily.

She had her pj's still on as she prepared breakfast; *always putting her family before herself.*

I pressed a gentle kiss on the top of her short, chocolate brown hair. Quickly, she turned around and hugged me with full force. Her round cheeks were a light shade of pink, a big smile on her beautiful face. Her arms could barely wrap around me.

Her head gently leaned against my chest, right under my chin. Her head rose and fell to the rhythm of my heartbeat. I wrapped my arms around her, and for a quiet moment, we held each other.

The best type of hug.

I gazed out the window, admiring the new day. The window was covered with a light morning frost. Dew covered the blades of grass.

"What's wrong?" Momma slightly pushed away to look me in the eye.

"Something I have to do thanks to Jer." I huffed out. I woke up with a feeling I couldn't pin point and I knew why. There wasn't an ounce of happiness within me because of the blind date, but I did it to get Jeremiah off my back.

After many years of being friends with him, I learned that Jeremiah can be very annoying when he wants to. Yet he never wanted anything bad for you. All he wanted was to mettle into your life.

She was intrigued by that statement. "Bless his soul, what did he do this time?"

I dropped my head back and breathed in a deep breath. Already prepared for her reaction. "He asked me to go on a blind date. I said yes to get him off my back because he was very determined to get me to say yes."

When she didn't answer, I looked down to see her with a

small smile. A few seconds of silence went by, which gave me permission to tickle her.

Her little frame jumped up. "You little rascal."

She playfully hit my arm. Her breath was heavy from all the laughter. I laughed along with her delighted in her happiness this morning.

She was also the most ticklish woman I have ever met. Just a breath against her skin would leave her giggling.

"You're still that little boy that pretended to be a cowboy while wearing nothing but a diaper." She placed her hand over her heart and sighed.

Her warm eyes looked at me with such warmth and happiness. I knew she didn't look at me like the twenty-eight year old man I was. She treated me like I was still her little baby.

We laughed at my childhood memories. We chuckled at all the times I ran around the house with only a diaper, yelling out loud, *"Faster boy."*

My momma said that she never wanted more children because I was the same amount of work as three. I always tried to imagine what it would be like to have a sibling, but if Jeremiah was a handful, then who said I could deal with a sibling.

She gripped both of my arms. Her lips tried to suppress a smirk but failed horribly. "Whelp, good luck. I have to start preparing everything for the banquet that we're hosting this year. A lot to do and little time to do it." She let out a big puff of air to try to shake off all the nerves. Her waves and curls bounced up and down. A single curl landed between her eyes.

I tucked it behind her ear and gave her a light kiss on the

head. "Don't worry, Momma, you can do anything that you put your mind to."

I believed that with all my heart. If she wanted to build an entire house by herself, she could do it. If she wanted to bake for an entire town in only three days, she could do it. If she wanted to be the next Ethan Hunt, then she could do it.

The soles of my cowboy boots barely hung on. Pieces of fraying leather at the sides signaled the good use I got out of them.

"Dang, I need to get new shoes." I examined them as I carried it to the porch.

My outfit today wasn't any different than the other days of the week. Dark washed jeans, t-shirt, and a cowboy hat over my freshly washed wavy hair. The brim of the hat kept the sun rays out of my eyes. The jeans protected me a bit more than sweats and a t-shirt was more bearable than anything else within my closet.

The list of what needed to get done multiplied as the hours of the day passed.

Did I have enough time to do this?

It wasn't an option to not get everything done. I needed to because it was my mission. My mission is to help my parents and to help those around me. Whatever I needed or wanted could be put on the back burner.

Each morning, I needed to milk the cows. I swear they are best friends because they were glued to one another. They gossiped among themselves, and when I was near, all of them would give me a bombastic side eye.

Today they were surprisingly quiet, and deadly still as I milked them. It was strange because they usually kicked the air and slapped me across the face with their tails.

"What's going on, girls? What happened to y'all?" Something had to be wrong for them to be this quiet. Then I remembered that I needed to call the vet; *remember to ask the vet about this.*

Slowly, to avoid any noise, I strolled around them to see if anything seemed to be unusual. There was no blood or an indication of pain. After I checked each one of them, I scratched the top of their heads. Their eyelids instantly shut as their tails swung side to side.

Strange.

I raced against the clock. The constant ticking sound of the watch slightly irritated me. The constant noise didn't match the slow minutes that passed. Time was against me, I needed it to go faster, but it didn't care.

I rode Sky across the property. My eyes glanced over all the animals to make sure everyone was okay. The longer we rode, I noticed something wrong with the fence. Even from afar, I could see the fallen and broken pieces of wood. It leaned against the floor, hung only by one pair of nails. Scratch marks covered the pieces of wood; *I know who this was.*

An evil minded cow; *Betsy.* She had a knack to try and leave this ranch, and the one thing I did every single day was trying to keep her inside. She acted like this place was a prison; *It wasn't a prison. It was a palace. And these animals are ungrateful.*

Quickly, I rode back to the barn to grab everything I would need. Only a few seconds later, a pre-cut piece of walnut wood and other little things were already in my hand. After years of headaches and lost time, I finally decided to have pre-cut wood. It saved me energy and time.

At this rate, having an iron fence would save me much more money. Who thought one cow could do so much damage?

Before I even could fix the first damage of the day, Betsy was already attempting to escape. Her body still like she complimented how much force it would take to break the rest of the fence.

Honestly, should I just give the freedom she craves?

I sighed because she is a constant headache. I don't know why we keep her, but my dad insists she doesn't give us trouble. He probably wanted to keep her because he never really saw the amount of damage she caused to the fence. I always fixed it before he ever saw it.

"Betsy. For the love of everything holy in heaven, go into the barn right now." She whipped her head around and stared at me. I thought my stern gaze would do something instead, she blinked at me and ran in the opposite direction.

I have to deal with a cow full of attitude.

I sighed and went chasing after her. Sky already figured and remembered Betsy's pattern. This wasn't something new, and riding after Betsy was a part of my day to day schedule. Betsy had absolutely deceiving limbs for an older cow.

At least she gave me an excuse to practice how to lasso a cow. I spun the woven rope in the air and threw it right around her neck.

Inside, my younger self had a small party. After years of practice, I finally started to get the hang of the lasso.

"Heavens, Betsy. You must not like it here, to be trying to leave every chance you get." I swear she gave me the stink eye as she trotted back into the stable. Betsy turned around so that her butt faced me.

That's just low.

I checked my watch again and sighed. All that chasing

made the clock pass too fast. With the little willpower left inside me, I rushed to get things done as fast as possible.

"You better not leave a mess in my garden at the end." My momma spoke that so many times that it engraved itself into my mind.

The lives of several weeds came to an end. They needed to be ripped, or it was going to destroy everything we worked so hard to build.

We were on a tight timeline with the annual *"Love Creek's Fall Banquet."* Each vegetation from here on out was very important and couldn't be wasted. Every fruit had a purpose. Feeding more than a hundred people wasn't easy. All this reminded me of the importance of life and what I needed to strive to do with my life.

This was for something greater than I could comprehend.

Our town wasn't just a group of people who lived in the same area or people who lived their own lives. We were an enormous family, and each one of us had to do a part.

AMELIA

CHAPTER 10

I stayed awake for hours. The heaviness of sleep on my eyelids wasn't enough to drift me to sleep. A constant ticking of the clock added fuel to the fire. Yet the temperature of the room was perfect. Warm, fluffy blankets made it close to impossible to leave. Everything should make me instantly fall asleep, or that's what I thought.

Every time the anxiety built up or the pain in my body intensified, I downed a handful of pills. A mix of painkillers with sleep pills. Nothing worked, which made me want to yell to the ends of the earth.

No peace.

One minute, ten minutes, five hours. Time rolled by like nothing. When slumber finally hit me like a truck, my phone rang non-stop. The day had barely begun so what was so important to ruin the sleep I desperately needed.

What is so important to wake me up before sunrise?

I cursed loudly. "Can it not wait."

I grumbled underneath my breath. Trying to cover the

constant noise with a pillow. My phone constantly vibrated with messages. My phone turned into a thorn in my side.

After a lifetime, it stopped.

Silence.

"Finally." I yawned and made sure that the ringer was silent and the vibrations were off. I needed sleep to conquer the day and nothing was going to stop me.

If aliens were invading the planet, they were going to have to wait until I woke up.

Knock, Knock

"Amelia, open the door." Lily hissed. Her voice was low and threatening; *she probably didn't want to wake up Jeremiah.*

Her hand knocked against the door in a steady beat.

I cursed again and sleepy went to unlock my door. I looked at her, barely making out her face. Even my eyes were heavy with the desperate need of sleep.

I guarantee that there were dark circles under my eyes. My hair felt like a bird's nest, hundreds of knots.

She was unfazed by me and my tired face. After several seconds, I realized her distressed expression on her face.

"What do you want?" I grumbled while walking back to bed. I let myself fall back into the comfort of a pillow and endless fluffy blankets. The soft cotton against my skin constantly called out to me.

She didn't respond, her lips formed a tight line. The moment the door locked behind her, she rushed beside me. Her eyes were frantic and worried.

"I guess you didn't see it." Lily whispered quietly to me.

"If you mean the hundreds of notifications I received before sunrise, then no." I grumbled like a cat. "I haven't really slept all night. Everyone can wait for me to sleep for a few hours."

"You probably should check it though-" She nervously responded.

I knew when she was nervous by the way she bounced her legs and fiddled with her fingers. Lily rarely got nervous. So for her to act this way right now, it had to be something serious.

"Why are you even awake at this time of day?" I questioned her.

I glanced at her and noticed she was now nibbling the side of her mouth.

Oh. Something did happen.

"Lily, you're scaring me." I straightened upright.

I took her hand in mind to help steady her nerves. She gave me the faintest smile. The lamp on the bedside table softly illuminated the room. Lily wore her silk pj's and her hair was braided for bed.

What could have possibly happened for her to wake me up this time of day? What has gotten her so nervous?

Her leg shook rapidly. Worry lines formed in the middle of her brows as she waited for me to look at the notification.

The moment I clicked on the notification, a huge picture of my parents appeared. They had a smile across their faces and wore the classiest suits they owned.

"Lily, I am too tired, lazy, and exhausted to read this. What does it say?" I yawned another time. My words blurred together, unable to speak clearly. Every hair on my body ached and every neutron in my mind was fried.

The words on the screen looked like one long line of

black blobs. I couldn't see anything defined and it aggravated me even more.

She fidgeted with her fingers for a bit before she responded nervously. Her voice trembled at the end of each word, "Your parents got a big account. So they did an interview together. When the interviewer asked who the legacy would be passed to," She hesitated to continue. I nodded that it was okay. With a slow breath she continued, "They said their most trusted assistant. The interviewer proceed to ask what about you, their child-" The moment Lily said all that, I woke up. It was like a heavy dose of adrenaline was inserted into my veins.

I didn't expect them to do such a thing.

"What did they say, Lily?" I pressed on. If I didn't force Lily, she would freeze up and stop talking.

Lily's eyes filled with a deep level of sadness and concern. I knew she was nervous about the way I was going to take it. "They said that they didn't have a daughter. Everyone knows that's a lie but no one asked further questions."

For a moment I felt numb, out of this world and out of my body. My heart twisted with rejection and agony. The hairs on my arm stood up, a cold chill trailed across my skin.

It's one thing to be rejected by your parents alone. It was a whole other thing to be rejected in front of the entire world. No one on the face of the earth could prepare you for that feeling. A feeling of desolation. A feeling of void.

No worse feeling than being disowned by your own birth parents.

It's not like I didn't see it coming but it still hurt. It was like a knife passed through the middle of my heart. That level of rejection couldn't be comprehended, yet I didn't cry.

Not a single tear ran down my face. Not a single yell of sadness left my lips.

Maybe I had become numb to this?

This only proved the point that they never cared about me. They chose fame over family. Money over love.

"Is that it?" My voice came out weak and small.

She hugged tight. Her arms wrapped around me like a big hug, not letting me go for a second. "Oh, Amelia, I am so sorry. This is far worse than what I thought it was.

She cried because of compassion. She cried because she was one of the very few people who actually cared about me.

We sat there for several moments without saying a single thing. Her compassion and love towards me was worth more than gold or riches. Our friendship gave me a reason to keep going. And even if she didn't do anything wrong, she kept apologizing over and over again.

I believed every word, and didn't doubt a single thing she said but I didn't want her pity. I didn't want her to be my friend because she felt bad.

"I am not your friend because of this." She pulled away from the hug. "I am your friend because Jesus taught me to be. I believe we are in each other's life for a reason," A small smile on her lips. "And I wouldn't trade this friendship for anything.

It's like she could read my mind.

Being rejected by my mom and dad, well-I don't even know if I should call them that anymore. At that point, I didn't even know what they were to me anymore. Everything turned into a constant headache. Constant fear of being betrayed and rejected by someone else. Every person that I didn't think would hurt me, always did. Now, I have little faith in people. Not having affection and faith felt like a safe place because you didn't expect anything. I didn't need to have expectations.

"I need some space." I gave her hand a final little squeeze and let her go. My eyes felt like a dam about to burst open. My body was tired from the emotional impact.

She nodded and slowly walked out but before she closed the door, she looked back. Lily looked deep into my eyes and the silence reassured me that everything was going to be okay.

"They don't deserve someone like you." With that, she locked the door behind her. And as I heard her footsteps fade away, tears slowly and quietly rolled down my face.

Lily's words replayed in my mind over and over. I wanted to listen to the news for myself but when I did, I completely regretted it. Hearing it come from their mouth felt different.

To make matters worse, they smiled while they held hands. I was a distant memory to them. They spoke without conscious of how heavy it was. The way it affected me wasn't something they were going to understand.

It would be an impossible miracle for them to apologize.

They truly cut me off from their life and from everything they built together. I was nothing. I had no worth and no importance.

I have no value.

I grabbed the med bottle that I had grown so used to and downed endless pills and laid on my bed in agony. The bottle had the engraving of my handprints from the amount of times I held it.

My breath got shallow and uneven. The room around me looked like it got darker and smaller. My lungs were unable to breathe the dark and heavy air. My heart pounded faster and faster like it was going to explode inside my chest. Thoughts and comprehension shattered into a million pieces.

I can't breathe.

I can't breathe.

I can't breathe.

I quickly sat up to see if I could get a fraction of air within my lungs. My body went into fight mode. My mind couldn't comprehend anything around me. The weight on my shoulders grew unbearable. Fear and anxiety crept quickly into my mind. Every thought or action overthought to the worst possible outcome.

What was I going to do?

Wasn't the med supposed to numb the pain?

Wasn't it supposed to make me forget.

"Breath Amelia, Breath." I whispered to myself. Trying to keep myself from going insane.

Later today I had a date to look forward to, but even that wasn't enough to make me calm down or get me distracted. I needed to focus on something other than this panic attack. Yet every possible thing didn't stand a chance against the terror.

"What will I do?" Tears puddled in my eyes, blurring my vision. Another level of suffering had a grip on my soul. A circle of suffering that seemed to have no end. I felt like I was walking in the same desert for the last twenty plus years of my life.

MATHIAS
CHAPTER 11

After endless hours, it was finally time for my blind date. I had gotten ready quickly because I hated getting there late. *"A gentleman always has to get on time to help the lady"* Momma taught me as soon as I reached the age to date.

Jeremiah picked a restaurant I was very familiar with. In fact it's one of my favorite places. The owners were close friends with my parents. My parents helped them build this place.

The owners were a sweet old couple that had retired from their desk corporate jobs and wanted to do something different. So they opened a small restaurant together and has been a go to spot for locals and visitors. I have been here before and never once did I think I would be here for a date.

As I strolled in the cozy space, Mrs.Stanford speed walked in my direction. Her arms instantly reached out and wrapped me in the biggest hug. She was several inches shorter than me which made me have to bend down slightly to be able to hug her.

Tall people problems.

"Hello sweetheart, how are you? How are your parents?" She asked happily. Mrs.Stanford talked a thousand miles per hour, not taking a second to catch her breath. She was one of those people who was a literal fire cracker and I loved that about her. Her personality made her who she was and I wouldn't ever change that, even if I didn't catch half of what she said sometimes.

"I'm good." *But I am really physically tired.* "My parents are well, rushing to get everything done in time." I responded and flashed her a toothy smile.

"Why are you here today?" She scurried behind the desk and looked at the reservations. Her fingers typed at lightning speed.

"Jeremiah set me up on a blind date." I sighed and gave her *"the"* look.

Love Creek had a few hundred people, so everyone knew everyone. Everyone knew Jeremiah. Every single person was a target to play match-making with.

"That goof ball set you up on a blind date?" Mrs.Anderson looked at me like I was joking. "I think I need to have a talk with Lily about how much romance movies they watch together." She giggled at her own joke.

She had a big grin on her face, "Follow me."

Our table had already been reserved, far away from the traffic of people coming in and out of the restaurant.

Great spot.

As I took off my jacket to sit, the nerves started to settle. I haven't been on a date in months; *Did I forget how to act or what to say?*

My right leg bounced rapidly underneath the table. I

made several rips onto the napkin, needing to do something with my hands.

The free bread sticks slowly disappeared as time went on. *Totally not nervous eating.* They were covered with garlic butter, a southern man's weakness. After ten minutes, the bowl was empty. The butterflies in my stomach fluttered non-stop.

My mind couldn't think straight, hundreds of thoughts passed through it. The couples and families around me faded away as I was consumed by my thoughts.

I mentally thought of a list of women that Jeremiah could have set me with. There was no one. Not a single person that I was interested in dating; *What does Jeremiah have up his sleeve?*

Then I thought of one person. Part of me hoped it would be her, but I wasn't going to allow my hopes get too high. After ten years of not being with her, I was more than ready to make up for lost time; *But I need to respect her space and time.*

It was straight out of a movie. I lifted my head to call the waiter, and there she was. Time slowed the moment she walked through the door, a spotlight only on her. *Amelia,* breathtaking and gorgeous in every single way.

All the people and constant chattering faded away in an instant. If beauty were a person, it would be her.

She looked gorgeous, and there was no denying that. Her hair pinned away from her face, showing off her features. It enhanced all the beautiful details of her God kissed face.

"I don't want a son who doesn't know the amount of time a lady puts in to look nice." Momma always taught me to compliment a lady when she took time and effort to get ready for something. *"Be the difference this world needs."*

Her dress hugged her in the right places, showing off her beautiful delicate frame. I didn't desire her that way but for some reason I couldn't take my eyes off her.

Her eyes made immediate contact with mine. A small laugh left her rosy lips. My cheeks burned from how big my smile was. I guess we both expected this without expecting it.

Her smile, I haven't seen a smile more beautiful than hers. "So you're my mysterious date." The corners of her mouth turned up in a small grin.

AMELIA
CHAPTER 12

It was Mathias.

It's not like I didn't expect it to be him because my friends were hopeless romantics. In fact, I didn't know what to expect. All Lily said was, *"You need to do something to get your mind off your problems."* And in a way I agree with her. I needed to turn off my mind for a few hours before I lost all my sanity.

The moment I saw him across the restaurant, time stopped. He looked handsome and that was just a fact. And even if I didn't have an interest in dating right now, I would be a complete fool to say he didn't look fine.

His tall frame hovered over me, making me glance up to look him in the eyes. His white shirt hugged every muscle; *he must have walked out of a romance novel.*

Mathias didn't respond but instead got up and stood beside me. For a moment, he broke eye contact which allowed me to take a deep breath. My knees were about to fail me; *He isn't supposed to have an effect on me.*

It was more than difficult to compose myself.

Don't say anything stupid, but I was bound to do that at some point or another.

He pulled out my chair and stood right behind me. His hands extended outwards, ready to catch my jacket. My breath caught the moment his calloused hands faintly brushed against my skin.

Mathias' spicy and wood scented cologne made the butterflies in my stomach flutter uncontrollably. I closed my eyes and took a deep breath in.

With each breath, I discovered a new layer. Hints of spice, musk, and pepper. I couldn't put my finger on what it was but it definitely made heads turn.

Mathias smelled as good as he looked but I had to step away before it got weird. The moment I sat

He has never stopped being a gentleman. Once was, always is... well in most cases.

As I slipped into the chair, Mathias whispered into my ear, "Hello Sunshine." It rang with his southern charm and accent.

He. Did. Not.

Sunshine was the nickname he gave me when we were children and it always made my stomach flutter.

His eyes locked with mine. His lips in a beautiful smile. Whenever Mathais smiled, his brown eyes shined. They were big, round, and beautiful. One of his best features are his eyes, they captivated anyone who looked at them.

"What are you smiling about?" I questioned. A small smile on my lips could never cover the rose tint on my cheeks.

His dimples made their grand appearance the moment he smirked, "You look absolutely captivating today, Amelia." His gaze completely focused on me. And the longer he looked at me, the more the nerves faded away. "Absolutely beautiful in every way."

His gaze stayed locked with mine for a moment before it fell to the red and white menu in his hands. Everytime he didn't look in my direction, I would look at him for a moment.

Is this a dream or is this real life?

He looked perfect. His shirt complimented his beautiful brown eyes. His hair damp, the curls and waves combed to perfection. He looked dashing in every way. The moment he spoke, my heart came out of my chest. My cheeks instantly heartened when our eyes met again.

Our eyes always seemed to find their way to each other.

"What would you like?" He questioned.

I looked down at the long menu. Everything looked absolutely delicious. From the juicy steak to the lasagna and to dishes I have never heard before.

My stomach rumbled in hunger, but ever since this morning I couldn't bring myself to eat anything. My stomach automatically grumbled when I read all the options for steaks. Yet before I responded to Mathias of what I wanted, I heard Brandon's voice in the back of my mind.

"You're a fat pig. Stop eating and maybe you would actually be pretty." He hissed at me when I was offered a hamburger at a dinner party.

I tried relentlessly to put Brandon in the past but his words were like a dog. They followed me everywhere and never left me alone. It haunted me everyday, evening and night.

Maybe I was fat. Maybe I did need to stop eating to be beautiful.

The painkillers weren't helping at all. I thought it would

give me a bigger appetite but instead, it slowly destroyed it. Maybe that was a good thing and I should be grateful but I don't know what to think.

My mind turned into a constant war field. There wasn't a single moment of silence and peace.

"Just a salad." I managed a small smile to try and seem convincing.

Tonight, my goal was to avoid any questions about my ex or my parents. I knew he wanted to know about them but I wasn't ready. The bruise was still bleeding and deeply tangled with my soul.

He placed the menu on the table and looked at me. Hands crossed over his chest as he examined every part of my face. Mathias didn't seem convinced but I continued smiling. His eyebrows knitted together like he was in deep comprehension.

I hope he can't hear the loud grumbles of my stomach.

I was hungry but wasn't at the same time and it made absolutely no sense. One moment I wanted to eat a cow and the other I could barely swallow water. Something inside me stopped me from eating like crazy.

The waiter strolled to our table. A notepad in her hand and spoke the warmest southern greeting, "Hey y'all. How are you this evening?" Her bubbly attitude was completely intoxicating.

How can someone be so happy?

The moment her eyes fell on Mathias, they went wide as the ocean. A rosy pink color rose to her cheeks, "Mathias. I didn't even see you! How are ya?"

Mathias looked up at her and gave her one of his greeting smiles. A smile that destroyed any sadness near. An attitude that could change someone's day.

There is another reason we don't belong together: He's perfect and I'm not.

I don't even know why I thought that. I wasn't interested in Mathias in any way or maybe that's what I am desperately trying to convince myself of.

Mathias politely answered, "I am good and how are you?"

She lightly giggled at the attention she was receiving. Her fingers played with the edge of the pen in her hand.

"I am good thank you for asking."

The waiter finally turned in my direction, I could tell she forgot that I was right beside her. The waitress' face dimmed when she met my gaze,"Could I please have a bottle of Cabernet Sauvignon? And a small salad with no chicken please and minimum toppings."

Her eyes widened for an instant. Her dominant hand speedily wrote my request. Without a thought, she spun in Mathias' direction. If desperate wasn't the word then I don't know what was.

"Can I have a plate with rice, beans, and a well done steak." His eyes trailed over the words on the menu once again, "On the side could I also have a bowl of buttermilk biscuits and tater tots. I would also like to have another plate of cooked mac and cheese. Some cornbread and a small plate of fried chicken please. That's it, thanks."

There was a bright smile on her face. She looked like she would worship any word that Mathias said.

"Well done, got it. What would you like to drink?" She asked.

Without missing a beat he added onto his long request, "Water with lemon."

"Gotcha." With a blushed grin, her legs speedily walked away to get our order started.

"Isn't your momma feeding you?" I spoke before thinking.

Embarrassed, my hands went up to cover my face.

I don't think I ever paid attention when my teachers said to think before you speak.

He laughed and it filled the space around us, it was sweet yet strong. His nose wrinkled the longer he continued to laugh.

Did I say something funny?

"No," He finally managed to say as his laugh died down. "She has been feeding me too much. I can't even put my foot down or I'll get a stink eye."

I remember Mrs. Anderson. She was the mother that I never had. Always ready to help and serve. She never turned down a moment to put a smile on someone's face. Mrs. Anderson always gave me advice and was the biggest parental support I had.

I COULD SMELL THE FOOD FROM A MILE AWAY. THE air is infused with notes of saffron, cumin, and coriander. Steam erupted from each plate the waiters placed on the table.

"Enjoy your food and please let us know if you need anything else." The waiter beamed before leaving us alone.

I gawked at the food on the table, my mouth watered and my stomach grumbled louder than before. When I looked up, Mathias' eyes were focused on me. My face reddened underneath his gaze.

"Ready to dive in?" Mathias asked excitedly. His hands rubbed together, barely holding himself from diving in.

Mathias prayed a quick prayer of gratitude before we dove into the endless plates of food.

This salad was basic and bland compared. And I wasn't going to say anything because I asked for it. Seasoning and flavor rarely touched my taste buds so flavorless food became the normal.

Between bites of food, he asked the questions I mentally begged he wouldn't.

"So how are your parents?"

I cleared my throat and desperately reached for my glass of wine. "Sore subject, next question."

He placed his fork and knife down on his plate and leaned in closer, "You keep avoiding that question. Why?"

Mathias, never afraid to ask hard questions and keep pushing until he gets an answer.

I shrugged to make it seem like it wasn't that important. "You'll find out sooner or later" My fork continued to play with the last piece of lettuce. "I just don't want to talk about them."

He looked at me for a second, trying to figure out anything he could by my face. The only thing he didn't know was that I became a master at hiding a lot of my emotions.

"Aren't you going to eat it?" I pointed to the left overs with my fork.

Curious why he ordered so much if he only ate half.

I give in. I am weak. I will try to be more firm on my diet next Monday.

"I'm full," He gave me sad puppy dog eyes. "It would be a shame if this all went to waste. Could you be a lifesaver and eat it for me?" A sneaky glimmer shined in his eyes. It took me a second to process and connect all the dots.

I chuckled, "You did this on purpose, right?"

He shrugged and played dumb. "Maybe yes, maybe no, you will never know." He pushed the plate closer to me. A light steam brushed against my skin. My eyes rolled to the back of my head with each deep breath.

Is this what heaven smells like?

I hesitated for a moment. And even from that small decision I had to make, the anxiety began to boil. My head couldn't think straight and the space around me grew thick.

For several seconds, I closed my eyes. Desperately trying to focus on each breath. But with each passing second, it got harder and harder to breathe.

My soul jumped out of my body the moment a hand brushed against mine. Immediately, my heavy eyes fluttered open. The longer our hands touched one another, the more I felt waves of electricity in my hand. His thumb brushed against my cold skin in a slow steady movement.

I closed my eyes for a second and a picture of Brandon came into view. And without a thought, I ripped away my hand from Mathias' touch. His hand stayed in the same place for a second, confused at the abrupt movement.

His smile dimmed as he removed his hand from the table. I don't think I needed to tell him that I am no longer the girl he once knew. The girl before him is broken hearted, in constant suffering, and hanging onto life by a thread.

"I know you, Amelia." *No you don't.* "You're one to eat.

And you can pretend all you want with me and act like you're different even after all these years but I know the true you," The edge of his mouth slightly lifted. "There is still a child deep down inside you. Don't feel bad about eating what your body needs, Sunshine."

He spoke each word with love and care. There wasn't any judgment in his statement. And the way he spoke to me, healed a small part of me.

Maybe you could lose a pound or two, it wouldn't hurt. Maybe just stick to salad, even I would be embarrassed to walk out in public with you.

Braydon's words replayed in mind and destroyed a flutter of hope I felt at that moment.

"It's ok, I'm full." I pushed back the food to him. He had a doleful expression on his face for several moments.

"LET ME DRIVE YOU HOME?" HE BEGGED AS HIS hand extended to the handle of the passenger door. Mathias stood there, waiting for me to go in.

"No, I walked. I'm fine." I took a step back.

"Amelia, please. It's dark and you don't know what is out there." His eyes pleaded. "You will be safer with me." He gestured towards the car.

"I can take care of myself. Thank you for tonight, see you later."

Mathias didn't know the amount of times I needed to take care of myself and stop depending on other people. It was difficult for me to ask for help, especially if it came from a man.

He mumbled something underneath his breath. A

minute later, he stepped into his truck and drove off. Mathias' pickup truck faded in the dark night.

"I need a drink." I whispered to myself and headed to the place that I knew all too well. A place that felt like home away from home.

"Hey John." I greeted the security worker. My hand deep into my purpose, frantically searching for my ID>

"Amelia, you come so often that I don't even need your ID." His laugh boomed in the alleyway.

Before I was immersed by the loud music, John whispered. "Are you alright? You know I am here if you need anything."

I shrugged. "It's okay. I have forgotten what being alright even feels like."

I arrived early the next morning. There were no lights on which I assumed that meant Jeremiah and Lily were sleeping.

I gently closed the door behind me. My head leaned against the door, trying to regain my strength. The world spun in two different directions. My feet were unable to hold my weight. The painkillers and alcohol caused a nauseating feeling.

"So the date went well?" Two voices spoke, breaking the dead silence.

For a moment, my heart left my chest and the strength in my body died.

I hated when they scared me like this.

I cursed under my breath and slowly turned around to look at them. My hand gripped tightly on the knob, the cold metal dug into my skin.

"You are so annoying." I grumbled under my weak voice.

"Cupids are annoying but they are always right." Jeremiah said in between his laughs. He wiggle his eyebrows like a fool.

I bet they were having the best time of their life and were enjoying this.

"But in all honesty, how did it go?" Lily excitedly asked. Lily dashed to stand beside me, her hands gripped onto mine. You could see that she silently begged for any fraction of information.

Well I wasn't going to tell her anything. Plus nothing happened that was worth talking about.

"I have a headache right now. Good night." I fumbled up the stairs.

I could hear Lily sighing, "Amelia, where were you? Were you at the date or drinking?" Lily took a step closer to me, a look of annoyance on her face.

I struggled to speak, my words blurred together. For an instant, I swore there were two Lily's looking at me. Yet the disappointment was inevitably there.

"I went on that stupid date." I hissed at her.

My body almost lost complete balance. Her hands went out to reach for me but I resisted it; *I didn't need anyone's help.*

"Then why are you drunk?" Lily's hands were placed on either side of her hips.

All the little patience in me instantly snapped. "My life is none of your business. Maybe you should leave my life alone and worry about yours."

The color on her face was completely drained. The color in her eyes faded as they welded with unshed tears. Without missing a beat, Jeremiah stood beside her. His long arms wrapped around his wife in a comforting embrace but his fiery gaze looked at me.

This is the first time I have seen him act like this.

"Stop treating her this way. We are only trying to help. God doesn't want this type of life for you."

I couldn't help but laugh out loud at that statement, "This God you speak of is just part of your imagination. I am fine on my own. Look at me." I pointed to myself to try and prove my point. "I managed to live for twenty-six painful years on my own. Without help from a mother, a father, or a God."

I slowly made my way up the stairs and Jeremiah gently said, "But God does love you. He loves-"

I yelled back at him. All the strength that remained inside me shattered into a hundred flames, "Your God doesn't love me. Even if he did exist, he left me a long time ago. I have no one, don't you understand?" My voice slowly died down. The voice cracks barely helped. "Everyone eventually leaves me and you both are bound to leave me as well."

Everything turned dark and distorted. "He hasn't helped me because I am too broken to be fixed. There isn't hope for someone like me. I will ask only one time, stop messing with my love life. Stop poking your finger into something that is still broken."

MATHIAS
CHAPTER 13

I am not perfect.

This entire week, I have felt like I didn't belong here. My mind constantly floated with the stars. A constant unsettling feeling intertwined in my stomach. My exhausted mind replayed every moment from the date over and over again. There was no stop button, a constant torment.

With one look, Momma told me to lay in bed and rest as long as I wanted. She didn't pressure or ask me what happened but knew I needed space to process everything.

My brain didn't want to wrap around the fact that maybe I didn't know her. Maybe Amelia did actually change into someone else.

She felt like a known stranger.

Her expression shifted every time I offered to do something for her. Amelia wasn't the girl I once knew and once fell in love with. The young Mathias was completely broken-hearted over that harsh truth.

Was it me?

Was I the problem?

Questions stirred in my mind and I wanted to know what I could do for her. I wanted to know the reason why she didn't want to share about her parents but my thoughts were interrupted by a knock at the door.

"Come in." I announced, shifting my body into an upright position.

Jeremiah slowly opened the door and closed it behind him. His expression closed-off and not a single word came out of his lips as he sat on the edge of my bed.

Every ounce of me that wanted to joke around with him died because I knew that he wasn't in the mood for that.

"What's wrong?" I sat up, worried for my closest friend. His mouth opened and closed multiple times, his eyebrows scrunched together. Several minutes passed before he even spoke anything.

"What happened on the date?" Instead of sitting, he strolled back and forth in my room.

"Nothing, it was fine. Why, what happened?" My heart pounded faster. My thoughts went a thousand miles per hour, thinking of the worst possible things that could have happened with Amelia.

I know I shouldn't have left her alone.

His eyes darted up to me and with a big huff he finally let it out, "She came back really drunk. Like the level where you can't even tell who she was," He shook his head in disappointment. "To the point where she said rude things that broke Lily's heart."

My heart sank but I was still slightly confused. "Is that unusual for her?"

Maybe she didn't really drink so that one cup of wine knocked all sanity out of her.

He faked a laugh, "That is far from unusual for her,

that's her normal. What is unusual is for her to go a day without drinking."

My body felt like it received a thousand punches at once. An unsettling feeling in my stomach made me grip onto a pillow beside me.

"What happened?" That was the only thing that I had enough strength to ask.

"She came home really drunk. Then said some pretty hurtful things to me and Lily," Jeremiah took an unsteady breath. "She wasn't herself, but I'm worried about her, Mathias," He rubbed both his temples. "You're the only one who can get through to her because you know who the true Amelia is. And right now she is full of pride, hurt, and pain."

That comment alone made me want to cry and I wasn't one to cry all the time. "I tried but she doesn't even trust me. She isn't the same Amelia I used to know. I knew the young Amelia, not the woman she turned into. I don't know what you want me to do."

He sighed, "I don't know either. It would be a miracle for her to change. Not just change but be healed from the torment she has gone through. Now she's in God's hands."

AMELIA
CHAPTER 14

I woke up with a heart full of regret and sorrow and instantly I knew why. My heart remorsed for what I had done under the influence of drugs and alcohol. My head felt throbbed constantly like my mind was going to explode at any moment.

Worse than any side effects, I remembered all the hurtful words I said to Lily and Jeremiah yesterday. I wanted to go back in time and stop myself from acting that way.

And after laying in bed for longer than two hours, I took a deep breath and started getting ready.

THE MOMENT I PLACED THE LAST PLATE ON THE table, gentle footsteps descended the stars. Quickly, I patted my hair and turned to face her. Lily turned the corner, her face swollen from how many tears she shed. When her eyes looked up, her feet locked in place.

"What is this?" She questioned. Her feet took small steps toward the tables, examining everything I had done.

I had prepared some french toast, eggs, chocolate cake and other breakfast foods. In the center was a big bouquet of pink flowers that I ran to the store to buy because I knew how much Lily loved the color pink.

Each detail was planned with careful thought. I was heartbroken with the way I treated her. In no way did she deserve the way I spoke to her.

She's letting me stay at her house for goodness sake.

I knew she was just trying to help like countless other times. This was my fault and it would be immature to blame it on alcohol.

"I made you breakfast to show you how sorry I am." I stepped to the side and stood in the farthest corner. I didn't know if she wanted silence, distance, or to be alone. But by the way she crashed into me with the biggest hug, I knew it wasn't either of those options.

"Don't make me cry again this early in the morning Amelia, it's not fair." Her voice cracked as she sniffled. A small smile on her lips.

"I am really sorry," I pleaded. "You didn't deserve the pain I put you through."

She pulled back and looked directly into my eyes. "I forgive you."

We stood there for moments, not feeling a need to speak a single word. Slowly tears ran down our faces. It was hard for me to cry at moments like these but this time it felt different. It was the first time I felt the aftermath of hurting someone.

When I finally let go, she was already fully back to herself. Her pearly white teeth flashed as she gave me the biggest smile she could manage. "How about you and me eat breakfast and then go for a drive?"

Even though I knew I didn't deserve her forgiveness and the kindness she continued to display, I still took her up on that offer. I knew she forgave me but deep down inside, I beat myself up for treating her that way.

AFTER BREAKFAST, WE DECIDED TO GO DO A BIT OF shopping. The house needed stuff and that was our perfect excuse. For the entire car ride, we barely said anything but the silence brought us a deep level of comfort. It didn't feel forced or awkward but peaceful in a way.

We arrived at the mall in Love Creek in less than thirty minutes. The chill air blew all around us, our noses and hands slightly numb from the cold breeze. The weather that Love Creek was experiencing was a reminder that winter was right around the corner.

In the middle of our silence, my mind thought of a hundred unanswered questions.

Was I the bad one in the relationship?

Was I wrong to leave the relationship the way I did?

Lily was beside me, our pace nice and slow. We enjoyed every breath, every leaf that fell, and I could tell that she was in her own little world.

"Do you think I was the bad one in the relationship?" My voice broke the silence.

It was a question that I felt that I couldn't answer for myself. In my eyes, I only saw what Brandon did wrong. Someone needed to tell me what they saw from the outside because I was blind in this situation.

Lily stayed silent for several minutes, picking her next words very carefully. She knew that I battled with anxiety and overthinking every single thing I did.

Her pace became slower until it came to a full stop before turning to me in the middle of the sidewalk. Her gaze was focused on her white and pink tennis shoes. They had small charms on the side of them and I was surprised they were still clean despite the weather.

Did she think I was the problem?

She took a shaky breath before answering, her voice calm and sweet like rushing waters. Lily approached the topic with care, "I don't think you were the problem but I think the relationship in itself was the problem. He was unfaithful and you were struggling. Two broken people that are together can't heal each other."

We continued walking, our pace slow and steady as I meditated on what she said. The relationship was the problem because there were problems and secrets hidden from both sides. We were both unfaithful in certain ways and didn't treat each other in the way we should have.

"But did I do something horribly wrong? Did I hurt him like he did to me?" I was genuinely curious. Surprised that I even asked her that question because I don't know if I was ready for the answer.

She could tell that I wasn't comprehending, so she gently grabbed my arm and pulled me to sit on the bench. It faced all the small shops in Love Creek. You could see people coming in and out of stores, smiles on their faces, and the joy of the autumn season in their hearts. Kids were having mountains of ice cream even though it was chilly outside. Their lips turned a light shade of purple not having a single care that they were cold.

"How many times did you wish to break up with him? How many times did you think about somebody else? How many times did you wish harm his way? How many times did you sell yourself to other things?" She asked me questions I never stopped to think about. "And it might be a hard truth but you weren't perfect either. He might have hurt you one way but you did in another way." Her eyes were full of compassion like she understood why I did those things but it didn't excuse the fact that it still was wrong.

"Why? Why didn't you tell me sooner or help me?" my voice cracked with emotion.

She explained to me the things she has learned over time. Lily was a Christian and never once did she force me to believe or think the way she thought. I never wanted to go down that path of being forced to do something because someone said so. And for a moment I stopped to realize that Lily has been changing. She has become wiser, smarter, and more loving to someone who has hurt her several times.

What was so magical about the Bible?

How did she find wisdom between the pages of a history book?

She took my hands in hers and started to tear up. Her eyes shimmered with tears, "I haven't said anything about church or religion to you because I knew you were too hurt to listen and you wouldn't care," Lily took a moment to put together her words. "No one can look at you and say you haven't been through the worst part of hell. A part of me didn't want to say anything because I could have lost you forever because of *the* truth," This conversation was doing something to my heart that I couldn't explain. "People in the church fail. A human's natural reaction is to fail and to sin. That's why we need him to heal and transform us. Don't judge Jesus by the way humans display him. We usually display his love wrong but that just proves once again why we need his grace over and over."

She gave my hands a light squeeze before continuing, "Don't judge God for my mistake. He hasn't done anything wrong but I have failed continuously. If I could go in the past and fix my mistakes, I would but then again, my past shows the faithfulness of God."

I nodded and told her that I faintly understood what she talked about. The truth stung but I knew that she meant well and that there was no harm in her words. Another failure of mine that I did constantly, I judged before I asked.

You could at least listen to us, my parents would tell me constantly.

You could at least listen to me and we wouldn't be in this mess, Braydon would yell at me.

I closed my eyes and tried to keep the tears in. I was growing weary of this circle. The same cycle with the same mistakes and the same mess. I felt like I had dug myself too deep this time and I needed to get used to it.

"Anyway, let's change the topic. How is drawing and painting going? Didn't you used to do that?" She was so giddy and excited to hear about my painting journey and I hated to disappoint her.

Months ago, I stopped making art. It was sucked out of me by the negativity around me. The joy, the passion, and the love to create something with my hands was all gone. My parents said that was for babies and toddlers, that I couldn't make a lifestyle out of it. Life would drain all my energy from me.

It was ripped away from me, and now I missed it so much. It's hard to go back to something that I used to love after rejecting it because of the influence of people. I don't know how to go back to something that made me feel like I had a purpose.

"I stopped." I whispered that harsh truth out loud.

She didn't hear the first time and asked for me to speak up. "I stopped."

Her face dimmed and instead of her bright happy smile she frowned. "Why did you stop? You never told me."

"Brandon and my parents sucked the life and joy out of me. They said it was for toddlers and that I couldn't make a living out of it. They also said it was useless and I had no talent," My heart felt like it was reliving those moments. "I got to a point where I got so tired of their hateful words and completely stopped."

She abruptly stood up and extended her free hand to me, "Well lets fix that, shall we?"

I laughed and grabbed her hand. Lily was a living ball of sunshine, always able to turn a heavy day into one filled with joy and happiness. I don't know how she could keep her head up high even when people threw hurtful words at her like I did.

Maybe this Jesus thing could do the same thing for me?

MATHIAS
CHAPTER 15

All week I tried to think of an idea to help Amelia but always would end up with nothing.

With each piece of wood that I shopped, my mind didn't stop thinking. I was so lost in my thoughts, my hands swung the ax in a repeated motion. The wood landed on the ground with a loud *thud* sound. A signal for me to get another piece.

My Pa startled me several times, he appeared out of nowhere and left in the blink of an eye. I told him that I was thinking of how to help Amelia. And all he did was give me a grin and walk away.

My father never judged me and was always supportive of whatever I decided. He always reminded me that I shouldn't try to resolve everyone's problems and that I shouldn't beat myself up when it didn't go my way.

That was one thing about me, I always wanted to help in everything that I could. I wanted to help with things that weren't even my fault and when things didn't go how I planned them, I would beat myself down.

I don't do it on purpose but after I almost lost my Momma and felt helpless in the process, I wanted to do my everything and anything for anyone.

I finished cutting the wood so I moved onto plucking the weeds around the flowers and garden. The weeds grew like crazy and the more we plucked, the more they appeared.

Then I had an idea. An idea that might actually work. These flowers reminded me of Amelia and for a good reason. I remembered all the times I would find a bouquet of wildflowers and Amelia would paint them afterwards. Every time she received a new flower, she said it was her favorite one but then again, she said that about all of them.

I don't think she knew why I got them for her, or the meaning behind them because I never told her. Those flowers reminded me of our secret place when we were children. The one place where we could run away from life. Where all our dreams were only a reach away.

It was a place where we could be ourselves and no one would judge us for it. A place where Amelia didn't have to keep listening to hurtful words her parents threw at her.

It was a small garden in the corner of a park. A place where people barely went to. We were free and there wasn't anything that held us back. A few years ago, the town raised money to clean it up and make it into a magical place for people to walk through and enjoy life. To some people it was something new. To me it was a home away from home.

That's where I will bring her tomorrow.

I knew she was going to love it and that only good memories were going to fill her mind. She might not remember it at first but I know once we sit on *our bench* all the memories will flood into her mind.

Now I just had to plan it perfectly and convince her to come with me.

MATHIAS
CHAPTER 16

It has been a week and a half since I last saw Amelia and my heart twisted and turned every time I thought about our last words. But today I was going to try to change everything. Take our new friendship back to what it once was.

A flood of people came into the church the moment the bell rang. Kids dashed up to me and gave me a hug around my legs. They all said *good morning* in unison. Boys and girls are excited for the holiday season approaching. It felt like they grew inches from the last time I saw them which was last week.

"Hey kiddos! How was fall break?"

"Fun!" They announced in unison before running back to their parents. The moment I turned around, I swore I was dreaming. It felt like it was out of a movie the way Jeremiah, Lily, and Amelia walked towards me. There steps slow and steady, Lily whispering something to Amelia which made her smile.

My eyes locked on Amelia, completely memorized by her. She hadn't even noticed me but I had already noticed everything about her. What she was wearing, to how her hair was, and the way she smiled at the children.

Our eyes finally connected and locked with one another. I continued to look at her as I hugged Jeremiah, but when he quietly spoke in my ears my gaze drifted away from hers.

"Be careful bro. She is brokenhearted and needs someone to hold her. What am I saying? Be that one for her, stop being a scaredy cat." He chuckled underneath his breath before backing away with a small grin on his face.

He stepped to the side so that Lily could hug my parents. He grabbed Lily's hand and walked to greet their other friends. The church was packed with people but my gaze was only focused on Amelia.

"Hello Sunshine." I said with a big smile on my face. I knew that she was still getting used to it again. My heart fluttered seeing here in church.

"Why do you still call me that?" She questioned with her arms crossed over her chest. She pressed her lips together like she was trying to hide a grin. I knew she liked that nickname but didn't want to admit it.

"Why do you blush when I call you that?" The tint on her cheeks grew rosier the moment I asked her that. My dimples hurt from how hard I smiled and how hard I tried to not laugh.

Her honey brown kissed eyes widened as I stepped closer, "Could I ask you a favor after church? I need help with something." I whispered the request.

The corner of her mouth quirked up, "What do you need?"

"Well I guess you are going to find out if you choose to say yes." I knew that she hated surprises but she was way too curious to say no.

Her breath went from still to rapid. Her eyes were beautiful in every single way. There was nothing better and more beautiful than her gorgeous face. And even though I have been told she's broken-hearted, Amelia still holds herself upright.

Even the briefest glimpse into her gaze made my knees weak and my stomach flutter.

"You Mathias, are a very mysterious cowboy. But my answer to your request is yes." She replied and took a step back. That one step back gave me enough space to take a deep breath.

I pretended to give her a mysterious look which made her giggle and it warmed my heart in every way. Her laugh was one thing that I would never get tired of listening to.

I had forgotten that my parents were right behind me. So I don't know how much they heard or saw. "Well I forgot to introduce you to someone. Momma, you remember Amelia."

Momma took a step closer and when she laid eyes on Amelia her face completely lit up. "I can't believe little sugar is here again. Oh my sweetie I missed you so much!" Momma hugged the life out of her and while she was over the moon, Amelia's face slowly turned light pink.

"Ok, Momma, you can let her go now. She needs to breathe." I reminded her because if I didn't she was going to squeeze the daylights out of Amelia.

They both chuckled and in their eyes you could see how much they missed one another. Momma gripped onto Amelia's arms and looked deep into her eyes. Momma has been with Amelia through thick and thin when we were children. Her first day of school, when she lost her first tooth, and so much more. I had never realized till now how she was the mother figure that Amelia never had.

"I've missed you so much, Sugar. We definitely need to catch up on everything." She took a step closer to Amelia and whispered something in her ear. I was right behind her so I still heard everything, "But someone missed you much more."

My cheeks instantly burned with heat the moment both of them looked in my direction.

"Amelia, it's so good to see you! How are your folks?" Pa asked her as he gave Amelia a fatherly hug.

Her eyes instantly dimmed, the edges of her smile dipped, "Well my folks, we don't talk anymore so I can't say."

My parents looked at one another but didn't push the subject. They both knew how hard her life has been and how neglectful her parents were. It felt like she lived mostly at our house. Her parents never really noticed when she was home or not. So she has always been with us at every party, event, vacation, and everything in between.

"Well sugar, it's amazing to see you and you're definitely coming home with us later. I need to feed you, you look as thin as paper." Momma announced with the biggest smile on her face. "But I will fix that right up, stuff you like a tick." Momma clapped her hands, happy that she was going to cook.

Her love language was food and she loved to serve all. She wouldn't let you stop eating until you had to roll yourself on the floor.

Amelia laughed loudly, her laugh brought warmth to my heart. Amelia turned to me, flashed a big smile and strolled away.

When everyone finally sat, the preacher came to the stage and church began. The choir sang a quick hymn before the sermon. The pastor prayed a quick prayer and then jumped into his message. My gaze drifted every few minutes to see how Amelia was taking this.

God please help her. Even if she doesn't believe in you, let her see your unfailing love and grace despite circumstances.

"Today's message is about the goodness of God in the most difficult of times." *Wow.* "A question everyone asks themselves is why do bad things happen to good people," The preacher cleared his throat as he glanced down at his notes. He looked up and continued, "Well John 8:36 says that if we turn to Christ, he truly will set us free. God states multiple times in the Bible that he gives us free will. But-this freedom should be used wisely because what we want isn't what we need most of the time."

From the corner of my eye, I could see that Amelia shifted around in her chair, unable to sit still. Her eyes focused on the pastor and then down at her lap. I wondered what was going through her mind. What was thought about the message so far and all the questions she had. I wanted to answer them but I knew I wouldn't have the response to half of them. I still didn't know the complete truth, there were still questions that filled my mind but I know at one point, God will give me an answer.

The pastor's voice brought me back to reality. "Well, we have the choice to walk in spirit or walk in the will of our flesh. It's not that God wants you to suffer and go through pain." He took a steady breath and glanced at Amelia for a moment. "It's because he gave us free will that when we choose the desire of the flesh, we must go through the conse-quences because of our actions. Free will is our choice, we can't expect God to give the answers on a difficult test when we are not willing to study."

He paced back and forth, looking at the bible in his hands and then back to the people. Everyone was immersed in the preaching. "We aren't any good. Nobody is good but by the grace of God we are made clean and whole. So to be protected, we must do what he wants us to do. Our desires must align with His and when we go through difficult times, He will be our judge and protector because we rested in him."

He gave what felt like a fatherly smile. "Jesus said that we were going to go through trials and tribulations in this life but for us to have good faith in the midst of it because he already overcame the world. Our choices will determine if those trials and tribulations will be easier or harder."

I thought about what he said for a moment. And with each passing day, I realized that we aren't as good as we think we are. If I look back at my life, most of my mistakes were because I thought it was the right choice. I didn't ask God and maybe I could have avoided heartbreak and pain if I would have just waited and asked.

The pastor continued on with the sermon and every word sank deeper into my soul. His words turned into a seed in my heart. My mind slowly processed everything he said.

Not only were questions answered, but new questions formed. It didn't make complete sense to me and the pieces seemed to not fit in my head but I knew that understanding would come with time.

Now the hardest part was to wait to find the answer.

THE CHURCH HAD JUST FINISHED OVER AN HOUR ago. My mind was immersed with the message and the pondering thoughts I had.

Amelia sat right beside me, the wind blowing through her brow hair. A peace came over me with the simple fact that the windows were rolled down and I was driving with Amelia by my side.

When I could, I quickly glanced at her. Amelia's eyes were closed and her head leaned back on the headrest. She looked peaceful until something flooded into her mind and her smile disappeared. Her face dimmed and I wanted to know why but I knew that I shouldn't keep pressing buttons all the time. She had to open back up on her own time and I didn't force her too.

I needed the kid I once knew, that I once loved. I needed the artist that I grew fond of and the person that made me forget problems and life. I needed her to smile every moment of every day. But healing takes time and after the message, I needed to learn to put it in God's hands.

God, please make Amelia come back to me.

AMELIA
CHAPTER 17

We arrived in a small parking lot and I couldn't put my finger on why this place felt so familiar. It felt like a distant yet familiar memory. I looked at Mathias and he had a sneaky grin on his face. He jumped out of the car and jogged to open my door, his hand extended forward for me to take it.

"I feel like I remember this place but I can't put my finger on it." my voice trailed off.

Slowly, I slipped my shaking sweaty hand into his. I hadn't taken my pain meds and my body was reacting. It was like clockwork and I knew it would only get worse if I didn't take my painkillers. Once I forgot to take them for most of the day and I was unable to lift a finger for the next three days.

He smiled at me, "When we get there, you will find out why you remember it. The town did a bit of fixing but it still has the same vibes and feeling." He gave a little shrug at the end.

We walked for a few yards before the memories came flooding in. Fifteen minutes later, I finally realized why it looked so familiar. This was *our* place and I couldn't believe I didn't recognize it sooner. Mathias and I practically lived here all our childhood. It's where we tell each other the answers to our tests. It was the place where we laughed, cried, and chased after one another.

The only person who knew about this place was his momma. So we could be here for hours and hours and no one would notice. My parents never noticed when I left the house, when I slept over at Mathias's house, or even when I was in my own room. They were constantly behind a desk and computer screen.

"Is it-" I asked him, not even finishing my sentence. Words failed how happy I felt that moment. This was a surprise I never in a million years would expect.

His dimples appeared as he took in the sight before us. "It is. It's our place"

Our place. A sacred place where fear and doubt were prohibited.

There were a lot of things that changed, but it still had the same essence. We walked deeper into the garden, surrounded by endless flowers. Each a different size, style, and height. The farther we walked the less I could see Mathias' truck.

There were sunflowers everywhere, they looked like little sunsets. Small golden marigolds looked like miniature suns. Different colored petunias brought life into the space. A different type of peace filled my soul as I walked in the garden. My cheeks burned from how long I held my smile; *There are no words.*

"What's wrong?" I asked Mathias. Focusing my gaze on him once again.

"Nothing." He walked slightly faster and pointed something in the distance, "We are almost there."

He was a few feet away from me which gave me enough time to quickly find the medicine bottle inside my purse. My hands fumbled as I tried to find the yellow bottle. And after much frustration, I found it. My hands sweated profusely as I tried to open the childproof bottle.

I really hate these bottles, I grumbled to myself and internally sighed when I got it open.

Mathias hadn't turned around so I quickly swallowed eight pills. In the beginning, I was only supposed to take three. Then my doctor told me to take one more if it didn't work.

Four more pills wasn't going to do any harm, right?

He turned around and yelled for me to pick up my pace. I was honestly so excited to be there but had no strength in me to walk any faster. Although, I knew the medicine was going to kick in any moment and I was going to run like never before.

When I saw that Mathias had stopped running and had his eyes fixed on something, I picked up my pace. As I approached, I noticed it.

Our bench.

A bench that held so many memories. It held all of our long painful yet beautiful stories. I was surprised to still see it standing after all these years. My mind wondered how many people have shared personal things on the bench over the years.

I carefully sat on it, afraid to break it. The moment I realized it could support my weight, I released a sigh.

It's like I had been brought back to my childhood and for a second, I could feel the child inside me alive again. It's like I got a piece of how I used to be, when life was more simple. And I didn't know how to express it in words, but those memories are what I needed to relax the anxious thoughts in my mind.

The flowers released a light aroma the moment the breeze passed through them. Notes from the marigolds and the aromatic smell from the herbs. There was a beautiful lavender and rosemary bush beside me which made me feel like I had just stepped into a spa. A refreshing and relaxing sensation filled my lungs.

I didn't open my eyes because I wanted to savour the moment. Every breath, every breeze, every crunch in the leaves. Maybe this was the effect of the painkiller but deep down inside I knew this garden healed a part of my broken soul.

"You remember everything that happened on this bench?" Mathias asked beside me.

I blinked several times, refocusing my vision. Giving me a moment to bring myself back to reality. My head and heart were far away, in the middle of the clouds.

He leaned back against the bench and looked at the beautiful view around us. We were surrounded by nature, surrounded by unexplainable beauty. Birds that chirred their own melody. Crushing of leaves that fell from the autumn breeze. This gave me inspiration, desire to paint once again. Yet I knew that you could never replace and replicate something like this.

"Of course I remember our long conversations." *Was that even a question?* "I also remember our laughs and our tears. This was *our* place, where no one knew about it." I spoke gently because my mind replayed all the bittersweet moments.

I turned and looked at him. His dimples are no longer there anymore. Mathias didn't have a smile anymore but he didn't look sad. He looked pensative, deep in thought.

"So many nights we sneaked out and would come here just to talk and look up at the night sky." I couldn't put a finger on the way he said that. *Admiration? Reminiscing? Regret?* "Those memories are what I hold onto the most, they give me hope." he spoke slowly, meaning every word that he said. Maybe this place brought me a level of hope but to him, it meant a whole other thing.

Hope. Such a fragile thing.

MOMENTS PASSED WITHOUT A WORD BEING SPOKEN but neither of us felt the need to fill that space. Just the sounds of the leaves and the whisper of the gentle breeze were sufficient for us.

For a second, I felt like we were our old self again. No adult responsibilities pressuring us to hurry up. A place where we turned off our minds and lived our own world.

"What's one conversation that comes to your mind?" he questioned, curious to what my answer would be.

I chuckled underneath my breath, "We've talked so much, Cowboy. How am I supposed to pick between endless options?" my eyes instantly widened.

I hadn't called him "*Cowboy*" in so many years and now it slipped like I never had stopped calling him that.

Sunshine & Cowboy.

His laughter echoed in the garden. A sweet sound that my soul ached to hear. My heart ached to have his laugh dance on my skin.

"You look petrified," Mathias glanced at me and burst out in laughter again. "I haven't heard that nickname in a while but back to the question."

My body heated with embarrassment because of the nickname that slipped so easily out of my mouth. It felt weird to say it again but at the same time it felt so right.

I replayed all the conversations in my mind but there were too many to count. When I finally came up with one, I shifted my gaze to the sky, unable to keep a steady gaze with Mathais.

It was still bright outside. It wasn't dark enough to see the shining stars but the sky was breathtaking in every way.

"I guess one that I still remember like it happened yesterday was when we were laying on the ground. Our eyes focused on the stars and my mind couldn't process anything.

Confused about my life and a hundred other things. I didn't even need to run or walk, my thoughts already beat the living daylights out of me," Tears blurred my vision because if I could only warn that little girl. "All I needed answered was: why?"

I took an unsteady breath in. My lungs ached with each breath I inhaled. "You were the only person there to help me."

Our eyes connected. Those eyes were stunning. When the sun hit them, they glistened. His eyes always brightened when he talked about something he loved. Someone might assume that he had won the lottery, but in reality all he ever talked about was how much he loved his family and friends.

I never told Mathias this, it was a secret I kept to myself but his eyes were something Leonardo da Vinci would have painted. They were perfect in every humble and beautiful way.

"You said that when God created heaven and earth and He saw my parents, he had to choose someone to come down and be their child," his words were a tattoo in my mind. "You said that God had hundreds and thousands of other people he could have sent but he chose me instead." I continued to look at Mathias, completely captivated by him. His gaze softened, an expression in his eyes that I couldn't pinpoint. I gave him a faint smile and proceeded, "You said that I wasn't chosen because God picked someone random or worthless. He chose me because he knew that I was the only one with enough strength to live this life. God knew no one would have the same values or qualities that I have," *What can other people see in me that I can't even see in myself?* "That this path was going to be hard no doubt, but God knew I was the only one that could handle the pressure."

Mathias smiled, the memory flashed into his mind. "God selected you. It didn't matter about the people who rejected, neglected, or abandoned you. Even if you abandon yourself, God's favor, love, and grace will always outweigh all opposition and fear."

Tears blurred my vision and my heart warmed with those words. And even if I hadn't thought about any of this for the last ten years, it was something that my mind would never forget.

That night, we didn't know that our days together were counted but we lived like there was no tomorrow. No matter what the next day held, we didn't want to regret anything. *I didn't regret anything during those years.*

I always told Mathias that he was wiser beyond his years and he always laughed at me but that night proved him wrong. No one knew the right thing to tell me except him. Maybe Mathias was put into my life for a reason. Maybe what I had convinced myself all these years weren't true.

"You were always there when I needed you and I didn't do it in return." My voice trembled with sadness.

I think that truth was finally starting to settle in. There was no worse feeling than someone helping you in your worst moments and you didn't do it in return.

"I feel like the worst person alive." I never thought I would confess those words to anyone, especially him.

When I was forced to leave that night, my life rapidly went downhill and everything slowly died in darkness. I was locked in the darkness and there wasn't a way out. Mathias was the light that I needed. And even though I didn't want it, allowing my parents to take me away from him was my biggest mistake.

They always said that he was a bad influence. *No.* Mathias only showed me the true path and value while they always wanted me to focus on money.

I kept my gaze glued to my laps and fidgeted with my fingers. Picking at a scar that never completely healed, a habit that I had when I was nervous or anxious. My mind always in constant fear, an unending battle.

A moment later, his calloused hand covered my own. His touch brought a wave of warmth and understanding. I don't know how you could feel all that with just a touch but I could. I focused my eyes on his hands. They had scars and bumps all over but that just made them perfect in their own way. Each healed scar told a story about who he was and how he got here. His hands told *his* story.

What told my story?

I looked up at Mathias, a kind expression on his face.

He gave a lopsided grin, "It wasn't and isn't your fault, Amelia. Don't blame yourself for your parents actions. I know you would have stayed with us if you could."

He gripped my hand tighter, his thumb rubbed back and forth in a continuous motion. "You are here now and that is all that matters. Forget the past, we can't fix that. It's me and you right now. It's only us. Nothing matters in this moment." Mathias spoke with such confidence and belief but I don't know if I was at that level yet.

For me there was still everything to think about. An endless list of things to get anxious over. I knew that it wasn't just my parents fault because look at what I have gotten myself into.

Out of all the problems I have, out of all the suffering I have gone through, the one thing I feared and dreaded the worst was to hurt Mathias again. I couldn't do that. I couldn't bear the thought, so I have to keep myself at an arm's distance. I had to keep space between our hearts as I tried to find myself again.

"Thank you," I muttered. Slowly, I slipped my warm hands out of his grip.

Mathias leaned against the bench. "I have to be the one to say thank you."

"Thank me for what? You're the one who brought me here." I acknowledged and reminded him. There was nothing to thank me for.

If I hadn't paid attention, then I would have completely missed his whispered response, "For being the light in my darkness."

"So it went well?" Lily asked with a shriek of excitement.

When I looked behind, she had a towel on her head, a pink robe, and a glass of wine in both hands. I grinned because it never mattered how tired she was, she would always want all the details.

Jeremiah had his hair pointing in all directions and the biggest smile on his face like he was just offered a big bag of candy. He sipped on his drink in between bites of popcorn.

"Did you kiss?" Jeremiah questioned, his eyebrows wiggled up and down.

They were so annoying yet this is the way they showed you that they cared. I haven't been here for long and they think that I am going to date, marry, and have a child in less than 2 weeks.

"You are so annoying but for your information we did not kiss." Just the thought of me kissing Mathias sent my mind on an emotional roller coaster.

Before I ran up the stairs, I turned around and looked at Jeremiah. "Why do you even care, Jer? You're a man, men don't care about girly lovey dovey stuff."

He laughed loudly, "I know but when you marry a woman who is obsessed with love, Valentine's day, and being a hopeless romantic, it kind of spreads to you. She is contagious but I love her and wouldn't want her any other way."

He gave her a very dramatic air kiss. Lily looked at Jeremiah and the world instantly faded around them.

"Where's your man card?" I asked.

He looked back at me with the biggest grin, "I don't

know but when you find it, you can throw it away. I have fallen head over heels for this woman and I don't want my life to change at all."

Before I closed my bedroom door, I heard Lily's voice whisper outloud, "She isn't drunk today!"

"We conquer a day at a time," Jeremiah responded before they silenced each other with a kiss.

AMELIA
CHAPTER 18

This week flew like a blink of an eye. It was finally Thursday and the bakery finally slowed down for a few minutes. At the end of the day, it's mostly just couples and old people sitting down for a cup of coffee or reading a cozy book.

I was in the kitchen preparing the batter for the pastries that Haven and Lily asked me. It's been a few days since I started and I love this job. Working with Lily is amazing and having Haven as a boss is a huge bonus. Apparently, she has an older brother who plays professional hockey.

My heart leaped out of my chest when I felt a vibration from my phone. I rubbed my hands together to shake off the excess flour and picked my phone out of my apron pocket. My mood dropped to the floor like someone had just poured ice water over me. A dying flame.

Multiple missed calls and text messages.

Ten Missed calls from Mother.

MOTHER

Please call me back

My body froze still as I read that text over and over again, unable to believe her request. My hands were shaky and sweaty. My hands gripped the marble kitchen island countertop to keep me grounded. The breaths in my chest went shallow and uneven. The world around me spun and the ground beneath me shook.

Maybe I was dreaming? I blinked several times and even pinched myself to see if I was dead but try after try, I was proven wrong.

I didn't want her to send me a message. I wanted my own mother to forget me for the rest of her miserable rich life. Not once did I need her so why is she asking me to call her now?

Why was there a message from her now?
After weeks, she finally calls?
What does she want?

My mind didn't process anything, completely paralyzed by a message. Eyes squeezed together, I blindly turned around to wash my hands. Quickly, my hands scrambled to find my purse underneath the countertop, searching for a familiar container.

A shaky breath in and a weak breath out. I took eight to see if it would do something and after an eternity, the woozy feeling filled me. It wasn't something permanent or long lasting but it was enough for me to keep pushing on for a few hours.

Someone cleared their throat as I reached for the dough again. The moment my heart rate lowered, it instantly spiked. Knowing that someone was watching me made me want to go into a coma. Because not only did I know there was someone watching me but I also knew who it was.

I looked up to see Mathias leaning against the fridge and glancing over at me. His lips were in a tight straight line. Mathias' eyes weren't brown today, they looked as dark as the night sky. They looked dark as burning embers.

My heart sunk to the floor, "Goodness, how long have you been there?" I placed a floury hand to my chest as if it could calm it down the desperate heart inside my chest.

Mathias didn't respond but walked closer. His arms continued to stay crossed, a look of disappointment on his face.

"What do you want?" I grew uncomfortable with the silence.

Maybe he just saw me gasping for air and didn't see me fill my hand with pills and down it like it was my last breath.

But maybe he did see me.

Is he mad at me? Why would he be mad, it's not his problem?

If he was mad, why would I care? My life isn't his to worry about.

Ahhhhhhhh!

His deadpan expression didn't give me a trace into what was going on in his head.

"What do you need?" I asked once again, hoping that this time he would answer and put my anxiety to ease.

"What was that?" Mathias demanded to know.

His voice was deep, arms crossed on his chest as he slowly walked closer to me. He waited for a truthful response but I couldn't seem to find my voice. There wasn't an ounce of courage inside me to respond to him.

Plus, I wasn't going to tell him that I've had an ongoing addiction with drugs and alcohol. I knew if I did, he would just judge me.

His breathing was sharp and fast. A piercing gaze directed to me, "What the hell was that?"

I mumbled under my breath, "Nothing."

I could feel him still looking at me. I sensed him studying my every expression, every move, so instead I put on a smile in hopes it would hide that turbulence inside me.

"I know you aren't alright so don't you try and change my mind. I will find out one way or another."

Mathias looked at me once more and for a moment, I had enough strength to look him in the eyes. I didn't have to ask or question anything. His eyes revealed the betrayal and hurt he felt. But a lie that I had convinced myself of is that Mathias doesn't need to know about my life.

Mathias doesn't need another reason to leave me.

The moment he stepped out of the kitchen, I released the breath trapped inside my throat. Slowly, I peaked around the corner to see if he had left. But instead, he was talking to Lily. Lily whispered something but Mathias didn't respond, all he did was continue walking towards the front door. Yet, like he could sense me looking, Mathias turned around and our gazes met once again.

I let myself cry silent tears for a moment. I don't know exactly what those tears were for but they were something from the depths of my soul. The medicine that I took wasn't because I even needed it but because it was the only thing that gave me some sort of peace. It gave my mind a temporary calmness. Even though it never lasted, it turned into something that I clinged onto.

Why did my mom call me?

Why did she text me?

Why would she bother with me if she said in public that she didn't have a daughter?

Why couldn't something be clear in all of this emotional mess?

MATHIAS
CHAPTER 19

I asked Amelia but she refused both times. She acted like there was nothing wrong but I knew better. I knew all too well about the feeling of wanting to hide your pain and suffering just to look strong

Amelia went from looking at her phone to searching for something frantically in her purse. At the end, she looked like she had seen a monster. Yet she was so stubborn and didn't let me help.

Why do people do that?

I wanted to help her but how do I help her if she won't tell me what she's going through. I felt like Amelia was so close yet so far.

When I was leaving, I told Lily what I had seen and asked her if she knew anything about it. All Lil told me was that Amelia wasn't doing too well but Amelia wouldn't let anyone close enough to help her. Lily's face etched with hurt and compassion.

"All we can do now is pray. God can help her in ways that

we can't." Lily whispered to me before heading back to work. The cafe busted at the seams with customers.

But my mind was consumed by Amelia. I replayed every moment we were together, every word her mouth spoke, and everything in between. Maybe I was paying too much attention to the space between the lines but I feel like she's hiding something very important.

Everything she said to me felt like the tip of the iceberg, and I was desperate to try and help her. I wanted to help Amelia. I wanted to help fight her inner struggles and be with her every step of the way. Yet, I couldn't fight for someone if they weren't willing to let me in. That's the downside of always trying to help everyone because the harsh reality was that not everyone wanted help.

I dragged myself through the rest of the day. Twenty-four hours felt like seventy-two. My mind felt like it had run a marathon this morning, unable to process simple information. My body felt like roadkill, aching at every joint.

Even if I didn't want to, I had to keep going because this Sunday afternoon was the Annual Love Creek Fall Banquet. We had more than a handful of things left to do and very few days to do it. But despite all the things I had to do, Amelia occupied all my thoughts.

"What am I going to do now?" I mumbled out loud to myself.

"I know you weren't listening to me. Those emotions don't match up with anything I just said." My Pa teased before drinking another sip of his lemonade. Momma makes a fresh pint every morning which makes all our hard work worth it.

Pa held a laugh back, his wide grin hidden behind the

edge of the glass cup. We were taking a much needed break. Our shirts were completely soaked with sweat and water. My hair was glued down against my forehead, sweat beads trailed the sides of my forehead. We were sitting on a picnic table that we made with scrap walnut wood. The picnic tables were almost done; *I think I can make picnic tables in my sleep.*

My momma wanted us to build rustic picnic tables that would be used for the Annual Fall Banquet and then later donated to the town. She decided to give this idea last minute so now we really had the work cut out for us.

My hands were covered with calluses and blisters. The baby smooth skin I once had was now completely gone. Instead, they were always sore, red, and in agony. Each scar on my hand had a story behind it, so I didn't mind them that much. It reminded me of how much progress I have made over the years. The scars were a gentle reminder that I worked for what I wanted, I wasn't given anything just because I asked for it.

"What is going on in that head of yours?" Pa looked at me before taking a bit out of his chicken sandwich.

"Amelia." I mumbled underneath my breath.

Pa always understood me. Maybe he could help me.

I knew that he probably already guessed it was Amelia and just wanted to keep the conversation going.

He hummed, like he was interested but waited for me to continue talking. His eyes focused on a single spot, which meant he was giving me his full attention.

With a sigh I gave in and told him what happened. "Today I went by the bakery to leave the supplies that Haven asked for. Lily told me that Amelia was in the kitchen and I decided to pop in and say hello. Amelia stopped kneading the dough in front of her and was glancing down at her phone. Instantly, her body language and facial expression changed. Amelia looked like she had received the worst possible news." I combed my hair with my fingers, unable to keep myself still. Desperately, I tried to shake off the emotions I felt at that moment. "When I asked her what was wrong, she ignored me. And I don't understand because I am trying to help her."

My Pa played with the last pieces of his salad with the tip of his fork. When he finally picked up his thoughts, he placed the fork down and glanced at me in the eyes.

"Women are complex creatures. When something is bothering them and you ask what happened, they say it's nothing. But one thing I have learned from living with your mamma for thirty-five years is that even though they say they are fine, they really aren't." Pa smiled. His grin stretched from ear to ear. "They want you to know that you're there and that you care but don't want to bother you with their problems. Yet at the same time, they want you to figure it out and solve it without them having to say a word." Pa spoke with a lot of experience after everything Mamma and him endured together. Her health problems tested their relationship to new levels. Endless hospital and doctor visits deepened their trust in one another. Although, despite all the hardships they came out stronger than ever. A bound that no storm can break.

His gaze shifted to the endless green field in front of us. After hours and hours of work, everything was starting to come together. The grass finally was thriving since the weeds had been plucked. Flourishing flowers in raised beds we built for Momma. Even the animals were thankful that there no longer were heatwaves.

The plantation constantly gave more fruits and vegetables. It was going to be enough for us, the fall banquet, the town and their still would be enough to turn into preserves. It all inched a certain part of my soul that I couldn't explain with words.

"My advice to you, my son, is to be there for her like you always were when you were children. Keep reminding her that you will always be there for her. And when you see that she's down, ask what's wrong and don't run away when she says the worst possible thing you can imagine." He only continued speaking after I agreed. "True love does not let problems, situations, or even an ugly crying session keep you away from someone. Love is when you do something despite what you feel. Continuing to love someone even if they hurt you or backstab you proves that you truly love the person."

He gave me a signature dad smile and continued to scarf down his food. I took several moments to look at Pa. Because every time I did, I was marveled by how much wisdom he had. From watching his true love fight between life and death and having to organize his parents' burial, it has made him appreciate life more and it changed his perspective.

I value his opinion and knowledge more than any other man on this earth. I say that he's my role model and this might be cliche but he has helped me turn into the man I am today.

Now that everything had gone "back to normal", even though our life would never be normal again, Pa has taken everything on top of his shoulders. He took everything as his own responsibility but still knows how to draw boundaries. I know a part of him wishes that he could have avoided everything that happened but he knows that God's plan will always be better than his.

So I know that his advice is worth more than gold because there's a testimony behind it.

Then I think about how I can bring this to my life. I hate to see Amelia and anyone I care about this way. I know the feeling of emotional distress all too well and I don't wish it on anyone.

Even if it has been ten years, the special place she had in my heart never faded. She never lost the love me and my family had for her because we had faith. We had faith that one day she was going to come back. And after ten years of prayer, she finally came back.

I didn't need her to be mine again, all I needed was for her to find herself. Allow herself to feel joy and happiness and be whole once again. She hasn't told me anything but by the pieces that I have collected, I knew she went through several things that tore her heart to pieces.

And even though none of us are perfect, I don't wish that type of pain on anyone, not even on my worst enemy.

THE DAY WAS FINALLY HERE AND ALL OUR HARD work was going to pay off in just a few hours. Every table had been sanded down with a new layer of wood stain. The lights had been hung, giving the space a cozy feeling.

Everyone was going to come right after church so I decided to stay back and finish the last details. That was the reason I gave my momma but in reality, I also needed some time to pull myself together to see Amelia. Just the mention of her name made me feel like I was in the clouds.

Pa said that you could see just by a look at my face that Amelia consumed my thoughts. And in no way, shape, or form did I want Amelia, Lily, and Jeremiah to see that. And petrified barely scratched the surface of how I felt to see how Jeremiah would react. He never had a filter and no boundaries when it came to my personal business and love life. Just by thinking about that, my heart sped up and my knees went weak.

I still needed to set up the dinner table, put decor out, and build the fireplace. Although, that did not include the day to day job. Clean the barn, feed the animals, make sure Betsy didn't break out, and a hundred other things.

A cowboy's job is never done.

MY RUST COLORED SHIRT WAS COMPLETELY stained with dirt, grass, and something brown that I didn't want to know what it was.

Betsy decided to throw a fit just before people began to arrive and I basically had to bribe an animal to go back to the barn.

I should call her Miss.Independent instead.

The weather felt more humid than it usually was. And silently, I prayed that the temperature would change before everyone arrived. I wanted this to be the best day ever and be able to enjoy everything my family worked so hard to accomplish.

All by the grace of God.

My hands dug into a piece of wood; *that definitely was going to leave a blister.*

Momma had sent me a message and asked me to move

the tables so that there would be more room. And with each table I moved, a small piece of wood dug into my skin. I needed this to be perfect or I never was going to hear the end of it.

When I finally added the last table cloth, I released the breath I didn't know I was holding in. Momma had just come back and was in the kitchen, adding her final touches.

"Mathias, come here." I heard my momma yell from the back door of the house.

Momma had a power house voice, you could hear it from miles away.

Health conditions might have taken her strength but it could never take her voice.

With a peaceful breath in my lungs, I mounted my horse and dashed to where she was. My legs felt like overcooked spaghetti and my arms felt like a beating like a drum. My knees cracked as if I was forty-eight but I wasn't even thirty.

I feel like an un-oiled iron door.

My old boots flew off my feet as I rushed into the kitchen. The clock was ticking and each second was precious gold. I quickly gave Momma a kiss on her forehead before washing my hands. "Yes momma?"

"People will start arriving soon so before you get in the shower please help me set up the tables in the dining room." She stated it like a request but I knew better than to deny helping her. She did so much for me and doing this was the least I could do.

Momma had decided to keep most of the food inside for now until everyone was here. There was a high chance an animal could break out-it likely would be Betsy-and try to eat the food. It has happened before and was a headache to clean afterwards.

When she turned around to place the pans of rice on the dinner table, I quietly shoved a spoon of food in my mouth. Her food always hits right, like a cup of cold lemonade on a hot sunny day. Her food was always better than any restaurant or fast food place. It melted in your mouth and left you wanting more.

"Mathias Anderson, you better not be eating the food before the party." She threatened without even looking over her shoulder.

I couldn't help but bark out a laugh because it's like she had another sense. Maybe she had another eye somewhere and never told me.

"I am an angel momma, you know that." I answered with the biggest grin on my face.

She turned around, her eyebrow lifted to her hairline. Momma took one glance at my huge grin and started laughing as well. "You haven't grown up at all, my little gremlin."

"I am a five year old stuck in a 6'2 body." I responded with honesty.

She slapped me lightly on my sore arm. Something in her snapped and began sending orders to both me and my father.

There never was a dull moment with her. Something about my momma was that when she is put to a task, she doesn't fall short. She went above and beyond, Momma truly lived that verse *"Do everything as you are doing it to Christ."*

Maybe it's because she didn't take life for granted anymore.

Maybe because he wanted to serve the person who gave her life back.

I don't know why she was like that but I wanted to be like her. Every time I asked her why she went above and beyond if most people didn't care or pay any attention, she always reminded me of what the Bible says. Since that day, I have tried to do my best in everything. Her obedience to the Lord has influenced me to do better.

Instantly, I heard a car lock in the distance. My heart started beating uncontrollably because I wasn't expecting anyone to arrive so early. The footsteps of a small family got louder and louder. Pa was already outside, welcoming everyone.

"Hey, how are you?" He loudly announced.

The family answered but their voices were too muffled for me to hear.

I scurried to the bathroom to take a shower because I knew I could kill anyone with just a hug or a whiff.

And I don't want to kill Amelia.

I QUICKLY STEPPED OUT OF THE SHOWER AND added curl cream into my dripping wet hair. Hurriedly, I scurried to my drawer to grab my hair diffuser to dry my hair before I left a puddle on the floor. I was not in the mood to have a bird's nest on the top of my head.

I cracked open the bathroom door, looked right and left and dashed down the hall in my robe, leaving a trail of foot-marks. The clothes I wanted to wear today were already laid out, ironed to perfection. A part of me really wanted to just wear a pair of sweatpants and lay in bed but my momma would give me a whooping if I did.

Another part of me wanted to look presentable and nice

for a certain someone. I tried to convince myself that it totally wasn't the woman who consumed my every thought. I should know better than to let a woman consume my mind all the time but Amelia was different.

I didn't see her as just another girl. I saw her as my answered prayer.

AMELIA
CHAPTER 20

Today I felt like a ticking bomb. Any moment I was going to explode and hide somewhere so I wouldn't have to go.

It took me hours to pick what I wanted to wear, what to do with my hair, and how to do my makeup. And when I couldn't make my mind, Lily came into the room and said that she would help me pick an outfit that would leave Mathias starstruck. When I told her that wasn't the reason I wanted to get ready, she just ignored my comment and shrugged her shoulders.

I had asked her to do my makeup because if I did it myself then I was going to turn into a clown. Lily had multiple talents hidden underneath her belt, and a part of me wished I was even a fraction of how talented she was. When Lily finished, she took a step back and said that she did her greatest work.

The moment we arrived, my breathing went rapid and short. Everything around me spun in different directions. A block of ice inside my stomach made me freeze up with every step that I took.

I knew that I was going to see a lot of people from my past but I didn't know if I was ready for that. I also knew that people were going to ask about my parents and I don't know how I am going to respond.

"Oh, I have an addiction problem to drinking and painkillers so I got disinherited because of it. My parents also said on public news that they didn't have a daughter but other than that I am fine," If I responded that to everyone who asked about my parents, everyone would look at me like an alien with three heads.

The moment my brain figured out that was a possibility, I wanted to run and hide in the car. But before I could make a run for it, Lily gripped my hand and pulled me to walk beside her. With each step I took, a deep breath filled my lungs and gave me enough strength to continue on. The moment we turned the corner, time froze. Lily and I stopped for a moment, taking in the beautiful view.

Everything looked like it was straight out of a movie, something from a fairytale. The first thing that I noticed were the twinkle garden lights that dangled above the space. It illuminated everything in such a romantic way.

The wooden picnic tables gave off a cozy and warm feeling. As we walked past the tables, I noticed the small details on them. The way the colors of wood swirled together, each table different from the other. I could tell there was a wooden stain on them, the tables shone underneath the sunlight.

Music filled the space, my skin constantly tickled with the warm breeze. Despite the large land, everything felt intimate. Then I remembered all the times I used to be here, but back then there weren't as many animals or vegetation.

I couldn't tell where their land started or stopped, unending green grass in all directions. The animals in the barn fast asleep, not a care in the world to all the people around them. The main house looked renewed. The fresh red paint on the outside walls made the house stand out from everything else. At that moment, I realized how much had changed since I last came here. A profound realization of how much I missed this place.

My childhood second home.

From the corner of my eye, Mrs. Anderson walked towards me. Her arms wide open and the sweetest smile on her beautiful face. You could see the overflowing amount of joy in her eyes, love radiated off her. Mrs. Anderson always loved hosting and you could see how much it made her happy.

"My little sugar, you came!" She squeaked in excitement. "I started to worry that you wouldn't come." She gave me the tightest hug and a kiss on my cheek.

That is one thing I love about Mrs. Anderson. She is the sweetest person you will ever meet. It doesn't matter where you are from or what you have been through, she will always have open arms for you. With her, I feel loved and seen by someone. I feel like I actually have a mother, someone who cares about my wellbeing instead of choosing money over me. I used to tell her that she had a super power but she just has a magical touch.

She gave two more tight hugs to Lily and Jeremiah while I continued to admire the decor. Spinning around and taking everything in. All the details, all the people talking and having the moment of their lives. People were already gathering in their corners and talking away. Some were dying of laughter and others were just chatting like old friends.

"You have really outdone yourself." I marveled at every single detail. There were even huge versions of board games on the floor so that people could play. Mrs. Anderson knew how to bring people together. She did everything with excellence and love.

"Thanks sugar, I couldn't have done it without my sweetheart and Mathias." She made sure that she added extra emphasis on Mathias' name. Her eyes twinkled with mischief. When my cheeks started to get hot, she rolled her lips to hold back her laughter.

When I was about to open my mouth to speak, someone began walking in our direction. Every atom in my body froze and I felt like I had forgotten how to breathe. He looked like an angel walking on earth, one of those men straight out of a romance book. I wasn't attracted to him in any certain way but it wasn't fair how fine he looked. It was hard to take my eyes off him, as he walked over with such confidence and style.

He wore a dark blue dress shirt that hugged him in all the right places, which made it hard to stay focused. His boots and jeans were his signature touch; *Nothing separates a cowboy from his jeans and boots.* Lily cleared her throat beside me, and instantly I was embarrassed. I was clearly gawking at him and for good reason. My eyes were solely focused on him; *Muscles. A woman's weakness.*

"Speaking of my honey bun, here he is." Mrs. Anderson extended her arm to give Mathias a side hug.

He kissed the top of her head and mumbled something to her that left her chuckling. Her cheeks were a bright shade of pink. *Such an angel. Please don't tell me that Jeremiah and Lily turned Mrs. Anderson into a cupid.*

"Momma, I am too old for nicknames." He gently told her.

Someone snickered beside me, "Honey bun, Ha!" Jeremiah snorted. "Mrs.Anderson, you can keep calling him that because he hasn't grown at all. Still a little child with that big sappy heart of his." Jeremiah barely could contain his laughter. Lily hit his arm but that made him laugh even harder.

"Look who's talking. All you watch are romance movies and romantic comedies. Gotta find a new bro to hang out with." Mathias crossed his arms and shook his head in such disappointment.

Jeremiah looked at Mathias in the eyes with a fake death stare before they both started laughing. Mathias then looked at Lily and gave her a quick side hug and quietly asked how she was.

"I promise I will try to keep him normal today. I think he had too much sugar." Lily stated and everyone laughed at that but Jeremiah pretended to be stabbed in the heart.

"That hurts love. Lucky for her, she has to deal with this hunky piece of meat." Jeremiah wiggled his eyebrows and flexed his arms. Everyone couldn't stop giggling with laughter; *Jeremiah was literally the life of the party.* We were all different shades of pink, constantly gasping for air.

Lily looked at him with the funniest expression. Her eyebrows knitted together and her button nose all scrunched up. She turned back around and mouthed, *"Help me."*

But before long, Jer scooped Lily in his arms and carried her off. When I turned around, Mrs. Anderson no longer was in sight. It was only me and Mathias standing together in complete silence.

Mathias' eyes finally found mine and my stomach released a cage of butterflies. The dress felt a bit tighter and my heart pounded faster. He looked me up and down, taking me all in with the biggest grin on his face. Mathias stepped closer, placing the lightest kiss on my cheek.

My skin danced underneath his breath. *My knees might give in at any moment.*

Mathias' sweet voice whispered close to my ear, "You look absolutely beautiful Sunshine."

He was so close that I could smell his shampoo and cologne. He smelled like wood and musk. A sweet blend of different notes that perfectly suited him. It wasn't something overpowering but definitely addictive. His hair was freshly washed, each curl was defined and placed perfectly.

"You don't clean up bad yourself cowboy." Allowing myself to take another look without being a total creep. He looked perfect in every way but that's a truth that I was going to keep to myself.

"That's it?" Mathias pretended to be offended at my vague compliment.

I chuckled and admitted that he did look nice but I would never say how good he actually looked. I couldn't put into words how attractive he was to me. Maybe it wasn't what was on the outside. Maybe it was something I saw inside him that lured me closer.

He put both of his hands on either side of my arms. A reassuring look in his eyes.

"You truly do look marvelous, Sunshine. Don't think anything less." He gave my shoulders another light squeeze before letting me go.

We stayed there for a few minutes and chatted about our day. He said that the only reason he stayed home and didn't go to church was because he still had things to finish. He then began to tell me about the adventurous cow that they had and her attempts in breaking out. By the time he finished that story, I was dying of laughter. My stomach started to hurt and my cheeks started to burn.

"Let me show you around." He glanced back and extended his arm.

I looked at it and then back up at his eyes. A gentleman through and through. There wasn't an ounce of rude nature in his body and that was new for me. I was used to guys mistreating me and playing with my heart but he never did that.

I took his arm and smiled the brightest smile that I could manage. "Let's go."

"You did not!" I squeaked like a school girl.

I squeezed Mathias' arm tightly. I jumped like a little girl, baffled that he remembered. S'mores were a staple in our childhood memories. It brought warmth to my heart that he remembered that; *To re-live the good old days.*

I was about to bribe him to let me make one before dinner but then my happiness died and my smile faded.

"You're fat because all you eat is junk. Close that damn mouth of yours and lose a little weight, actually a lot of weight." Brandon sneered at me when I wanted to eat a small piece of cake.

I loved sweets and had the biggest sweet tooth but forcefully had to train myself to reject it. I had to learn not to eat sweets despite really wanting to. His words replayed in my mind, completely stopping me from asking Mathias to let me make one. I know that I shouldn't worry about Brandon and what he said, but it was hard to form new habits and break old ones.

I shook myself back to reality and when I looked up, Mathias had worry lines on his forehead and eyes. He gently placed his hands on my shoulder and stepped closer. His touch made me feel grounded.

His eyes searched for a response, but before he could ask, a lady called out his name. She came dashing in our direction, desperate to get Mathias' attention. Despite the woman calling him, Mathias kept his eyes glued on mine.

She was probably near my age, maybe a little younger. Her pony tail swayed right and left as she ran, a big smile on her face.

"Mathias, are you trying to run away from me again?" her bright bubbly voice asked as she extended both her arms to hug Mathias.

He let go of my arm and wrapped his arms around her and spun her around. She giggled at the embrace; *I'm not jealous.*

Saying that she was gorgeous would be an understatement. Her bright blue green eyes added to her beautiful complexion. Maybe I was a bit jealous.

Are they together? Were they good friends? Maybe they are engaged?

I felt horrible for thinking questions like that. I was in no place to get up in their business. If she was his girlfriend then good for them.

"Little cuz!" Mathias grinned. "How have you been?" Mathias asked after settling her onto the ground.

When he said *cuz*, a part of me relaxed. My lungs could

finally breathe again. Although a part of me felt ashamed in thinking they were anything else except cousins.

You shouldn't be this jealous, I reminded myself.

"I am great but I do wish you would stop calling me little. I am only three years younger than you." She scrunched her nose. Her arms were crossed over her chest, her foot constantly tapped against the floor.

The woman turned and looked at me. Her pearly white teeth appeared when she flashed a bright and big smile. I never thought that teeth could be that white and gorgeous.

Was it a thing to be jealous of white teeth?

"Howdy. How are you? My name is Samantha, Mathias' cousin." Her greeting was a big hug. All the air was knocked out of my lungs the moment she wrapped her arms around me.

"My name is Amelia." I greeted with a smile of my own. It wasn't as pretty as hers but I managed.

Her eyebrows shot up to her hairline. Samantha's eyes went huge. She looked at me, then Mathias and then back at me again. "*The* Amelia?"

Mathias cleared his throat, giving her a *Cut this conversation now* glance.

I guess she understood it because she let out a huff. Their interaction left me curious about how she knew who and I didn't.

"Come with me. I am going to introduce you to everyone around here." She grabbed me by the arm and started pulling me away.

I WAS ALMOST EATING MY SALAD. I DON'T KNOW IF it's even considered a salad if it only had lettuce, salt, and olive oil. In my right hand, I had a cup of wine. The guy who passed it around said he grew it and made the wine himself. Each person that I met today had a unique talent.

I wish I had talent.

I sat on the bench, admiring the colorful sky. The sunset sky caught my breath, leaving me completely and utterly speechless. The sky was a mix of beautiful colors. There were colors from magenta, lavender, rose, pale yellow, and orange. My mind thought of the endless possibilities of replicating it but I knew you could never replicate this artwork. Each sunset was always different from another one. They could be similar but never the same and that was the best part.

A few feet away, there was a dance floor that was right beside the fireplace. Old couples danced to their own beat, taking small steps to the left and right. Kids ran around, desperately trying to win the game of tag.

Haven, Samantha, and Lily immediately got up and started dancing. They begged me to join but I refused.

"It's ok, I prefer to sit and watch." I waved them off with a smile on my face so that they wouldn't feel bad for me.

I searched the entire crowd, admiring how each person made themselves feel at home. This felt like a big family, no one rejected anyone.

Was this too much to ask for?

Then I saw a man that stood out like a star in the night sky. Matthias was talking to a guy and instantly started laughing from something that they said. His face was filled with joy.

Calm down, heart.

He then excused himself and searched for someone in

the crowd as well. A part of me wondered who he was searching for. Maybe he already knew who he wanted to dance with. My heart twisted with slight jealousy at the fact that it might not be me.

Then our eyes connected. The world faded away and it was just us. There wasn't anyone or anything that would rip me away from his gazes. His eyes captured me and I was beginning to like that feeling.

When he reached me, he smiled one of those blinding smiles and extended his hand to me. "Could I have the honor to dance with you, Sunshine?"

"I would but I can't."

His hand dropped to his side. "May I ask why?" He frowned like a little child.

I squinted my eyes and tried to keep a straight face.

"Well cowboy, I can't dance." His frown slowly turned from a frown to a grin. "I would feel bad for your feet if I tried."

"You got me worried for a second. Well it's easy to learn." He extended his hand out again and with a warm smile, he asked slowly. "Sunshine, would you give me the greatest honor to dance with you for the first time in a long time?"

All the times we used to dance together flashed through my memory. A smile came on my lips at the sweet memories. We danced in his living room, the kitchen, and even underneath the rain.

I took a shaky breath in and placed my hands in his. Our hands always fit perfectly together.

His fingers enveloped mine as I whispered, "You may."

WE SWAYED SIDE TO SIDE FOR SEVERAL MOMENTS. Neither of us felt the need to speak, silence in that moment felt comfortable.

Our bodies gently touched each other as we danced. His breath tickled my skin which made me lightly shutter. When he noticed, he pressed our bodies closer together and smirked.

"So how is your night so far?" He whispered close to my ear.

I looked past him, not having the strength to look him straight into his dashing eyes.

"I made a few friends, so it hasn't been all that bad. And what about you?"

"This isn't my first rodeo, so it's fine." He shrugged his shoulders. "This year is better because of one thing." I waited patiently for him to continue on. "This year is better because you're here. We are here together."

I melted into his embrace, desperate to hide the blush that slowly appeared on my entire face. He chuckled near my ear. Mathias rested his head on mine as we continued to sway to the music. My head rested on his chest, the even beats of his heart was a drug.

"We haven't seen each other in a long time so please bear with me." His arms gripped onto me tighter and I knew for sure that Mathias was never going to let me go.

"Do you have any new hobbies? What about your painting and art?" I knew that he was going to ask that question. Mathias loved watching me paint as much as I loved doing it.

I stiffened in his arms. "What's wrong?" He asked. Small fine lines formed in between his eyebrows.

"Thinking about how to respond to your question." I took a steady breath and decided to jump in head first. "I haven't painted in a while. Something happened which took that joy away." *I regret how other peoples opinions affected me as much as it did.* "Then I came here and I thought it would come back if I bought a few supplies but it didn't." The day me and Lily went out to pick some art supplies would forever be one of my favorites. "The supplies are still untouched on the desk back home. I haven't made anything new in a few years. I don't even remember if I know how to do it."

"*Interesting.*" were the only words he managed to gruffly say.

I tried to change the subject to not dampen the moment. "Ok my turn, what are your hobbies?"

I knew what he was going to say because Mathias never changed. He didn't change for anyone and once he found something he loved doing, he stuck to it.

"Well I mostly stay here. Mainly I try to keep Betsy from breaking out. It's hard for me to go out but I try. This is what I need, nothing more. I am satisfied with it and so I have nothing to complain about."

He takes a few moments before talking again. "My parents are getting older and the land is getting bigger which means there's more responsibility and work. My family needs me so I always put them first."

His eyes connected with mine. "Life isn't about partying, buying, and taking advantage of everything because you only live once. You have to know what comes first and what is important. I ain't gonna regret my life when I die because I know that I lived it in the best way."

I played with a long curl in the back as we swayed to the music and drifted into our own world. His hands were wrapped around my waist. My legs already started to give in but I didn't want to stop because in a way this felt like what my soul had been searching for. A type of peace that I can't explain. Something beyond what drugs and alcohol could do.

His heartbeat went along with each beat of the song. Mathias' breath slowed as I rested my head once again on his chest. Few people were still dancing. Every few minutes a couple would leave the dance floor and head one.

What time was it?

But I didn't want to know. I wanted to live in this moment like there wasn't a tomorrow.

Nothing to fear.

Nowhere to go.

Nothing to run from.

I would have completely missed his question if I hadn't been paying attention.

"Sunshine, tell me something." He whispered. His voice was like the sound of an autumn breeze.

I hummed so he would know that I was listening and that he could continue talking.

He hesitated for a moment before finally asking, "What happened?"

MATHIAS
CHAPTER 21

"My ex took advantage of me in ways that I didn't expect." Amelia lifted her head to look me in the eyes. "My parents disowned me because of my choices. You know them, they never cared about me anyway so it wasn't really a surprise."

"Could I ask you one more question? If you're not up to it then that is completely fine." My voice was barely above a whisper. My heart crushed at that truth and no wonder she didn't open up so easily.

She was broken and needed healing.

She nodded which felt like permission to continue on. I guess today was the day we both felt enough bravery to talk about everything. "Why do you take medicine?

She stopped dancing for a second. And if I wasn't so focused on her I would have missed it. She didn't respond and I thought for a second I felt like I had crossed the invisible boundary. "I was in an accident a few years ago. They're pain killers."

If someone punched me in the stomach, it wouldn't be

anything. I felt like my heart was being burned alive. My emotions instantly became a mess, a turmoil inside my mind. And that feeling could kill someone alive.

My brain completely froze. I couldn't think of a single thing that would bring her comfort.

After what felt like an eternity, it finally hit me. All of those moments where I wasn't in her life and I thought she was having a wonderful life, was all a lie. The lies I thought were true were being completely destroyed in the matter of seconds.

"I am not the girl you once knew. She's dead and I don't know how to get her back." Those words made more sense to me. Back then I lacked understanding and now everything changed.

I looked down at her for a moment and saw the vulnerability written across her face. I saw something in her gaze that I hadn't before. Something inside her was changing and I couldn't put a finger on it. Maybe the heaviness of her past was catching up with her and all she wanted was change.

I hugged her even tighter and pulled her closer to me. "I am so sorry sunshine. I am sorry you had to go through all that. I am sorry I wasn't there." With each word I spoke, I felt myself gripping onto her even tighter.

Maybe it was a natural reaction to try and protect her from further pain.

She chuckled and pulled back to look into my burning tear filled eyes. Whoever said that a man couldn't cry was lying.

Amelia smiled, her eyes glassy and red as mine. What surprised me the most was when she gently placed her hand on my cheeks. For a moment I felt like a lost man.

The feel of her hands against my sore skin instantly made

all the pain fade away. I could be lost in her touch forever. My eyelids could barely open with the power her touch had over me and she didn't even know it.

She whispered. "Cowboy, it isn't your fault. I don't blame you and you shouldn't either. Things happened in both of our lives that were beyond our control."

TODAY I FINALLY SAW THE SIDE OF AMELIA THAT I longed to see. That moment made me long for more, want more. Nothing in this world would rip that away from my heart.

I needed to help bring back the person who loved to paint and draw. The one who loved to find new places to eat and explore. That person was *my* Amelia and no pain she went through would change her value to me.

Even if the world was against me and people told me that it wasn't going to work, I wasn't going to listen. I was going to prove every lie in my head wrong.

A FEW DAYS HAD PASSED SINCE THE FALL BANQUET and our lives were finally going back to normal. I finally could continue on doing my morning workout and morning swim in the lake. When I finished my morning routine, the roster crowed; *on time.*

After a fulfilling morning, I rested on the grass for a moment. I loved to admire the sunset and the beautiful shades of blues that were painted across the sky. It was gorgeous and each day I was baffled by how God created such perfect things.

Once again, my thoughts went back to Amelia. I couldn't help but think about my Sunshine. I had given her that name years ago and it stuck. I don't think she fully understood why I called her Sunshine. I started calling her sunshine because that's what she was in my life. She brought happiness and radiated sunlight where there was darkness and loneliness.

I called her after something I loved to admire. I loved to adore and gaze at her. She was more beautiful than any other living person or thing that walked on this earth. And after ten years praying that somehow our paths would cross with one another, they finally did in a way that I never expected. She was my answered prayer and I was marveled by how God connected all the pieces together.

"Sky come here." Her head peaked up from eating the grass and looked at me. Slowly she walked my way and allowed me to pet her semi-soft coat.

I leaped on top of her and rode to check on all the animals. Luckily no cows were on the loose, no chickens were trying to MMA fight each other, and the sheep were happy because they had food. The other horses were covered in the barn, sleeping from a hard day of work.

From afar I saw my pa wave his hands like crazy desperately trying to get my attention. I tapped my foot against Sky for her to ride faster and before she came to a full stop, I hopped off and rushed inside, the door shutting behind me. When I rushed to find my parents, Momma was on the sofa, her beautiful face the color of snow. Pa tried to check if she was ok but she just kept hitting his hand.

"You two are off your rockers. Thinking about who

knows what," Momma huffed out loud. "I am fine! Look at me!" She pointed to herself to prove that there wasn't anything wrong.

From the shiver to the light purple lips she had, I don't think she was fine. Her hands trembled every time she moved them. Pa extended to her a glass of water and the moment he let go, she barely could hold the weight of the cup.

"Your momma thought it was a good idea to start cooking, cleaning, and carrying boxes around the house by herself," Pa responded. His fingers went over his temple in a circular motion. Pa couldn't talk clearly, his words jumbled together and his cheeks a bright red color.

Oh. He was upset.

PA HAD THE SAME PROBLEM AS I DID, WE BOTH over thought everything. So I could tell that he thought of every worst possible thing that could have happened. And even if he was upset, he still treated his wife with kindness and love.

I gazed and looked at the mess around the house. There were dusty plastic boxes everywhere labeled *fall and Christmas decor.*

When it came to this time of year, mamma went all out and she didn't waste any time to start decorating. There never was a countertop, wall, or room untouched. Sometimes I was convinced that she was the queen of Christmas.

I couldn't help but smile because this was who she was. She loved doing all of this and it was something that made her happy.

Ever since her medical accident, she has been under strict orders. She wasn't allowed to pick up heavy boxes, push herself too much, or stay on her feet too long. If she exceeded her limit, she could pass out or lose her strength for several hours and maybe even days.

I walked to where she was laying on the sofa and glanced at her tired eyes. They were swollen and red, sensitive to all the dust around us. They glistened with unshed tears and one glance at them broke my heart into a million pieces.

How can I be mad at her?

She has gone through so much and when she wanted to do something she loved, she couldn't. "Momma, you almost gave me a heart attack. You're doing too much." I gently said. "You have to give yourself a break every few hours."

I could feel the tight worry lines form on my forehead. The veins tightened and my hands were sweaty and clammy. An unsteady feeling settled into my heart.

What if something did happen?

What if something happened and we weren't here to help her?

She took her trembling fingers and lifted my chin. It took a moment for my eyes to find hers again but once they connected, tears began to overflow. Momma gave a tiny weak smile, putting on a brave face even though I knew she was a bit scared herself.

Her eyes were beautiful portals to how her soul felt. And at that moment, I knew she was tired. The tiredness finally caught up with her body. Momma's eyelids drooped, heavy with slumber.

"I am fine, my boy. I am just tired, that's it. Maybe I did carry too many boxes but all I need is a little rest and I'll be good as rain." She said with confidence.

She opened her arms and I melted into her embrace. I melted in her arms because no one had the same affect on me as she did. No one knew me as well as my momma did. She was my best friend and her arms were home to me. Her embrace was somewhere I could run to and never be let go of.

Before letting me go she whispered in my ears. Her voice was a light brush against my ear. "Don't blame yourself for anything that happened to me. I don't get hurt from heavy boxes but what hurts a mother's heart is when she knows her son blames himself for things he never did."

With a gentle and final squeeze, I stepped away from her to give Pa space. He picked her up and carried her up the stairs. And once again I was alone. Tears that threatened to slip finally did. Each tear that rolled down my face, left a numb feeling in its wake.

I weaved my numb and cold fingers through my hair, distracting myself from the past. Distracting myself from the memories that haunted me day and night. But it was like a flash. I couldn't stop it from happening.

"She might not make it tonight." the doctor croaked in the dead silence.

The doctor didn't even look into my eyes. His expression had no ounce of remorse or sadness.

He cleared his throat and continued to speak quietly. "She must stay here until her body can work on its own or..."

He didn't need to finish his sentence because we all understood the unspoken words. There were so many things going on that all my brain wanted to do was shut off.

There's too much going on for my brain to process.

I looked left and right, but there wasn't anyone beside me, my Pa, and the doctor. The dark halls looked threatening and scary. The smell of clorox no longer burned my nose hairs. An endless hall full of doors that led to people who were fighting for their lives. A hospital is no place for someone to be in, it's filled with torture and darkness. Instantly, a shiver went down my spine like I could feel darkness creeping over my shoulder.

"Please take the boy away from here, this is no sight for a young boy." Quickly, the doctor started pushing me out of the waiting room.

I GASPED FOR AIR, BEING TRANSPORTED TO THE dark past made me feel inferior. My forehead dripped with salty sweat. My blood pressure went to the floor. My chest gave in and the lack of oxygen made me dizzy.

Time ticked slower than usual, the world faded away from my grip. Today wasn't even as close to that horrible week, but it reminded me of every cry, every medical beep, and every code blue.

It all came back to me even like a storm even though I tried so hard to keep it away, to hide it, and forget about it. I tried to run from it but it never lost its grip on me. The faster I ran, the tighter my past pulled.

There wasn't a loophole.

My mind whirled in all directions, that I almost hit my Pa when he started shaking me.

"Sorry Pa" I used the back of my hand to rub my eyes, trying to get rid of those memories as quickly as possible.

A second wave of tears threatened to spill. My vision burned. It burned with pain, suffering, agony, and troubles.

"Did it happen again?" He looked at me with worry, pain, and unending patience. He continued to rub his hand on my shoulder, keeping me grounded until I blinked back into reality. His silence was the best remedy.

I always admired Pa. Every time something happened he knew how to deal with it. Never yelled, never screamed, and never panicked. He knew what had to be done and never let his emotions get the best of him.

How many times has he gone through this?

He quietly broke the silence. His voice was barely a whisper, "She's sleeping now. I can thank God for that but today she pushed herself way past her limits."

"But our words go in one ear and out the other. She doesn't want her past to stop her from living her future." I mumbled back.

His sigh was the only answer that we both needed.

I need fresh air.

When I opened the door, Sky was lying on the ground. Her eyes peacefully closed as she bathed in the glorious golden sunlight.

The moment she noticed me, she stood up and strolled closer to me. "She is pushing herself too much."

I wrapped my arm around Sky's neck and then we walked side by side.

Amelia

Chapter 22

Lily and I have been bonding a lot. She has helped me find myself again. Several times she advised me to start painting again, but I didn't know if I was ready for that quite yet. I wanted to paint because I felt the passion and the love for it again. I didn't want to paint just because I needed to, but because I wanted to.

After work, my feet begged for a break. They were swollen and red from the constant hours of being on our feet. Our backs creaked like an iron door.

"You know what Amelia," Lily turned to me during an ad break. "I am very proud of you."

Her comment took me completely off guard since we were in the middle of watching Pride and Prejudice for the hundredth time.

"The hand flex scene never gets old." Lily always said to anyone who questioned our movie choices.

"Why?" I was genuinely taken aback from her statement. Something I didn't expect but my soul needed to hear.

She turned her body to look at me directly in the eyes.

Her eyes were a bit swollen, her pupils barely visible. "Because you are improving. Notice that you're not drinking as often. Your addiction is getting better. And you are forcing yourself to be better."

I swear that my vision got instantly blurry with clogged tears.

Never in a million years did I think someone was going to be proud of me.

No one ever appreciated anything I did so this meant something. It gave me a bit of hope that I still had meaning in people's lives and that there were a few people who still cared about me.

"You don't know how much that means to me." I leaned in and gave her a hug.

Our hugs expressed things that words weren't sufficient for. Every step that we have taken together has demanded courage where there is none. And I knew I couldn't do any of this without her by my side.

"I am so sorry that I wasn't there for you like you were there for me."

She smiled. A single tear rolled down her pink cheeks. "You helped me more than you know. When I felt like no one needed me, you were always there to remind me that someone needed me. God pairs two people for a purpose and we are living proof of that."

TOWARDS THE END OF THE MOVIE, LILY AND I WERE laughing like fools. Mr. Darcy was very awkward at times but very swoon worthy.

One moment we cried and the other we laughed uncontrollably; *We are weird*. After the movie finished, I laid in bed and stared at the white ceiling. I don't know how or what happened but something in my perspective changed.

I started to find worth in things, places, and people that I never had before. Desire to be in places that I shouldn't, began to fade away. I wanted to be closer to Lily, Jeremiah, and maybe Mathias.

Mathias and I still had mountains in our new friendship. Miscommunication here and there. Neither of us knew how to express our emotions all the time which made it difficult to understand the other person's point of view.

Despite whatever I tell him or what I do, Mathias is always there for me. Maybe I have been a stuck in the mud but maybe the change was to open up my eyes. Open my eyes to a new reality, a new perspective, and new ideas.

Over the past few days, the walls I had built slowly crumbled. I have been slowly opening myself and so far nothing bad happened. I just hope that in the end, this will all be worth it. I don't think I could stand another heartbreak or betrayal.

Today I worked a normal shift. I was up on my feet at the crack of dawn and back home at sunset. After work, I took a shower, ate food, and stared at the wall for several minutes.

I'm so bored.

I looked around me to see if there was something I could do but there wasn't a single thing that peaked my interest. It was just me and a silent house. Lily and Jeremiah decided to have a night out so there wasn't anyone for me to annoy.

So I just laid on the sofa, contemplating life. I wondered about my accident and how I got here. Everything felt like a lifetime ago, a distant memory.

I remember the accident like it was today. I was driving back home from the bar and was very tipsy. Now that I think about it, I should have called someone to pick me up.

I had stopped at a red light and everything was fine until the light turned green. The moment that light switched was when my future changed forever.

I pressed on the gas pedal and when I glanced to my left, a truck came rushing in my direction. It drove with full force towards me and in that moment, my life flashed before my eyes.

My car flew by the impact. The car landed several feet away, several other cars impacted by it. Waves of shock flooded every sense in my body. Warm blood trickled down the sides of my forehead and down my face. And when everything went quiet, I thought I had died. Every fiber of me was convinced that I had just gotten a one way ticket to hell.

But despite the suffering I was in, doctors and police officers rushed to get me out of my car.

Their voices sounded like they were miles away. People touched my face and arms. They opened my eyes and told me to wake up but I couldn't. The light at the end of the tunnel called me.

"I don't know if she's alive."

"Her body is barely working."

"She has a gushing bruise on her head."

Each person who looked at me was baffled that I was alive. The accident would have killed me in the matter of seconds. They said it was a miracle and I agreed. And even though I don't believe in God, there isn't a single thing that could explain how I still came out alive after the accident. There wasn't an explanation to how I wasn't dead.

Several hours later, they took me to the hospital and prescribed me with medical drugs to help with the pain. The doctors were unsure how long the pain would last since I had sprained my feet, broken several bones, and taken severe head damage.

That was about three years ago. And instead of going back for a check up, I have been giving myself higher doses.

Ever since the accident, my drinking addiction got worse. It was the only thing I found comfort in, temporary relief.

And after all these years, drinking and drugs were catching up with me. I was beginning to realize that maybe I have been doing this all wrong. A different type of conviction formed in my heart. The church sermons rang in my mind non stop. Lily explained the answers to all the questions I had.

The only conclusion I had come to was that I needed to change. Change needed to happen before I killed myself. Before the pain and suffering killed me from the inside out.

I wasn't living a happy and full life. To this point, my every breath depended on pills. Three days ago, I tried to stop but when I did, my heart ached and twisted. It was like even my body knew this was going to be hard.

Lily told me that I should try to take one pill away at a time until I didn't take anymore. So that's what I have been trying. It was a constant war between and success. A constant mental battle.

I was fighting myself.

With each passing second, my thoughts turned into a

snowball. I wanted to throw up everything I had eaten. My stomach constantly turned, sweat beads formed. Waves of cold shocks overtook my entire body.

Today I felt brave, so I only took four pills but my body hated me because of that.

Was I having a heart attack?

Was the world ending?

I felt the sofa gripped onto me, not letting go. A suffocated breath filled my lungs as I desperately tried to get up.

The world spun in different directions, the earth crumbled beneath my feet.

Darkness crawled on the walls, demons whispered in my ears.

With unsteady breaths, I took a step forward and fell to the floor. A ringing sound erupted in my ears and an agonizing silent scream in my mind.

The corner of the side table scraped and bruised my arm. My phone landed flat against my face. Despair filled me because I didn't know what I was going to do.

Maybe I was going to die? I deserved that more than anyone.

I felt paralyzed on the floor. My heart was desperate to burst out of my chest. The cries of hell filled my ears. It lured me but I was petrified to follow the voice.

What if what Christians say is actually true?

The medicine was supposed to give me a reverse reaction. A numbing and calming sensation was far from what I felt at that moment. The torture of a heart and anxiety attack burned me alive.

I tried calling Lily and Jeremiah, but neither of them picked up. A sense of defeat came over me because there was no one else to help me.

Not everyone.

I looked at Mathias' name on my phone and debated for several moments if I should call him.

Was I going to be a bother?

Was Mathias going to hate me?

The third ring didn't even sound before he picked up the phone. Several moments of silence passed before either of us decided to say something.

I didn't know what I was going to say or how I was going to say it. I couldn't just say "Hey Mathias. So I am calling because I am having a heart attack and Lily didn't pick up the phone."

"Hey Sunshine, how are you?" Mathias asked.

His voice wasn't as cheerful as usual which made me regret calling him. Maybe I had just called him in the middle of a date or something.

"Oh nevermind, I will figure it out by myself."

"Don't worry, I always have time for you. What do you need?" He assured me.

I fumbled over my words because there wasn't a single way to start this conversation. Words weren't sufficient. The silence couldn't express the cry my soul felt.

How would I explain the harsh truth that I had become an addict of sorts and needed help. How would I explain that I felt like I was being killed alive?

The world slowly faded away and turned pitch black. Unable to keep myself awake any longer, I used the little strength I had left and whispered, "Help."

MATHIAS
CHAPTER 23

My body automatically went into fight mode the moment Amelia whispered help.

I rushed to get in my truck, desperate to reach her. My mind thought of a hundred different scenarios of what happened to make her call me. But she called me. Maybe she didn't want to call me but she still did and that fact did unspeakable things to my heart.

From my house to Lily's house was a thirty minute drive but somehow I got there in fifteen. Each red light made me want to curse proud. My fingers gripped onto the steering wheel, the rubber burned into my skin.

Whatever happened I knew she needed help. And if she called me then that meant she had no one else to call. Lily and Jeremiah must not be around; maybe she actually didn't want to call me and just did because I was her last resort. Doubt desperately crept into my mind and with barely enough strength, I pushed those thoughts away.

Once I got there, I quickly searched for the hidden key that Jeremiah always had hidden underneath a pot.

I struggled to open the door, but once I did I swung it open.

And the first thing that I laid my eyes on was Amelia passed out on the floor. She had her phone in her hand but there was no moment in her body.

Lifeless.

God please don't let this be true.

I rushed over to her, letting the keys and my phone fall on the floor. I didn't care if my phone screen would crack, all I cared about was Amelia.

Gently, I brushed the hair away from her pale face. Even if she was white as snow, Amelia was still beautiful in my eyes. And at that moment, I was grateful that I had passed things like this before.

I don't feel useless.

I used the back of my hand to check her temperature; *She is hot but sweating at the same time.*

Her body was weak and fragile. As I picked her up, her body was lighter than usual. Her arms swung side to side as I walked up the stairs to her bedroom. She didn't move or wake up; *How long was she like this before she called me?*

My heart pounded at an unrhythmical beat but I tried to keep myself composed. I needed to keep myself together for Amelia.

I went around the house and began to grab things that I knew I needed. The first thing that I needed to do was turn down the temperature. The temperature was eighty degrees which was a major cause of her fever.

Maybe she passed out because it was too hot?

. . .

THEN I GRABBED MEDICINE, SALTY SNACKS, AND some water. Quickly, I rushed to put everything inside a basket. My legs have never run so fast.

My lungs felt like they could breathe because I noticed that Amelia had moved. Even if it was a fraction, she still moved.

AMELIA TURNED AROUND TO LOOK AT ME, UNABLE to comprehend what was going on.

"Hey." Her weak voice broke the silence. "What happened?"

I gave her a faint smile. "You called me and then asked for help and passed out on the floor." Finding her on the floor has been replaying in my mind for the last few hours. "I'm the one who wants to ask you what happened."

Amelia tried to move but a shock of pain went through her body. She closed her eyes for several seconds and stayed still before she continued to move.

She described how her day went and what she did when she got back home. Amelia said she didn't feel well and started to get hot and when she tried to get up, she fell on the floor. Neither Lily or Jeremiah picked up the phone so she called me instead.

I nodded and paid careful attention to every single thing she said. But after she said everything she remembered, I was still left confused as to why she fainted.

"But something made you unwell and sick." I mumbled. "Nothing you said would have made you that sick. It's something else."

After years of helping my Momma with her health problems, I learned a lot. I might not be a doctor or have a degree but I knew how to help someone.

Amelia instantly froze. She closed her mouth and looked into the distance.

Did I say something wrong?

Maybe she did remember what caused her to get so sick. I didn't have a single hunch of what it could be but once she started talking again, all the pieces connected.

"About three years ago, I got into a car accident and the hospital gave me some painkillers." I could tell she barely wanted to talk about the subject. *Maybe it was something still sensitive to her.* "They told me that I could only get a higher dose if it wasn't working and I needed something strong but instead of going-"

I put the pieces together and finished her sentence. "You gave yourself a higher dose and your body is reacting against it." I dragged my hand down my face; *Now I know what she desperately tried to find in her purse that day.*

Amelia nodded and took another sip of her water. "I have been slowly taking the pills away but I did take it today. Maybe I accidentally took it on an empty stomach?"

I sighed. I wasn't mad at Amelia but I just wished she would have told me sooner. I wished she had enough faith in me to trust me with this.

"And who is helping you with this?"

I might regret asking.

Amelia didn't respond at first. She distracted herself by slowly tying her hair in a ponytail. "The sermons at church and late night talks with Lily."

What?

Her answer completely took me off guard. I was surprised that the sermons had been speaking to her as much as it did to me. Even though I was happy for her, I felt back stabbed because she didn't let me help.

Did everyone except me know about her problems?

"Why didn't you let me help?" Maybe that question was too much to ask at that moment but I needed the answer.

Amelia looked deep into my eyes. "Because I was scared. I was scared of what you were going to think and how you were going to react." Her honest response broke down the walls of my pride. "Plus we just saw each other again after ten years. I don't think it would be a smart move to info dump all this at once."

She was probably right and maybe I even slightly agreed with her. Maybe I wouldn't have known how to deal with it and what to do. Maybe this was God trying to protect us from our friendship being broken again.

God works in mysterious ways.

Now she has opened up with me and I feel like we have made progress. And even if this was a small step to most, it was a huge leap to me.

"Why share this with me now?" I wondered out loud.

"You did help me, didn't you? I think I owed you at least an explanation."

FOR THE REST OF THE AFTERNOON WE TALKED about what she was going through and all the problems she constantly faced in her life. Amelia admitted that she wanted to change but only for her sanity. She said she wasn't ready to accept a God she didn't fully trust in but soon that was going to change.

God was going to come in and open up her eyes in the

blink of an eye like he did with me. We talked for several hours, time flew by like it was nothing. And each moment we spent together, was another moment our friendship deepened. Another moment where I admitted to myself that I cared a whole lot about Amelia.

But this isn't love.

I wasn't going to allow myself to fall in love if I didn't know if it was God's will. I wasn't going to allow another heartbreak in my story because I wasn't willing to ask and wait.

When Lily and Jeremiah arrived, I explained everything that had happened. The only thing I left out was our conversation. Amelia trusted me with her life story and I was going to prove to her that she could trust me.

Jeremiah and Lily were in complete shock when I finished explaining to them what happened. Lily said that Amelia was fine the entire day, she didn't see a single problem.

After Amelia reassured me several times that she was fine and was feeling better, I went home. During the entire drive, I thought about every single thing she said. Every detail she opened about would forever be stuck in my mind. Despite all the bad choices she made over time, it was undoubtable that Amelia was slowly changing.

I was proud of her in a way that I couldn't explain. Amelia slowly had less shame to talk about her mistakes and addiction which made me admire her even more. It wasn't something easy to talk about.

Maybe I just had to wait all along.

Maybe I need more patience than I thought.

I had to learn to be satisfied with the baby steps. It was necessary that I accept the good and the bad, the hard and the easy, and the victories and failures. It took me a while to learn that God was a God of baby steps.

He did everything in his own timeframe. God worked everything for the greater good. God wasn't, isn't, and never will be a microwave. He's a crockpot who takes His time to create a masterpiece. Even if something would take a long time to finish, I needed to have the fruits of the spirit during the entire process.

If Amelia was supposed to be mine then so be it. If she wasn't, then I needed to learn how to be happy with that as well. All I wanted was to help Amelia realize that she would only receive change and transformation in Christ.

In her words, *"I wanted to be strong enough to face the challenges in life and not hide behind drugs and alcohol. I don't want to be a coward anymore."*

AMELIA
CHAPTER 24

These past few weeks have been eye opening. The sermons made me curious, it made me ask questions. Curiosity had gotten the best of me. It had gotten to a point where I didn't want to know more, I *needed* to know more.

Everything that Lily talked to me about, brought me to my knees. The love of God, the plans He had in store for me, and the sacrifice Christ went through broke me. It shattered my pride in a way that nothing ever did. Whenever we talked about the bible, it filled me with a peace that I always searched for.

My soul twisted and turned because of my wrongdoings. Yet despite all the wrong I do, God still loves me?

What type of grace is that?

What type of grace is just given freely and doesn't expect anything in return?

Sermon after sermon made tears roll constantly down my face. I gave up wearing makeup or looking pretty because I learned it wasn't about that. I didn't need to be pretty to go to church, I could go as I was: Broken, unhealed, and constantly suffering.

All God wanted was a relationship with me like father and daughter.

All I wanted was to be loved by a parent figure. Lily explained to me that God wanted that. God wanted a relationship with me and that baffled my mind.

He loved me before I even knew him?

Today, I read a verse that said, *"Even if your father and mother forsake you, I will not forsake you."*

I cried uncontrollably for hours because that moment I felt seen and loved. I felt like I belonged to someone. I belonged to someone who actually wanted me.

I am such a fool.

I am a fool for turning my back to someone who never stopped loving me. I searched for peace in a world that destroyed me instead of going to a father who waited with open arms. A God who sent his only son to die on the cross for my sins and sickness.

All the excuses I ever gave were pointless. His word told me to come as I was and he will make me new.

I didn't have to change myself to be ready for him, he would do that miracle himself.

I decided that I was going to stop giving excuses and stop living in the constant lie that I was in. I was going to change my life even if everyone hated me for it.

I decided at that moment that the medicine bottle I currently had would be the last one I ever bought. I was going to learn how to live without it. The drinking was going to have to stop, it was going to have to die from the root. Anything that ever caused me to fall or give me a fake sense of peace would be out of my life once in for all.

Life was way too short for me to keep living like this and I have had enough. I have wasted twenty-six years of my life and I wasn't going to do that anymore.

I talked to Lily and she instantly cried. She reminded me that it wasn't going to be easy but I should keep pushing on because it was going to be worth it in the end

I knew that the devil had a tight grip on my heart for most of my life but I decided that I wasn't going to live in the darkness anymore.

Run and hide, Devil.

You just lost another one.

MATHIAS
CHAPTER 25

My momma told me that in a few days Amelia, Lily, and Jeremiah were going to come over for dinner and help organize Christmas decor. This meant that I only had a few days to be able to finish the project that I had started. It was going to be a surprise but now it was me against time.

Over time, Amelia slowly opened herself. She wasn't completely open or healed, but I was grateful for the progress that we have made so far. And for the first time, Amelia asked questions about God. She wanted to know answers and that overfilled my heart with joy.

Amelia explained everything to me. She told me a bit about her relationship with her parents. She also talked a little about her past abusive relationship. I told her that we didn't have to talk about it if she didn't feel ready.

"If I allow fear to rule over me then I'll never be ready." The moment she said that, it hit me like a ton of bricks.

Maybe I needed to learn a thing or two from Amelia.

When I asked her about why she stopped art, she

explained to me briefly about all the negativity she received. As Amelia talked, I noticed she missed it. You could see the missing sparkle in her eyes, the longing feeling of having a paint brush in her hands once again.

When she told me that, I felt like I needed to help her. There wasn't ever a moment where I didn't want to but this time it felt necessary. She was in a healing process and needed an escape. Something where she could be herself and no one would judge her for it.

I wanted to bring that back to her in some way because I know how important it was to do something that you loved doing. It was important to have an outlet from the world. That night, I stayed up late thinking of different ideas. There were multiple ideas but none of them stuck out to me.

Then when I went to sleep, I dreamt of an art studio. It was perfect and I knew it was a sign from heaven. Ever since that day I built it slowly. Each day I worked on it a bit more, making sure that everything was perfect. Even Pa helped me here and there. He constantly leaned over my shoulder to check my work and give me pointers when I needed them.

I wanted the building to be as simple as possible, her paintings needed to be the center of attention. So I decided to make the walls out of bricks and walnut wood. The support beams and trim would be white, which would give it a cozy studio feel.

With Momma's help, she helped me decide on furniture pieces. She said that I should decorate it just enough to make it comfortable but leave most of it up to her.

So after much thought, I grabbed a note pad and some paper to sketch the idea in my mind.

I do not have the talent for art.

In the sketch, there was a table with just enough space for her to create her beautiful artwork. It was going to be placed in front of the two windows that looked over the hills. The sunlight would give her the light that she needed. She could also watch the sunset or sunrise when she wanted to.

Nature would be her inspiration.

I hope she would find the same amount of beauty in a sunrise and sunset as I did.

On the other wall, I was going to build a rustic table with glass doors. She could store all her paint and extra canvas. On top, there was enough space to lay her drying paintings. Momma also said that woman loved space and storage and that's what I intended to give Amelia.

Everything was planned to perfection. It was going to be hard work and I knew I was going to get a scar or two on my hands but it was going to be worth it. Every second and every sweat bead was going to be worth it because it was going to be for her. It was going to be my gift to Amelia and maybe it would remind her of me.

I wanted her to remember that I would always be by her side no matter what. I let her leave once and I wasn't planning on letting her go again. She was stuck with me forever. Lovers or friends, whatever it may be, I wanted and needed her in my life.

I TOOK A FEW STEPS BACK AND ADMIRED THE progress. I had just put the roof on and it was finally starting to look like a studio.

Part of me wanted to make the walls and ceiling transparent to be able to see the rain, but I knew it wasn't going to end well. I needed this to be safe.

I needed my artist to be safe.

After several cups of lemonade and a huge lunch, I went back to work to make sure I didn't waste a single second of my time. I had three and a half days to finish and I was beginning to doubt it would be enough time.

I was so close to the finish line but at the same time I felt like it was so far away. After admiring it, I began on the furniture. Whatever I could make by hand, I would.

The music on my speaker helped the time pass. Pa helped out every few hours. Momma made sure that I wasn't pushing myself too much, so she fed me every couple of hours.

When it was finally sunset, I began to put everything away. The saw and the tools were covered in sawdust but I was way too tired to clean them.

Maybe this was too soon but at the same time, I felt like I had wasted enough time. Maybe it wasn't a lover's love but it was a childhood love. And after everything she has been through, I think she deserved an act of kindness.

AMELIA
CHAPTER 26

"Sugar, this house starts decorating for Christmas the day after thanksgiving." Mrs. Anderson said before turning around and looking at me with mischief in her eyes.

She lowered her voice so that only I could hear. "Even though Christmas really starts on November first, two people think I am insane for thinking that. Bless their hearts, they don't know what they are missing out on."

I covered my mouth with my hands to keep my laugh as quiet as possible.

Today I was at Mathias' house because Mrs. Anderson kindly invited me over for dinner and to help decorate the house. Lily and Jeremiah were going to come over later. It felt like a small get together.

"Mamma, you would decorate for Christmas if it was the first day of July." Mathias yelled from across the house.

"Y'all haven't heard of Christmas in December, have you? No, you haven't. It's called Christmas in July, so even I am behind schedule." She responded with a sneaky grin on her face.

"Don't let her fool you. She's a crazy woman, but I am still madly in love with her." Mr. Anderson said, hugging Mrs. Anderson from the side. He gave her a gentle kiss on the head, completely obsessed with his own wife.

After much hesitation, he let her go so that she could continue making dinner. I told her that I could help, but she insisted that I was a guest and she must do it herself. She wanted me to kick my feet back and, in her words, *"She wanted to stuff me like a tick because just by looking at me, I was going to float away."*

She had a constant smile on her lips as she cooked. Mr. Anderson would be in the kitchen one moment and then outside and later sitting on the couch, he never stayed still. Mathias had gone outside to do who knows what while I sat on the sofa doing nothing. Once in a while, Mr. Anderson would whisper something in her ear. All she did was nod or glance outside with the smallest smile, their little exchanges made my heart happy.

"Please let me help. I can wash the dishes." I stood and rushed to begin the dishes.

Above the sink, there was a beautiful white framed window. It over-viewed their wonderful backyard; *this is a dream.* The kitchen was spacious enough for a few people but still felt cozy and small.

"I love that spot right there," Mrs. Anderson whispered, her gaze focused on the view. "It's beautiful."

It was beautiful for many reasons, but the natural beauty of nature always baffled me. And as each day passed by, I was more convinced that there was a God.

We stood side by side in comfortable silence. Neither of us felt pressure to say anything. Several minutes later, Mrs.

Anderson asked me a question I knew she had been waiting for.

"Can I ask you a question, Sugar?" Her southern accent rang with class and love.

"Anything for you, Mrs. Anderson." I grinned because I knew how much she hated my calling her that. Mrs. Anderson always preferred me to call her *"Momma"* or her actual name, *"Mabel."*

She softly bumped my shoulder with hers. "I ain't that old to be called Mrs. Mrs was my mother." She laughed and took a steady breath before asking a question.

"Why did you come back?" I knew she was dying to know the answer to that question. "After all this time, why did you come back to the small town of Love Creek?" I could feel her steady gaze looking at me.

It surprised me that she didn't know the answer. I had expected Mathias to have told her everything, but he didn't. And that was worth so much to me; *he respected my boundaries.*

I turned off the tap water but couldn't bear to look her in the eye. Mrs. Anderson and Mathias had the same eyes, the same gaze. And every time I looked at Mathias' eyes, it made my stomach flutter. He was the only guy who ever cared about me, and that did unspeakable things to me.

"I have a minor problem with addiction to two things," a nervous chuckle left my lips. "My parents warned me several times about my addiction and then disowned me for it because I would always be at home drunk or out drinking." I remember those days like they were yesterday. "It was my way of forgetting the pain."

Tears blurred my vision, and I turned to her to show her how much it hurt. She didn't say anything, but her own eyes filled with tears. She whisked her hand up and down my back, giving me a sense of comfort.

"It hurts so much. I don't have somewhere to call home or parents to call mine. The only thing that I had was a toxic ex that abused me both verbally and sometimes physically." I know I was on the path to being cured of all that trauma, but it still hurt. And every time I talked about it, I felt like something inside me was set free.

Suddenly, I felt like someone dumped a bucket of cold water on top of me. My arms were covered with goosebumps, nervous about continuing the conversation.

This wasn't something that I liked talking about, but I knew I had to if I wanted to overcome it. I wiped the tear on my cheek with the back of my soapy hand.

"It isn't easy, and Lily was my only way out. But now, memories have come back. Feelings for certain people came back." She instantly knew who I was talking about. "And people whom I never thought I would see again are the same people I am constantly around."

Mrs. Anderson nodded in silence. She understood every unspoken thing I didn't say.

My departure all those years ago didn't just affect me. It affected all the people who loved and cared about me. Relationships were put on pause, and friendships were frozen in time.

"I searched for help in alcohol, but it never resolved the problem. It only made the pit deeper and darker." That truth was hard for me to admit to myself. "I searched for people but they left me even more broken. I'm starting to find the truth but it's hard and I feel like I don't know myself anymore."

I lowered my voice even though there wasn't anyone

around us. "I lost the passion and love that I once had. I don't even paint anymore because of everything that happened but I miss it so much." I couldn't believe that I was about to admit something that I swore to never tell a soul. "I missed him more than I thought I did. Every time I looked deep into his eyes, I saw the person he had became, it's like-"

I stuttered as I tried to find the right words. "It's like I am looking at what I lost. Yet I'm looking at what I want." I didn't want Mathias to leave my life. I wanted him to be in my life, one way or another. "Maybe I was too young to know what love was, but he showed it to me and always loved me despite whatever I went through."

She gave me a warm smile, and without speaking a word, she wrapped me in a big hug. Both my hands were still hanging over the sink, covered with water and soap. I let my head rest on her arm and let the rest of the tears roll down my face without any restraint.

She had just asked me a simple question, yet somehow she could take out everything from me. She was the mother figure that I've always wanted and always needed.

"I am here for you. Think of me as your momma. Come to me with your tears, your laughs, your problems, your joys, and I will be with you through it all."

She pulled back and looked at my face. Our faces were swollen and red from the tears. Mrs. Anderson didn't make a single sound as she cried.

"About Mathias. He never had a simple life after you left. My health problems and his failed relationship were like a boulder that hit him with full force. He could barely get back up after everything that had happened. But let me tell you-"

She squeezed my arms. "He never once forgot about you. He never once hated you." That brought me so much comfort. "He was here, he waited, he hoped, and he prayed that you would eventually come back. He cares about you so much that there aren't enough words to express his emotions. You are something super special in his life, and sometimes he doesn't know how to say that."

"I thought he forgot about me." More tears ran down my face, my heart skipped several beats.

"I know that boy would give up his life to save yours and not just yours, everyone he loves. I don't even know how his chest holds that big heart of his." We both chuckled and looked at each other. We didn't need to finish the conversation. Our gazes and hearts spoke together.

Mathias was always there for me during every single moment of my life. He always made me laugh when I wanted to curl up into a ball and cry. Mathias calmed me down when I wanted to hide and die. He hugged me when I wanted to push him away.

The door creaked open, and our eyes instantly widened. We wiped the wet tears off our faces and continued doing our tasks. She gave me a side glance, and both of us erupted in laughter.

Could men hear their names miles away?

"What are you two laughing at?" Mathias' voice was deep and captivating.

He stood right beside me and washed his hands. Our arms brushed, which instantly brought warmth and a type of peace that I was falling in love with. I trailed my gaze to his face. He wasn't even looking at me, but had the biggest smile on his face as he talked to his mother. I could tell that the tension that was in his body not long ago had completely faded away.

Then our eyes finally met, and it was like time itself stopped. His chocolate brown eyes completely captivated me. It looked like milk chocolate, different shades of brown swirled together. He smiled, and little creases formed around his eyes. My gaze dropped to his lips for a second, and for a brief moment I wondered what it would be like to be kissed by someone who actually loved me. A person who would kiss me because he loved me. Kiss a person who respected my boundaries.

Mathias spoke in a raspy, gentle tone, "Thank you."

Before I could ask why he was thanking me, Mathias rushed up the stairs to freshen up.

I don't know what that thank you was for, but I had a hunch it was something to do with his mom. Whenever she felt stressed, Mathias couldn't relax. He only calmed down when he saw that his mother and father were okay.

That was another thing about Mathias Anderson. He put everyone before himself. He put everyone's health, problems, life, and joys in front of his own. That's Mathias' true essence.

I continued washing the last few dishes in the sink and couldn't help but think about everything that happened for me to get where I am now.

Every awkward conversation and funny joke we had led up to this moment. And over time, my feelings were changing. Maybe, just maybe, I was beginning to have feelings for Mathias again. I was ashamed of the fact that I forgot about what we had for so many years. Now, I realized how much I needed him in my life.

Mathias was back in my story, and I needed to learn

how to organize my feelings and emotions. Nothing was black and white anymore. The lines were being blurred, and when I was around him, my mind couldn't think straight.

What if I actually was falling in love with Mathias?

WE LAUGHED SO HARD DURING DINNER. DINNER was apparently the best time to talk about embarrassing stories about me and Mathias. There were things that Momma said that I didn't even remember. My cheeks hurt so much from the constant laughter. My lungs and stomach begged for a moment to breathe, but I just ended up laughing even harder.

Mr. Anderson said nothing, he was more of the silent type. All he would do was hum when he would agree with something that was said. He simply listened to all the surrounding chaos.

Mathias sat right beside me, and he laughed as much as I did. He protested that I didn't want to listen to stories about him. Mrs. Anderson—actually Momma—ignored his request and continued telling stories.

"It wasn't my fault the sheep were let loose." Mathias responded, shoving a spoonful of dinner in his mouth to stop himself from laughing even harder. He had the biggest grin on his face, and I knew he loved this moment as much as I did.

Mr. Anderson sat right in front of me and gave the biggest eye roll known to man.

He cleared his throat, "It must have been a ghost then because somehow he was the only one who had gone outside. And somehow, he ripped his jeans from all the times he struggled to get them back."

Then, Mathias' knee and hand slightly touched my leg. I glanced at the soft touch underneath the table. It felt like electrical beams flowed through us. I looked up at Mathias, completely oblivious to what his touch did to me.

The logical part of me would have scooted farther away and ignored that minor exchange, but I didn't. I stayed there, frozen by a single touch.

My insides were melting. His thumb brushed back and forth against my kneecap.

Someone turn on the fan, turn up the air conditioner, someone do something! I couldn't even focus on what everyone was talking about. My mind danced in the middle of the stars, the butterflies in my stomach were released.

I didn't want to raise suspicion, so I laughed and placed my hand above his.

Now it was Mathias' turn to be surprised. He looked at me, but I ignored him. We interlaced our fingers underneath the table, and that was the moment reality struck me.

I have feelings for Mathias.

Electricity couldn't be compared to this. There weren't enough words to describe the flicker between us.

"I am stuffed as a tick. No more food for me." Mr. Anderson announced.

He gave Mrs. Anderson a small kiss on her forehead and thanked her for dinner. Everyone rubbed their stomach and was beyond satisfied with what they had just consumed.

As Mr and Mrs Anderson cleaned up, Mathias and I didn't stop looking at each other. Our hearts spoke a deep, silent conversation.

I smiled like an idiot, my cheeks hurt from the constant

grin on my face. Mathias had a soft smile, his dimples barely visible. I loved every smile Mathias ever showed me. I saved each smile in my memory for any gloomy day.

"I have a surprise for you."

My eyebrows rose to my hairline, completely caught off by his comment.

"Oh?" I responded.

He smirked, "I have been working on it for a few days, and if you don't like it, then please just give me a fake smile."

I sighed and glanced at him. "You have known me for basically my entire life. I know I will love it."

Time slowed, and everything around us faded away.

Man oh man, Mathias has an effect on me.

He took my hand from underneath the table, and slowly lowered his lips to my hand but never once broke eye contact. I couldn't put into words to explain how I felt at that moment. All I knew was that there wasn't a greater feeling than to be cared for by a man who actually knows you.

To be loved is to be known.

Mathias pressed the softest kiss on the back of my hand, my lips parted in an *oh* shape. My lungs desperately searched for air.

Mathias Anderson could swoon any lady he wanted to. He probably could have anyone he wanted, but he wasn't that type of person. Mathias was nothing less than a gentleman.

He wasn't demanding or too much, rude or egotistic.

Mathias is perfect in my eyes. I hope he finds true love.

The thought of him finding love made my stomach twist and turn because I wanted him to find love and happiness, but at the same time, I didn't want him to find love or happiness with anyone else.

Whatever I felt towards Mathias, felt scary and unpredictable, but I guess that's what love does to someone.

"Are you ready?" He looked at me with the sweetest sparkle in his eyes. He held onto my hands, awaiting a response.

I trusted Mathias more than I trusted myself. Nervously I answered. "Yes."

MATHIAS
CHAPTER 27

"What's up your sleeve?" Amelia questioned, a suspicious look on her face.

Our hands were still intertwined together. *I have been dreaming of this for so long.*

All the times I wondered what it would be like to hold Amelia's hand were finally answered. Her hands were soft and small, it fit perfectly in mine. The way her arm brushed against mine as we walked side by side made my heart leap and jump.

Someone might need to resurrect me after this.

"Nothing." I whispered. The corner of my lips lifted in amusement because I realized how much Amelia hated surprises.

She hadn't noticed the studio only a few feet away. The small little space I built just for her. Her eyes were focused on either her feet or on me.

We finally stopped walking, but I didn't look at the studio. My eyes were fixed on her and her reaction. I looked at Amelia's side profile, trying to read her reaction, but there was nothing. Her expression was completely blank for several moments as her brain tried to put the pieces together.

"What is this?" Amelia's eyes darted all over, trying to understand what the surprise was.

She let go of my hand, and instantly I missed the warmth of her hand. Amelia took baby steps, proceeding the studio with caution.

"Come on." I ran to the entrance before she did so that I could open the door for her.

Even the door handle had her name written all over it. It was a transparent acrylic knob with a small paint pallet inside.

She hadn't even noticed that minor detail, but I knew she would later. The moment she stepped in, her mouth dropped wide open. Amelia twirled around and admired everything. The greenery, the books, and the sketchbooks.

Many types of pencils, colored pencils, and watercolors. I bought every single art supply that I could get my hands on.

The desk faced the windows, a light glow illuminated the space. Everything was organized to perfection, grateful that I had a mother who loved to organize and clean.

I stood by the entrance of the studio, my eyes fixated on her. Amelia's reaction was priceless.

One moment she teared up, and the other moment she bounced on her toes, excitement radiated off her. She looked like a kid in a candy store.

"You made an art studio for me?" Amelia looked at me, her eyes welling up with tears once again.

Amelia is a ball of emotions.

I had to pick my next words meticulously, or Amelia would burst into happy tears.

"All of this is for you." I admitted. "I made it myself, but I will admit that my parents helped out." My voice was thick with emotion, unable to speak clearly.

She took a step closer to me. My mind couldn't think with her this close.

I have very little self-restraint when it comes to Amelia Johnson.

"But why?" She questioned.

"Because I know how much you love art, Sunshine. You deserve to be happy and do something you love. Your happiness is worth more than gold to me. So if there's something I can do, then I will."

Amelia took one long stride and wrapped her arms around my neck. Her flowery perfume infused the air around us. It was sweet, flowery, and intoxicating.

I officially have my favorite scent.

"Thank you. Thank you. Thank you." Her sweet, gentle voice whispered in my ear.

Her voice. Her voice made all the anxiety melt away. Amelia's voice could calm any agitated storm inside me. Her laugh was my drug.

I hugged her tightly, not wanting to let go, not even for a second. Her arms wrapped perfectly around me; *this is the best thing ever.*

All the dreams and questions I ever had about how it would be to hold her in my arms were all answered in less than twenty-four hours.

Money couldn't be compared to Amelia's happiness. Her joy and the big smile on her face made me feel like I had won the entire world.

She tried to pull away, but I wasn't ready to let her go. Our faces were mere inches apart, and I couldn't help but look at her beautiful lips.

They were rosy pink, and I never realized how much I wanted to kiss them. They were perfect. At that moment, I finally admitted to myself that I wanted something more than friends. And it might be too early, but I didn't care because I still wanted her.

I wanted only my name to be on her lips and only hers. Even after my failed relationship in the past, that never amounted to what we had.

With much struggle, I brought myself back to reality and gave her a warm smile. "You're welcome."

She looked around once more and whispered, *"Amazing."*

She is beautiful. And this is where she belongs. She deserves to do something she loves.

Amelia took another glance out the window. The window had a beautiful view, but it could never be compared to her.

Her arms were wrapped around my waist, her head pressed against my chest. She clung onto me like she didn't want to let me go; *don't worry, Sunshine. I don't plan on leaving.*

Also, were we dreaming?

If we were, then I never wanted to wake up again.

"What did I ever do to deserve you?" She asked.

"I know I am one of a kind." I quipped.

Amelia looked up and gave me those looks, *why are you ruining the moment?*

"I am so grateful to have someone as beautiful and smart

as you in my life." I couldn't say *friend* because it would be a lie. *Friend* was far from what I saw her as.

She blushed at being called beautiful. "Thank you." Amelia stood on her tiptoes and gave me a feather kiss on the cheek. The skin under her touch erupted in a hundred flames. "You're the best."

She stepped back and smirked. "Last one back has to string the popcorn."

With that, she dashed away and ran as fast as she could. Her small legs struggled to keep a fast pace; *What happens when you pair up two competitive people?*

I knew I would beat her, but as the gentleman I was, I let her get several feet ahead of me, and in the end I would beat her by a hair.

I am not competitive.

But by the time I reached the front door, she was still several feet away. I could tell that she was exhausted from running so much, so I decided to run back and walk slowly beside her.

When she got to the house, she started jumping. "I won! I won!"

We laughed in unison, pure bliss. There wasn't any pressure on us to act a certain way or say specific things. We were free to act like children with no judgment.

"Well, I guess you two are having fun" my heart jumped to see Jeremiah and Lily standing beside us. They had the biggest grins on their faces.

"I won because I am a champion, and now he has to string popcorn." Amelia struggled to speak.

"Yeah sure Amelia, we have seen you in sports before." Jeremiah laughed before Lily hit his arm and gave him a stink eye.

"You're amazing!" Lily gave Amelia a high five as they walked back inside.

"What were you two doing out here anyway?" he asked with curiosity. Jeremiah, always curious about my business.

"I was showing her something." I shrugged my shoulders so he wouldn't ask anything else.

"You're a lovesick puppy, you know that, right?" He wiggled his eyebrow.

"Shut up." I pushed Jeremiah on the arm, which made him take a few steps back.

The unrealistic part of me fell in love with Amelia. It hasn't been long since she first arrived, but that didn't dim my feelings towards her. The only thing I worried about was her not feeling the same way towards me.

MOMMA HAD ALREADY MADE SOME HOT chocolate and already popped the popcorn. Christmas jazz music played in the background. Jeremiah and I were helping my Pa get the rest of the boxes of Christmas decor.

How many boxes of Christmas decor do we have?

Lily helped Momma unpack the boxes to organize what we had. I looked around to try and find Amelia and noticed that she was sitting on the sofa with hot chocolate in her hands.

I admired her profile once again.

She is the definition of beauty.

Amelia threw her hair into a messy bun, a Christmas mug in her hands. My eyes couldn't stop looking at her because she looked like a dream. A dream I never wanted to wake up from.

"Take a picture, it'll last longer." Amelia repeated my words all those nights ago. But I was actually going to take her word for it.

I jogged to the kitchen and grabbed my phone and plopped right beside her. My arm wrapped around her shoulders, our heads lightly touched.

At that moment, I felt a hundred butterflies in my stomach. I felt like I was dancing among the stars, and there was no way to bring me down. Happiness wasn't sufficient to describe how I felt. No words explained the complexity of my joy.

"I can't believe you're actually doing this," Amelia said with a small giggle

That's another thing about her. I love the sound of her voice, it was amazing. No, it was perfect. Her voice sounded like a hundred angels singing at once. It sounded like waves crashing against the shore on a hot summer day. A cup of hot chocolate on a rainy day. It was perfect and intoxicating.

"If I don't do it, then who will?" I looked at her through the phone camera.

Her perfect pink lips were in a beautiful upright smile. A while ago, she said that there was no reason for her to continue to smile, but now, Amelia smiled like there was no tomorrow.

I believe in a God of big miracles. All it takes is a bit of time, patience, and faith.

I tried to smile as brightly as she did, all I wanted was to display the happiness I felt inside my heart.

My dimples were on full display because I knew how much Amelia loved them. I never had a reason to smile that big, but today I did.

"I love when you smile like that. I love when you smile and your dimples show. Just don't smile before breakfast." Her face serious for a second before she broke out in a giggle. "They are too bright and cute." A sneaky smirk on her face.

"I remember when you used to say that it was your favorite feature on my face. Is it still your favorite?" I asked, curious if she was going to avoid the question.

She playfully hit my chest with her hand but then left her hand there. I instantly panicked, worried that she might feel how my heart beat rapidly for her.

"Smile more, like genuine smiles. And maybe, just maybe, I still adore them." Her big doe eyes went wide, and they instantly melted me.

"I will try." I didn't have to try. Just being around her was a good enough reason to smile all the time.

I RUSHED TO FIND MY PARENTS, WHO HADN'T appeared in the living room for several minutes. Both of them were in the garage. My dad had a hand on her lower back and whispered to her, "Breathe. Relax, my love."

Even from afar, I could hear her rapid breaths. Then her eyes locked with mine, and instantly I knew she didn't want me to see her like that.

"Momma?" I took a step closer to her but stayed far enough so she didn't feel suffocated.

"I am fine. Go back and have fun with your friends." she mumbled and tried to put a smile on her face.

"What is going on?" I asked Pa, but he didn't say anything. Instead, he gave me a familiar gaze.

"Your mom has been working and stressing her body too much. She collapsed with a box in her hands and fell on her back."

The stress Pa felt in that moment made me feel even worse that I hadn't noticed earlier. He cradled Momma against his chest, gripping onto her for dear life.

My eyes went wide, but before I could ask anything, she spoke, "I am fine, my boy, just a little hiccup."

"A hiccup that could have led you to the hospital." My voice came out harsher than I wanted.

Quickly, I rushed to kneel beside her. My hands on either side of her arm. "Let's get you to bed. You need to rest."

She nodded her head in agreement. My lungs finally breathed again, grateful that she didn't insist on staying.

We walked right past everyone, me on one side of Momma and Pa on the other side. We helped carry her so she would avoid carrying herself.

I could feel everyone's eyes. The question in their minds was louder than the silence.

"WHAT HAPPENED?" JEREMIAH, LILY, AND AMELIA asked in unison.

"Nothing, she's just tired." I struggled to make eye contact with everyone.

Before they asked even more questions, I rushed into the kitchen. Horror like memories flashed through my mind. Anxiety and fear crept into my bones. The kitchen felt like it was slowly shrinking around me.

"Cowboy, what really happened?" Amelia's hands

touched my back and calmed down the raging fear inside my heart.

I closed my eyes for a moment and took several small breaths. She rubbed her hand up and down my back. She didn't pressure me to say anything, or push me to open up.

I turned around, and a few more tears fell down my face. I guess I didn't know how much this actually affected me. This was just a painful reminder that a few Christmases ago she couldn't decorate or do anything. Momma was stuck in the hospital, and her going back there petrified me. That wound barely closed, too painful to even think about.

"She pushed herself too much and fell with a heavy box on top of her." I let out a huff of air. A struggle to keep an even, steady breathing.

Amelia didn't say anything at first. All she did was use her hand to wipe the tears off my face and cradle my cheeks.

"You know you don't have to pretend you're strong and that you can handle it all by yourself. We are here for you, you know that, right?"

My mind couldn't think straight. Doubt, pain, suffering, and fear invaded it.

"But what if y'all leave again? What if I have to learn how to take care of myself and my family on my own, with no one to lean on?"

Her face shifted at that comment, and instantly I regretted saying it. I didn't want to hurt her, that was the last thing on my mind.

Amelia told me a few weeks ago that she regretted not staying and leaving when I needed her most. Her eyes went glassy as well.

"That won't happen. Never again. I am your friend, and this," she waved her hand between us. "Is more than a genuine friendship. Friends don't leave each other at difficult moments like these."

I wrapped my hands around her waist, my head leaned against her shoulder. But not long after, the dam opened, and I silently drenched her shirt with salty tears. Amelia gripped onto me even tighter and played with a curl. Her touch slightly distracted me. Her hug kept me grounded as I melted into her arms.

We stayed like that for what seemed forever, and I didn't want to leave. I didn't want to let her go, I didn't want to go out and pretend it was all okay when, in my mind, it was a battlefield.

I was a mixture of emotions, and it overwhelmed me. I feared losing my mom because I don't know what life would be without her. She was the first person who taught me what love was. My momma had been through thick and thin with me. Life without her would be dull and lifeless.

"You know what I love most about you, Mathias Anderson?" Amelia softly spoke.

I chuckled, "What could you possibly love about me? I just cried like a baby in your arms."

Her hands dropped to mine. Our fingers easily intertwined with each other.

"No. You put everyone in front of yourself. Mathias, you have the biggest heart this world has ever seen. That is one of many things I admire about you, Mathias Anderson."

I smiled and gave her a light kiss on her forehead.

"Thank you for being here with me and knowing when I ain't okay. You said all the words that I needed to hear."

Amelia pulled me in for one last hug. The scent of her shampoo turned into one of my favorites. It smelled like her in so many ways.

"I think I am ready to go back." I whispered. My voice completely broken and frail. I don't know how long we stood there, but I never wanted it to end. Being in Amelia's embrace had officially become one of my favorite things.

She nodded, and we walked back into the Christmas chaos that was happening just a few feet away.

AMELIA
CHAPTER 28

Lily and Jeremiah were nowhere in sight.

Strange.

I looked at my phone and then at Mathias.

"They left." Lily had left a message on my phone not too long ago saying it was late and they needed to head to bed.

Mathias laughed. "With those two, you don't know what to expect. One moment they are here and the other, they aren't."

We played Christmas music on the television and continued to organize the Christmas decor. The vibe was perfect, and it even gave me inspiration for a painting.

I was still shocked that Mathias had built me an art studio. Never in a million years would I think that was the surprise. And not only that, it was absolutely perfect. The studio felt like a dream, complete perfection.

"Ok the tree is almost finished. There is only one thing left." He turned to put the plug into the wall.

For a few seconds, my mind only paid attention to one thing.

Wow, look at those arms.

I didn't even realize how much he worked out or how buff he was until now, but they were perfect. It was hard to stop looking at them. *Muscles are a woman's weakness.*

Mathias stepped back as I admired the lit tree. The warm Christmas lights gave a magical feeling.

"It's beautiful." I whispered, completely captivated by the tree.

"Sure is." he answered softly.

I looked at Mathias, his eyes solely focused on me. I don't think he saw the tree light up.

He had the faintest smile on his face, a content smile. Those smiles that you gave when you were happy and satisfied with life.

"Can I ask you a question?" Mathias took a step closer to me. Our arms brushed against each other, time instantly froze.

"Sure." my voice stuck in my throat.

"Would you ever consider going out with me again? But not forced by friends." A small step closer. "But because we want to."

He rubbed the back of his neck as if he already anticipated rejection.

"We want too?" I needed to tease him just a little bit. I already knew what I was going to say, but I couldn't tell him that easily.

His eyes went wide, his body slumped. "I don't know about you, but I want to. I want to go out with you, but I won't force you if you don't want to."

I smiled. "It would be my honor. A woman would be a fool to say no to you. Plus, you did just build me an art studio." A blush came to my cheeks. "I also might want to go out with you as well."

He looked at me surprised, his arms easily found their way around my waist. Mathias spun me around, overjoyed.

THE HOUSE WAS BEGAN TO FEEL LIKE A ROMANTIC fairy tale. Everything glistened with Christmas lights. The air smelled like cinnamon and pine. The boxes were pushed to a corner because both of us decided to leave most of the decorating to Mrs. Anderson. It wouldn't be Christmas without her personal touch.

There was so much holiday cheer all around us. We also packed all the fall decor into their designated boxes. I never knew Mrs. Anderson had so many boxes for just decorations, but it just showed how fond she was of hosting people.

"The house is looking amazing so far." I looked around with awe at what we had accomplished so far.

"This isn't even half of what she does. She decorates the barn, the outside, and everywhere she can get her hands on. It's become a problem." Mathias' laughs. "But I wouldn't change anything."

When we finished putting the boxes away, we decided to watch a movie and eat some popcorn. Mathias and I decided to watch Home Alone because it was a classic we would watch with one another during the holiday season.

When we were teenagers, I would always crash over and watch a movie or two. Mathias would make the craziest snacks for us to devour in seconds. Those moments were filled with happiness and a carefree spirit.

WHEN THE MOVIE ALMOST FINISHED, MATHIAS turned to me and before speaking, he shoved a handful of popcorn in his mouth.

"Could I ask you a question?" Mathias asked with curiosity.

It's been an hour and a half, since we began stringing popcorn. For every popcorn kernel that we stringed, about twenty would go into our mouths; it was about balance.

"Wow, so many questions today. What do you want to know?" I responded, focused on stringing the next kernel.

It was a miracle how only a few weeks ago, I couldn't stand the thought of opening myself up to someone. It petrified me to tell Mathias anything because I didn't want him to judge me, but he has proved otherwise. Mathias has shown time after time that he will always be by my side no matter what. And he deserved a truthful story from me. I was beginning to think that he deserved to know what I went through for the last ten years. Each time we talked about it, I explained it in more detail.

"I wanted to know what else happened in the last few years." He put up both hands in surrender. "But I am not here to force anything out of you."

Mathias shifted closer. His gaze steadily on me. And just by a look into his eyes, I already could tell what he wanted to know.

Mathias was a transparent person when it came to serious moments like these. He never had an ill intention. All he wanted was to understand, he wanted to help. I hope he is strong enough not to blame himself for what I am about to tell him.

"My ex was toxic and abusive with his words and sometimes actions." I played with the edge of my shirt. I wanted to do anything except look him in the eyes.

"My parents were neglectful after they became successful. They were also verbally abusing me with words that I don't wish to talk about. And because of those two things, I started drinking too much." It felt like a lifetime ago. "I hung out at the bar almost everyday to try and escape my world."

I blew out a hesitant breath. "So imagine my surprise when I was way past my conscious state, I looked outside and saw someone I hadn't seen in years. That made my mind go absolutely bonkers."

He cleared his throat. "I needed some fresh air to think."

I nodded understanding all the unspoken words.

"They got really angry at me because I was constantly drunk, and they provided everything for me. House, car, food, and clothes. So they kicked me out with nowhere to go."

I struggled to take deep breaths because I didn't expect to say all of this in detail. "They didn't even give me time to find somewhere to stay. So I am thankful I had Lily to back me up and give me a place to stay. Because without her, I don't know where I would be."

Lily was heaven sent.

Mathias cleared his throat but was unable to speak. His words failed him and I couldn't blame him. I don't know what someone could say after saying all that.

I left Mathias speechless; that's a first.

I continued on, "So after being with you guys, I have

been drinking less and less. But now I have to be careful because if I start again, I don't know if I will have enough strength to stop. Oh, and my ex cheated on me by dating his coworker while he was still with me."

His mouth dropped open and I swear he swore under his breath. We both stayed silent for a few moments because I knew what I had just said felt like a punch to the stomach.

When his mind finally caught up with his body, Mathias looked up at me. His eyes lightly shimmered with tears. Worry wrinkles around his eyebrows and eyes.

"I feel even worse. I feel like the worst person on earth. I feel like a prisoner that committed a crime and is still free. How was I not there when you needed me?"

Why did I tell him all this?

Now I had to fight against his doubt and anxiety. Mathias had a tendency to blame himself for things that he didn't have blame for.

"None of it is your fault. My pain isn't yours."

His eyes darted back up to me. "I should have held onto you closer. I could have tried to find you and bring you back. But I didn't." Mathias looked into the distance. I could see the battlefield his mind turned into.

Firstborns. Only child. They all felt like everything was their fault. That they were alone to resolve problems that didn't even belong to them.

"If I truly wanted to, I would have. But now, there is no going back and changing that."

I could see a lonely tear run down his slightly swollen face. But that's one fault I saw in him. He beat himself for problems he never caused. And if you weren't careful, it could destroy you.

"Mathias Anderson, you look at me right now." His eyes

darkened and his lips turned the color of snow. The color of his eyes weren't as bright as usual.

"Mathias freaking Anderson, it is not your fault and it would kill me at the thought that you think that," I desperately tried to calm the storm inside his mind. "That after ten years, you think that what I went through and what I still go through, is your fault. It's not, I promise you with my life. In fact you and your memories were the only piece of hope in my dark life."

I grabbed his hands and intertwined my fingers with his.

"You are literal joy. You are amazing and wonderful for simply being you. I admire all you do for me, your friends, and your family. But you should blame yourself for other people's failures. You shouldn't kill yourself mentally for the mistakes of others."

He squeezed my hands, "Thank you Amelia."

He pressed the lightest kiss on my forehead and then leaned his forehead against mine. Our hands still intertwined together.

"After all these years," I whispered into the heavy silence. "After all these years, I finally realized how much I really missed you." My voice trembled at admitting that truth. "I thought I lost you forever. And now I realize how much it would have killed me to never have you in my life again."

I squeezed my eyes shut and silently cried as he talked. His voice soothed the sadness within my heart.

"I thought I lost you forever. And now I realize how much it would have killed me to never have you back in my life." Matthias softly whispered.

I slightly opened my eyes, our foreheads still leaned against one another. Mathias had a smile on his handsome face; *that smile was worth everything.*

As if he could read my thoughts, he opened his eyes.

Oh how I love those brown eyes.

"Part of me thinks I am living in a fantasy. I feel like I am dreaming." I admitted to him.

This dream didn't haunt me, or torture me. Was this the feeling that people said life was worth living for?

"Can I show you something to prove that you're not dreaming?"

I nodded, his hands reached out to cup my cheeks,

"I am going to kiss you Amelia" our lips mere inches away from one another.

All the thoughts in my mind instantly faded the moment his lips touched mine. His lips were light and sweet against mine. And I practically melted in his arms; *now this is a dream I never want to wake up from.*

I shifted closer to Mathias. My arms wrapped around his neck, my fingers interlaced together.

I never felt love from a simple kiss. The chemistry this kiss ignited couldn't be compared to anything I had ever experienced.

My ex couldn't compare to what Mathias made me feel. His strong hands were wrapped around my waist, and he didn't let me go for a single moment. Without thinking, I shifted closer. Desperate for another touch, another kiss. But this kiss wasn't just for pleasure, our hearts spoke to each other. We showed our desire for one another, how much we missed each other, and how this was meant to be.

I was meant to be with Mathias and there wasn't a single doubt in my mind. I could feel him pulling away but I wasn't ready. I needed to savor this moment because I was beginning to think it was going to be the first of many.

This did way more than alcohol could ever do.

"Was that alright, Sunshine?" His voice deep, thick with desire.

My response was to kiss him again. He chuckled and proceeded to express a thousand other things. If I ever had doubt that Mathias Anderson loved me, I was going to remind myself of this moment.

There was a complete difference from trying to find love to love finding you. You could run for miles but it would always be there. There was no running from it. I could admit, wholeheartedly, I had fallen in love with Mathias Anderson.

I pulled away. My lungs gasped for air.

"You are so much cuter when you blush." Mathias chuckled, his finger brushed the loose hair away from my face.

I thought it was weird in romance movies but it was much more romantic when it happened to you.

Sheesh. Someone please turn on the air conditioner. Get me a fan. Where is the fridge?

I shoved my face into his neck and tried to hide my blooming smile. I knew I was smiling like a fool.

I was happy. I was dreaming. I was living. I was alive.

All those church sermons, all those preachers, and everything in between finally made sense.

God won't give you something you want until you learn the value of it.

Mathias squeezed me even tighter, a gentle kiss pressed against the side of my head.

I feel loved, protected, and free.

AMELIA
CHAPTER 29
(FLASHBACK)

No one dragged me to church. No one bribed me, but I felt like I needed to go. My heart ached and my stomach was as cold as ice. Something inside me longed to be within those four walls. Somehow those walls brought me more comfort than any other place I set foot in.

Wear something comfortable.

Sweatpants and a hoodie were the first things I laid my eyes on in my closet. My hair didn't want to work with me today, so a messy bun was the only option.

Lily questioned when she saw me leaving, "Where are you going?"

"Church." I responded before I shut the door closed behind me.

Church this week was on Saturday, but the pastors had said the door was always opened to those who needed it.

I needed it more than anyone.

There was a desperate cry within my heart to be in the church. To rip open my heart and have a moment with God. I didn't want eyes or ears to judge me. All I wanted was to talk like no one was watching or listening. God brought comfort to my heart as he began breaking down the walls of my pride.

Not everything needed to be exposed to everyone. The hidden place was worth more than any treasure the clamoring world could offer.

So the moment I stepped foot into that church, my heart began writing a card to my heavenly father.

AMELIA
CHAPTER 30

"He did what!" Lily shouted with excitement.

She looked like a child who had ants in her pants or was being offered an entire candy store. Her eyes wide with excitement, her body radiated joy.

I explained every romantic detail to her. It felt like I was watching a movie, a movie I would never get tired of.

"Mathias is a romantic cowboy who I have fallen for." A small smile as I took a long sip of the hot coffee in my hands.

Lily had more questions than I had answers to. For every question I answered, she managed to create ten more.

"Take my advice and snatch him up before another girl gets any ideas." She wiggled her eyebrows up and down.

I hadn't told her about the kiss yet because imagine if I did. *If she got this excited over a hand kiss, imagine a pucker on the lips.*

"And this is why I am called Mrs. Cupid. Think of what would have happened if I hadn't left." She formed her hands into a heart. A big grin on her face like she had won the lottery.

Now, I was glad that she had left because it gave us a moment. It allowed us to be vulnerable and to be ourselves.

An itching feeling burned inside me. It burned because I hadn't told her the best part of the night. And several times, it almost slipped. But before it could, I shoved a snicker-doodle cookie into my mouth.

Haven wanted to try new recipes at the bakery and my sweet tooth wasn't complaining.

"You're hiding something." She crossed her arms and a suspicious look was written all over her face.

"We kissed." I mumbled.

"What? I couldn't hear you." Lily shouted louder.

Out of nowhere, loud footsteps ran down the stairs. By the sound of it, I had a deep feeling it was about to get crazy.

"They kissed, Lily! They kissed. I told you it was a good idea to leave!" Jeremiah came into the living room gasping for air.

His eyes went back and forth between the two of us, everyone quiet for a moment.

The silence before the bomb explodes.

Lily's head whipped back to him for a moment and started laughing. "Sure, that's funny. Nice prank you two."

Jeremiah and I looked at her with blank faces. Her eyes darted back and forth between the both of us, several expressions were written all over her face. You couldn't tell what was happening in her mind.

"Wait, you kissed?" Lily finally asked.

I slowly nodded, my heart left my chest the moment Lily let out the biggest squeal. She jumped up and down and ran around the house. A dose of adrenaline had been deposited into her veins.

"And how was it?" She came running back, almost colliding into me.

"If I tell you, you'll fly to the moon." A big smile on my lips. No attempt to try to hide the butterflies fluttering in my stomach and the hearts in my eyes.

She looked at Jeremiah and he raised both hands into the air. "Mathias told me what he felt, but that's bro code. I already revealed more than I should have."

Lily looked at me once again. Her eyes desperate for even a smidge.

"It was amazing." I finally gave in.

Her giggles filled the room, and my heart softened at her happiness.

Having someone support you and be happy for you was worth so much.

When it's true friendship, they get excited over the smallest things. Even if it's nothing beneficial to them, they celebrated like it was one of their own victories.

"I told you. You're falling head over heels for that man!" She squealed once more. "It's been weeks of pure torture. Both of you are like peanut butter and jelly. Coffee and whip cream. Fries and ice cream!"

I scrunched my nose. Peanut butter? Who in the world likes peanut butter.

"First of all, I hate peanut butter. And second of all, who in the world even eats fries with ice cream?"

She laughed, "Don't knock it until you try it."

"I have to go, but I am happy for you Amelia. He's a good guy." Jeremiah gave me a rugged smile and dashed back up the stairs.

"Now I want to know the juicy details." She rubbed her hands together.

Now, it was my turn to get all googly and turn into a puddle.

"He is everything. He is sweet, generous, kind, amazing, and a good kisser." Mathias could make me forget my name with just one touch.

She hit my arm lightly and leaned in to hear more.

"He isn't even comparable to my ex and thank God. Oh Lily, you were right, I am falling for Mathias."

Instead of laughing or saying I told you so, she flashed me a warm smile. "Let me introduce you to something. That is called true love and it's one of the greatest things ever."

A FEW DAYS HAD PASSED SINCE OUR FIRST KISS AND it was hard not to constantly think about it.

I sent Mathias a message saying I would be in the studio. He responded me with a kissing face emoji and a heart.

I sat in that seat for half an hour to admire everything around me. Every detail was planned and made with love and care.

I tied my hair into a messy bun, loose strands everywhere. I had kicked off my shoes the moment I stepped foot into the studio.

I glanced down at the countless trays of paints. Several shades of the same color; *the organization made my heart happy.* Brushes were organized by size and thickness.

With every brush stroke, a part of myself came alive. Every color I dipped my paint brush into, made the creativity blossom. Art was not just work, it wasn't just paper and pencil. Art was when you expressed your feelings through something you loved.

After mindlessly painting, I took a step back to admire the work. It was absolutely perfect to me. Art was my purpose and no one would ever take that away from me again.

"AMELIA." SOMEONE WHISPERED MY NAME SO softly. A calloused hand brushed up and down my back.

"Oh my goodness!" I jumped upright when I remembered where I was.

The entire whole world spun, but before I could fall, a pair of strong arms held me.

"It's just me" Mathias' warm voice soothed the anxious thoughts in my mind.

"Oh." A big yawn left my lips. "What's wrong?"

"It's almost midnight and I started getting worried about you, so I came to check in on you. I'm not surprised to find you asleep and snoring."

Playfully, I hit his chest. "Ladies do not snore"

He laughed once again. "Sorry sunshine, you snore and it's super cute."

Mathias let me go and turned around to grab something. "And I know you're going to say you're not hungry, but you need to eat. So I brought some dinner."

He extended a plate of food that made a part of my stomach turn but it looked so good.

"No thanks."

Mathias took a step closer. His voice dropped even

though we were the only ones here. "If you won't eat for your sake, then can you please eat for me?"

I looked at his brown caramel eyes. *I needed to learn how to accept other people helping me.*

"Thank you." Mathias pulled up a chair beside me. "So what did my artist create?"

My artist.

Those two words made butterflies flutter in my stomach.

"Well I made a few paintings, I couldn't stop."

I glanced at the table, covered with paintings. Mathias pointed to the first painting. "That's my favorite."

"Be careful, it's not fully dry." I held my breath as he picked it up and examined every detail. Oil paint took forever to dry but it was amazing to work with.

"This got me thinking." he rubbed his chin after setting down the painting.

"What?"

"What if we paint something together? Like when we were little kids?"

"Sure, when?"

He looked down at his watch, "How about right now? It's too late for you to go home and I ain't tired. I'll grab some wine and snacks and we can paint here."

I stepped closer to him and whispered gently, "Is this a date?"

He smirked, "Gosh darn it. You read between the lines."

BY THE TIME HE CAME BACK, I THOUGHT HE brought the whole house with him. Mathias brought drinks, snacks, blankets, and pillows. I couldn't help but laugh when I saw him struggling to carry everything.

"What's wrong?" His eyebrows furrowed together.

"Now I understand your definition of snacks and a drink. Did you bring your whole house or something?"

He grinned and explained how it wouldn't be a date if we didn't set the ambiance.

There were twinkling lights hung on the ceiling, making everything even more romantic. And everything was pure bliss.

My hands and apron were completely stained with different colors of paint. I glanced at Mathias, and couldn't help but fall back in laughter.

"What? Do I have something on my face?"

Streaks of blue covered his nose, streaks of orange and yellow on his brows and cheeks. Pink on his chin and lips.

"Just a little" a chuckle left my lips.

"Wait, you have something on your face." He reached over and touched my face. My cheeks, forehead, and lastly my lips. His fingers stayed a fraction longer, desire in his eyes.

Without him noticing, I dipped my hand in the paint and splattered it all over his clothes. He looked at me with disbelief.

"You have started a war and I am not one to lose." he responded.

I felt alive like never before. It was amazing; *incredible.* At the end, both of us were covered head to toe with every color of the rainbow.

Thank God this is washable acrylic paint.

The pillows, blankets, and even the wine glasses had splatters of color on them.

Even if we looked like a mess, Mathias still looked hand-some to me. Without thinking, my hands reached over to add even more paint. But before the tips of my fingers brushed against his skin, Mathias leaned back and I fell on top of him.

The laughter instantly died and all I wanted to do was kiss him and get lost in his touch. But I knew better than to do that. It hasn't been long since we opened up about our feelings; *good things take time.*

"You look irresistible. Prettier than the Mona Lisa."

I scrunched my nose because I didn't know if it was a compliment or an offense. "In my personal opinion, she isn't very pretty."

Mathias laughed. His laughter vibrated off the walls, making me feel immersed in his voice. "Then who do you think is pretty?"

I pretended to think long and hard. "Any princess, queen, actress, or model. The list is endless."

"Well sunshine, even if you mix them all together, they can't reach a fraction of your beauty."

"You're just saying that. You probably have said that to all the girls you dated or flirted with."

"That's where you're wrong." one corner of his lip lifted. "Between all the women I have gone out with, dated, or talked to, no one compares to you, Sunshine."

I looked down at his lips and gave him the sweetest kiss. It was just to tell him how much his words meant. And if he read between the lines, that kiss also showed how hard I was falling for him.

Without hesitation, he wrapped his arms around me and fervently kissed me back. So simple and sweet. Not harsh, demanding, or overpowering in any way.

Love wasn't meant to be harsh and demanding, instead it was supposed to be unconditional.

And whenever I looked or talked to Mathias, that's what I saw in him. And with each day that passes, I wanted what he had. The ability to love and care for people without measure was what I desired.

"You can't kiss me and expect me not to want more." Mathias' raspy voice answered, the dim light barely illuminated his face.

My body was still on top of his. My hands were pressed against his chest as he held my waist. It wasn't comfortable at all, but I was willing to stay like this just because of how close I was.

"It's not my fault, you started it." I got up and gazed down at my clothes.

"Really? Is it my fault?" He took a step closer in my direction. Eyes locked with mine and a glisten of mischief in his gaze.

I stepped away from him, slowly opening the door behind me. "Mathias, what are you doing?"

He took a steady step closer. "Nothing. I am just talking to you. Is there a problem?"

"With that look in your eyes, maybe." Before he responded, I darted out the door and dashed towards his house.

I wasn't made for running.

Me and running were like water and oil, we never mixed. The longer I ran, the less strength I had to breath which made me slow down to the speed of a turtle.

Seconds later, a pair of strong arms wrapped around me and spun me around in circles. Laughter exploded out of my chest; *I felt like a child again.*

"You were never good at running." Mathias chuckled beside my ear. A wave of tingles danced up and down my skin as he breathed against me.

"It's not my fault that you have long legs and strong lungs. It's also not my fault that you were raised on a farm and your lungs were made for this kind of stuff."

"Can I use your bathroom first?" I pleaded because even though I loved paint, sometimes I hated the feeling of it on my body.

"Of course, but before you do, let me grab you something." Mathias jogged into his bedroom.

"Here. Use my shirt and these sweatpants. My momma will throw a fit if she sees paint stains all over the house."

Mathias handed it to me and without him noticing, I placed it right beneath my nose.

It smelled like him.

The light musky scent with deep notes of cinnamon, wood, and pine. I adored his signature scent.

After a quick shower, I changed into his clothes, and looked at myself in the mirror.

A whisper yell, "Pull yourself together, Amelia. You can't have fallen this hard already."

The light gray sweatshirt he gave me had, *"Family. Jesus. Nature. Repeat"* written on the back with the design of cowboy hat and boots.

I wondered where he got this, but then I reminded myself that there was no way he was going to get this sweatshirt back.

It's mine now.

Hesitantly, I took another deep breath and opened the door.

I walked to see if he was in his room, but there was no trace of him there. And instead of walking downstairs like a normal person, I snooped into his room and looked around.

There wasn't a shadow of a doubt that Mathias decorated his room. Because if Mrs. Anderson got her hands on this, it would be decked out with every type of Christmas tree.

The only colors were brown, black, and white. The walls with pictures and quotes. I glanced to the corner and saw his completely torn and broken cowboy boots.

If it is unusable then why did he still keep them?

"It might seem hard to believe, but I actually am getting a bit bored of this basic room." my heart jumped out of my chest the moment I heard Mathias' voice behind me.

"You don't have to change it if you don't want to."

"I know, but this isn't me anymore. But I am letting the idea boil in my mind." Mathias shrugged his shoulders and stepped further into his room.

That's when I noticed he had taken a shower. He had sweatpants and a t-shirt, making him absolutely irresistible.

"Why do you keep those boots if they are unwearable?" I pointed to the boots

Even from afar, I could see the places where he tried to glue it.

"Memories, I guess. It's hard to let go of them. It was the first pair of boots I ever got. Those boots mean a lot to me and so do the memories." he chuckled and sat on the bed beside me.

"I have been meaning to get a new pair, but I feel selfish if I spend money on myself, so I never did."

Keep that information for later.

"So, I can't go home because it's so late. What do you want to do?"

He smirked, "You can't go home because it's late or you don't want to?"

I ignored his question and repeated my question, "What should we do?"

"I have an idea." he stood up and extended his hand for me to take it.

MATHIAS
CHAPTER 31

Do you know how hard it was to see her with a messy bun and in my clothes? The hoodie almost swallowed her whole. Amelia looked cuter than a litter of kittens or a newborn foal. She looked breathtaking without even trying and it was hard to keep my hands to myself.

We both sat under the stars, and consumed some peach pie and wine. Our gazes focused on the sky above as we admired all the stars.

I looked over at Amelia and noticed she was slightly shivering from the cold. Without hesitation, I shrugged off my jacket and placed it around her shoulders. Luckily, I also brought a blanket so I used it to cover our legs and arms.

Neither of us felt the need to keep talking or invade the silence. Silence was much needed after everything that happened. The light breeze made the leaves crunch and fall.

"How are you liking life here, honestly?"

The silence maintained a bit longer before she responded. There were several layers to the answer of that question. "It's definitely different from city life. The style, schedule, the people, and just life in general. It's all different. But there are more good things than bad."

"Is there anything in particular that is better here?"

She turned her head and gave me a little smirk, "Probably the people. I didn't have this when I lived in the big city. There were only lights and noise all day, every day."

"Interesting."

She shifted closer and leaned her head on my shoulder. Amelia was basically a cube of ice even under the blanket and the jacket. I wrapped my arm around her and held her close against me.

I am never letting this woman go ever again.

"Why didn't you ever move from here?" Amelia questioned, curious at my answer as well.

I really thought about that question because no one had ever asked me before.

Love Creek was the only place that ever felt like home to me. Yes, maybe when I was little a part of me wanted to explore the world. But now, I just wanted to be close to friends and family.

I have had countless problems over the years, but none of them were big enough for me to move on. I also felt obligated as an only son to stay and help on the ranch. But the biggest reason of all was when my Momma got sick and she needed me.

"I never really had a reason to leave. Everything and everyone I knew lived right here. Problems came and went, but it never was big enough."

Her response was a little head nod against my chest.

"Would you leave all this behind for someone?"

I knew Amelia was asking from a deeper point of view.

I never thought of the answer to that question because

the answer was simple to me. The only reason I would ever leave was if my significant other wanted to.

When I was engaged, my ex-fiancee left me and I didn't feel the need to go after her. She went to the city to find more money, fame, and success. There was a point where she even threatened if I didn't abandon everything and followed her. It also answered the restless question in my mind: *did she even love me?*

No, she didn't and that took a long time to admit to myself. But my soul felt instantly free the moment I let her go. There wasn't a burden on my heart or shoulders anymore.

"I would give up everything in a heartbeat for the right person. If they ain't for me then there is no point in giving up my life and desires for someone who won't even see it."

With that, Amelia went silent.

AMELIA HAD JUST LEFT AND WENT HOME AFTER MY mother forced her to eat breakfast. I told Amelia that she could go home and I would clean up our mess. And the rest of my day continued like normal. There wasn't going to be anything fun or entertaining so I was startled the moment I received a phone call from an unfamiliar number.

"Hello, who is this?"

Silence. And then the person spoke and I never thought in a million years I would hear this voice again.

"Hey Mathias! It's me, Isabella."

My blood pressure dropped, the world faded away for a brief moment. The floor beneath me felt like it was going to crumble any moment. Suffocated only began to describe what I felt.

"What in the world are you calling me for?" my voice engraved with irritation. There wasn't an ounce of patience in my body to deal with Isabella.

"I miss you."

I huffed in disbelief. A laughter almost escaped my lips, "That's how it always ends and starts with you. You find something, you abandon it, and then leave. I ain't falling again."

"But I do miss you babe." Isabella complained like a six year old.

No she didn't. I could already tell by the way she was talking to me.

"Don't call me that. We ain't together and never will be. Not in this lifetime or the next." When I was about to press the turn off button, she blurted out words I never expected to come out of her mouth.

"I messed up and I am sorry. Please, at least give me a chance to explain."

"Let me think about it." And turned off before I said or did anything I would later regret.

"Help me, what should I do?" I whispered a silent prayer in hopes that the God I believed in could hear me.

For the rest of the day, I thought about all the reasons that prompted her to call me after so much time.

Why did she call me?

Why does she miss me?

What was her motive, her reasons?

I didn't know any of the answers because my brain was jumbled at the brief interaction I just had with Isabella. The ache in my chest made me want to scream. My room spun around me, it left me dizzy and clinging onto something sturdy.

God allows people from your past to reappear in your present so that you can forgive them, fix any mistakes, and learn a lesson.

"God, it's hard to trust you but I'll try."

AT THE END OF THE DAY, I CALLED JEREMIAH AND asked if he wanted to go out and have a drink or two. WIthout hesitation, Jeremiah was up for it

When the bartender came with our drinks, we both took a long sip of our beers and slammed it on the table.

"What do you want to talk about?"Jeremiah asked as he shoved his mouth with french fries.

"How do you know I want to talk about something?"

"Whenever you want to go out, it's to talk and try to make a problem fade away." he laughed and proceeded to drink the rest of my beer.

We rarely ever went to the local bar and when we did, we never got drunk. Jeremiah and I knew our limits so we kept each other accountable.

"My ex called."

The cup froze mid air. He didn't blink for several moments, completely paralyzed from what I just said. Slowly, Jeremiah turned towards me. The wooden barstool creaked at his movement. He slowly chewed the food inside his mouth, careful to not choke.

"Oh, and she called me babe."

That was the last thing it took for Jeremiah to slam his cup onto the table and focus his eyes completely on me. Jeremiah met Isabella once and didn't like her. Now, her name repulsed him.

"What did that woman want?" He asked, disgusted that we were mentioning her again.

When Isabella left my life, Jeremiah told me that we would never mention her name again, yet here we were.

"She said she missed me and wanted to see me. Her excuse was that she needs to apologize."

He whispered a foul word and rubbed both his hands over his face.

"Dang, and isn't it funny that this happens right when you're falling for a girl?" He gave me *that* look.

"I don't expect anything less from that woman."

The bartender put a new drink in front of me and a burger. The four ice cubes floated on top of the drink, condensation formed on the sides of the glass. Droplets of water dripped from the glass onto my hand; *it's cold.*

I took a deep shaky breath and looked back at Jeremiah. He didn't say anything and a part of me was glad because I don't think I was in the head space to keep talking. Nothing had happened but it has already given me a huge headache.

"What are you going to do about it?" Jermeiah looked at me with a question in his eyes. I knew he wasn't asking about Isabella, but instead was asking about the girl who captivated my entire heart; *Amelia.*

I had no feelings for Isabella and I knew I never was going to. The moment we broke up, there was no going back. I am way past that chapter of my life and I never want to go back.

But Amelia, she is the best thing that has ever happened to me. And now, we were starting to get some-where. So I have the chance to continue what is blossoming between us or relive the past. But that never was a hard decision for me.

"I don't know man. She left me. Isabella didn't break the engagement, I did. So in her mind, she thinks this is still salvageable."

Jeremiah huffed and started tapping his fingers on the bar table. This guy has been with me through thick and thin.

He never abandoned me when life was tough, but instead, he carried the pain with me.

Jeremiah has never complained and he was honestly the brother I never had. He always had a listening ear and a shoulder to lean on. Whenever I needed to make a hard decision, he would always put himself in my shoes to help me out.

"Well if I was you, I would tell Amelia asap before she thinks you're using her. Avoid any problems or miscommunication." He gave me a side eye. "Miscommunication is the downfall of love."

"Thanks for the advice, Cupid" I hit his shoulder and asked him if he wanted to play a game of darts.

I always beat him and Jeremiah always insisted that I cheated which was never the case. Jeremiah just hated the idea of him losing.

HOURS AND DAYS PASSED BY AND I HADN'T SEEN Amelia again. It killed me. And every time I texted her to see if she could talk on the phone, she was always at work or about to go to sleep. My stomach turned every time I reminded myself that I hadn't told her about Isabella.

I wanted Amelia by my side every second of every day.

My heart was in desperate agony to feel her touch and listen to her voice.

There were only twenty something days until Christmas. Everyone gossipped about the latest news and what each person was going to do for the holiday season; *the town was alive.*

People invaded the stories, desperate to buy the final details for their holiday celebrations. Kids bursted with excitement to finally figure out what they would get for Christmas. Couples strolled up and down the sidewalk. The crisp air turned everyone's noses and ears bright red.

Today I needed to do a few errands for my Momma. She needed groceries for dinner, a few decor pieces, and some other random things. Momma only had a few touches left before our house looks like it came from out of the grinch movie. There were Christmas trees everywhere and an unfathomable amount of lights hung on every possible surface.

She needed a distraction after a week of health problems. The hospital was the last place I wanted to go to so me and Pa made sure we did every possible thing first. So when I started to see signs of improvement, it was like I could breathe again.

After I bought everything that she needed, I drove to the church. Today wasn't Sunday but I felt like I needed extra time with God. My relationship with him had been failing so I felt all my burdens bring me down and drag me across the mud.

"What do you want from me?" I huffed out a long breath and looked up at the ceiling.

I knew that God would never abdomen me but sometimes I felt like He was so far away. There were times I thought He abandoned me, but in reality, God was always there for me.

"What do you want me to do?" my voice weak and thick with emotion.

Like the rushing of many waters, calm and still, He spoke to me. I knew it wasn't me because it was too clear, too perfect.

Trust in the LORD with all thine heart; and lean not unto thine own understanding

Lean into me, my child and I will take care of the rest.

My strength automatically renewed at the mention of those words.

AMELIA
CHAPTER 32

Today, we were having a Christmas themed girl sleepover day. Samantha, Lily, Haven, and I bought movies, games, and way too many snacks.

I never knew how much I needed these girls until they came into my life.

"But it was so not funny." Haven kept blushing as she told the story.

Haven isn't dating anyone, but there is a cute guy who keeps coming to the bakery. When Haven went to take his order, she said she had flour all over her hands and face. This mystery guy always smiled every time he saw her. But there was no way they would work out. Haven had a protective hockey brother and team behind her. They scared off any guy who came in close proximity.

"And I am not lying when I say that the bag of flour exploded right before he said hi. I looked like I aged sixty years in three seconds."

My lungs hurt from how hard I kept laughing. Lily had

toppled onto the floor, and Samantha kept clutching her stomach.

Haven shook her head in disbelief. "It was humiliating, but I will admit it was a bit funny. Glad I have an entire hockey team to save me from further embarrassment."

We all had facemasks on and were enjoying girly conversations. Jeremiah wasn't even at home, so he crashed at Mathias' house for the night.

"Me and Jeremiah have been through some embarrassing moments, but that's what makes life all the more fun." a big smile on Lily's face. "Like the time where we went boiling. It was my turn, and right when I let go of the boiling ball, I fell on the ground. Jeremiah came rushing to help, and right before he reached out for my hand, he fell right beside me. It was embarrassing but absolutely hilarious."

All our cheeks were bright pink, and our hearts were filled with laughter. All the problems and worries that had been invading my mind were completely gone.

"Popcorn and movie time!" Samantha said with excitement as she rushed to go to the kitchen.

As we waited for the popcorn and hot chocolate to finish, we sang like no one was watching. The TV played Christmas karaoke music, and with spoons in our hands, we sang our hearts away. Lily left a cinnamon candle burning, and Haven baked some sugar cookies.

This is perfect.

For the rest of the evening, we watched movies and played board games. Everyone laughed because they noticed how competitive I get at board games.

Samantha insisted on playing several rounds of UNO until she won. We kept playing UNO until three in the morning, and after much determination, Samantha won.

Lying in bed, I gazed at the ceiling, reflecting on my progress over the last few weeks. I know I'm far from perfect, but I knew for sure that I was getting better.

And maybe being kicked out by my parents hurt me, but that helped me become the person I am now. They didn't know that kicking me out caused me to push past my fears and pain.

I am also thankful for the new friendships I've made. Everything felt like it was heaven sent.

God sent people to help heal me.

I'm constantly living a miracle, a miracle that I don't deserve. Because I would have died years ago, but it was by His grace that I am still alive.

Without my parents kicking me out, I would have not met Mathias again. And he was one of the greatest blessings in my life. I don't think Mathias knows the impact he has had on my life. He taught me several things without even knowing.

"What are you thinking about?" Samantha whispered, not wanting to wake up anyone.

I shifted on the floor so that I could see her. Samantha laid down on the sofa, her face illuminated by the Christmas tree lights.

"Are you thinking about Mathias?" my cheeks instantly blushed at the mention of his name.

"Do you love or like him?" She asked.

"What's the difference?"

Samantha shifted closer and whispered, afraid of waking up the other girls.

"Liking someone is when you simply like the person for who they are, for what they do, say, and who they are as a person. The appearance, if you will." She took a slight break before continuing on. "Being in love with someone is when you see the person as someone you can't live without. You feel a need for that person to be in your life. A person who brings out the child in you and makes you dream among the stars."

Samantha sighed again. And instantly I knew there was history there. Has Samantha ever been in love? What was the story?

"Someone you can't even bear the thought of losing. Where gifts aren't enough to express your love for them."

I thought about what she said for a moment. And when I looked into her eyes, they were soft and sweet. I knew Samantha meant every single word she said, truth intertwined in her speech.

"Well then, I might love him."

She giggled and tapped my arm. Her smile as big and bright as the sun. "Well then, don't lose him. Hold on to him with all your strength because you never know your last moment together."

We said our final goodbyes and went to sleep. It was already past four in the morning, and I knew we had a full day ahead of us.

I don't plan to lose Mathias, not even for a second. I was going to do whatever I had to so that I could keep him in my life forever.

MATHIAS PROBABLY DIDN'T KNOW I WAS IN THE art studio because he hadn't come to check on me. Maybe that's another match made in heaven. I looked up every so often to see if someone was approaching.

I bought Mathias a new pair of cowboy boots and painted them. I tried not to make it super girly but still have my touch.

I painted flowers and vines around the sides of the shoe. His name painted on the back; *perfect*. I couldn't think of anything that looked more like Mathias than this.

It was like I could already imagine his big smile. I could bet money that he was going to spin me around and whisper how thankful he is. And maybe a stolen kiss or two. Quickly, I grabbed a black pen and a piece of paper.

Dear Mathias,

Thank you for always being the friend that I need. You make me laugh when life gets too hard. You're amazing, and I am forever in your debt.

When I saw your cowboy boots, I knew you needed a new one. And I thought it was finally time for you to have something for yourself.

So, I got you these boots and customized them just for you. I put everything that reminded me of Mathias Anderson. I hope you like it, and if you don't, then please just put a smile on your face. Thank you for helping me face my fears, and even though I am not completely healed, having you by my side is the best thing ever.

And this might come as a surprise, but I am grateful that my parents kicked me out because without that, I wouldn't have met you again.

I don't comprehend everything, but I know it's going to be alright.

Enjoy this new pair of boots and hat,
Amelia

I reread the note a hundred times to make sure it was as close to perfect as possible. Satisfied with the final result, I put on my jacket and headed towards the house.

Each day, it felt like the temperature dropped even more. The frigid breeze made your teeth chatter and your nose turn bright red. It hadn't snowed yet, but I was counting down the days until we had snow. People in the big city hated the snow. They said it stopped them from getting to work on time, but I loved it. I loved how it made my nose and hands turn bright red. And how it was the perfect excuse to have hot chocolate.

MY HAND REACHED UP TO KNOCK ON THE DOOR, but I heard muffled responses coming from the other side.

"It's annoying that you keep calling me. You left me in case you forgot." Mathias said.

The door slightly cracked open, which allowed me to peek inside. I noticed Mathias pacing around his room. He looked aggravated and annoyed; *what's going on?*

"I don't love you anymore. I am in love with someone else." he shouted on the phone and huffed.

Silence.

"Fine, coffee only. Nothing more than talking, and I am only saying yes so that you'll stop annoying me. I don't need anything from you." Knots formed in my stomach because by the pieces I picked up, Mathias was talking to his ex.

What did she want?

He threw the phone across the bed, and when I finally mustered enough strength, I knocked on the door.

"Come in." he mumbled. Clearly annoyed by the phone call he just received.

The moment his eyes connected with mine, his attitude completely shifted.

"I didn't know you were here." Mathias took several steps closer to me.

Why did she call him? We weren't official, so I shouldn't be jealous.

"I was in the studio. I made this for you." I extended the box to him. He looked down at the box and then back at me.

"It's not a snake, right? Last time I took something from someone, it didn't end well."

I giggled. "No, just open it." There were a hundred ants in my pants.

His mouth dropped, and time froze. Mathias went minutes without blinking, completely stunned. My heart fell to the floor, and my stomach grew cold.

Did he like it?

Did he hate it?

Give me something!

He slowly opened the envelope. His eyes read the letter quickly, a small smile grew on his lips.

"Do you like it?" I was desperate to know.

He wasn't saying anything, wasn't doing anything and was just looking at the box.

Mathias turned around and placed the gift on the bed. And with long strides, he placed his hands on my cheek and gave me the sweetest kiss. It instantly melted all my worry away. He pulled away for a brief moment and then pulled me in for another. And another and another.

"It's beautiful. I love it." Mathias whispered before pressing a kiss against my forehead. He took several steps back, a huge grin on his face.

"Gift wars. Oh Sunshine, it's on."

"What?" My mind was completely confused.

"I built you the studio. You gave me these. So now it's my turn. You're on, Sunshine."

I laughed at his silliness. "I guess you're on then, but be prepared to lose, Cowboy. This girl never loses."

We instantly had a poker face competition, but neither of us won.

This is joy.

This is healing.

God constantly healed me in ways I never expected him to. Each day that passed by, I realized that I had been wrong all along. Back then, I made the mistake of allowing pain to define me. Now, I wanted God to rewrite my entire story.

MATHIAS
CHAPTER 33

I glanced at the clock and noticed it was one in the morning and Amelia still hadn't called me. I twisted and turned in bed, desperate to know if she was okay.

Ring. Ring, Ring.

Without thinking I picked up the phone and answered it. Relief instantly washed over me the moment I heard Amelia's voice.

"Hey." Amelia's sweet voice flooded from my phone.

I blinked several times, trying to wake up my brain from the haze it was in.

"Hello Love. How are you?" I roughly asked.

She hummed, "Actually, I have never been better."

Instantly, every cell in my body woke up. "So it went well?"

Amelia had told me a few days ago that her mother called her and after much hesitation, she decided to pick it up. Apparently, her father got a heart attack and was in the hospital, fighting between life and death. Amelia rushed to the hospital, and said she would keep me updated.

Amelia cleared her throat, and all I wanted to do in that moment was give her a huge hug. *Today has probably been a very emotional day for her.*

"We apologized to each other. They told me they started going to church and wanted to rebuild our relationship. I invited them for Christmas dinner, but they already have a vacation planned, but they said they wanted to come over for the new year."

I hummed because I was completely speechless. This whole time, I expected them to reject her, but to my surprise, her parents did the complete opposite.

"God is good all the time and-" I paused, waiting for her to finish.

"And all the time God is good."

For several minutes, Amelia explained what happened. She said her father was getting better, but still wasn't perfect. The doctors said that if everything went according to plan, then he would go home soon.

Getting a heart attack was no joke and despite every-thing, I still felt bad for her father. He was getting to an old age and wasted most of his life in bitterness.

God forgive us all, for we do not know what we do.

"So, can we hang out today?" Amelia asked over the phone. Her sweet voice a sweet lullaby.

"No, I can't. I am busy."

Today, I needed to confront my ex. A woman who left me heartbroken. A person who had no regard for my feelings or personal life. I needed this to be over with once and for all.

I don't want my past to haunt me any longer.

"Oh." Her voice cracked, and my stomach twisted.

EVERY TIME I GLANCED DOWN AT MY WATCH, IT felt like not a single minute passed by. We were supposed to meet thirty minutes ago, and Isabella still hadn't shown up.

And if she didn't arrive in the next ten minutes, then I was going to go home. My patience was drawn thin today.

I needed a distraction.

I focused on the small details around me. Couples who held hands with each other. My mind instantly pictured me and Amelia doing that. Children had chocolate all over their faces; *were we ever going to have children?* Old couples gazed out the window and sipped on their lattes; *I wanted to grow old with Amelia.*

In the corner of the coffee shop sat a couple who were living in their own world. Passion burned in their eyes, love radiated off their bodies. The guy looked at her like he had won the biggest prize in life. He looked madly in love; that's how I feel with Amelia.

But my mind couldn't help but imagine me and Amelia like that. Grow old and live life to the fullest. Where we lived like there wasn't a tomorrow.

I wanted a future with her.

Amelia was the only thing I was certain of. She was the one person that I wanted with me for the rest of my life.

I was brought back to reality when a tall frame blocked my view. She had a black little dress and I instantly knew what she was trying to do. But I wasn't going to give in, my heart already belonged to another woman. But maybe my heart has always belonged to Amelia and I just never knew.

My stomach twisted when Isabella's icy cold fingers brushed against my arm. "Hello baby."

Shivers traveled up and down my spine as Isabella sat in front of me. She carried herself with so much pride that it disgusted me. And the way she waved over the waiter, I knew she hadn't changed. Isabella was as self centered as the day she left me.

"I ain't your baby." I shot back, pulling my arm away from her touch.

Her eyes barely opened since the botox covered any sense of emotion. Isabella didn't even look like herself.

"Aw don't gotta be so harsh, babe."

I growled, "I am not your babe. I belong to another woman and am happily in love."

A sense of nausea punched me in the stomach the moment she said babe. Isabella left me because she wanted money, she never wanted me. I never fit into her stereotype, so why did she come running back?

When the waiter came back, he could sense the tense conversation and turned right back.

Me too, me too.

"Cut straight to the point, Isabella. What do you want?"

She finished chewing her food, patted a napkin on her face and placed it on her lap. She acted like she was royalty, "I am here to win you back."

I couldn't help but throw my head back in laughter at her words. A part of me wished I was dreaming, that this was just another nightmare.

"You must be joking. May I remind you that you left me." My arms were crossed against my chest, not a single part of me wanted to entertain her ideas.

"I left because I never thought you would make something of yourself, but you didn't turn out too bad. Plus the city life doesn't have any men pleasing to the eyes."

There was no interpretation needed to know her intention. I was just another piece to her plan, another desire on her wishlist. Sometimes I felt like a pawn in her game of chess.

"You're delusional." I hissed loudly.

Isabella lost me a long time ago and I was beginning to think it never was love. She wanted me for money and I wanted her just to get over a woman who walked away.

We never loved one another.

We both made mistakes and at least I regret mine.

"I needed you and you left me. We are done. And there will never be anything between us."

I couldn't just sweep all the pain, suffering, and self doubt I had to endure for months because of her. I wasn't going to rid of what I now had for something I knew that wasn't going to work out.

It's a plan for disaster.

"You won't even give me one more chance? Who is the other woman in your life? What is her name?"

Unshed tears blurred her icy blue eyes. Isabella always had a way to manipulate someone into doing what she wanted; I wasn't going to fall for this again.

"I won't give you another chance because you traded me for fame and money. And who says you won't do that again?"

I let her speak and nothing. Not a single word came out of her mouth because she knew I was speaking the truth.

"For your information, yes there is another woman that wants me for who I am. She never has asked me to change into something for public appearances."

The floor creaked underneath me as I pushed myself out of the chair. Eyes drifted to our direction for a split second before they noticed it wasn't anything interesting.

"I don't hate you but you hurt me. You hurt me enough to know that I can't be with you again. So I pray and hope you find a man that will treat you well. And may he teach you that life isn't just about money."

I gazed down at her for several moments in silence. She fiddled with the plastic straw, contemplating what I had just said.

After what felt like an eternity, Isabella stood up and looked at me with a sad smile. "If this girl means as much as you say, then don't let her go. And don't let her let you go either," she took a step back from the table. "I am beginning to realize what precious thing I threw away."

My lungs could finally breathe. "Go to church. It will do you some good.

She nodded and that was my signal to walk out the door. And the moment my fingers brushed against the door, my soul felt free. My past didn't feel like a heavy burden anymore. The constant grip on my heart no longer was there.

Now I know my next mission. The one person that ran through my mind day and night. My Sunshine has made me into a better man and she didn't even know it. And despite all the fear and doubt that I knew ran through her mind, I was more than willing to fight for her.

AMELIA
CHAPTER 34

The sky felt darker and gloomier. Dark clouds covered Love Creek. A downpour was bound to happen any moment. Yet despite the heaviness outside, everyone found refuge inside the cafe.

People gathered near the fireplace and chattered endlessly. The kids were completely immersed in the Christmas movie playing on the screen, letting their parents talk in silence.

My puny fingers were tired from the amount of sweeping and cleaning I was doing. Constant mud tracks all over the shiny white tiled floor. My hands gripped the red rod of the mop, swaying back and forth. The motion had become second nature to me, my mind a blank slate.

My day was going great until someone purposely stepped on the mop and froze me in my tracks.

Those boots look familiar.

My eyes slowly trailed up the body until I met a pair of stormy black eyes. Eyes that haunted me for years and years, someone I never thought I was going to have to see again.

Brandon slowly wrapped his fingers around my wrist and gripped onto me. He pressed my body firmly against his. Brandon smelled disgusting, and I wanted to throw up from the smell.

My skin burned under his touch. Everything in me wanted to run away. Trapped in his embrace. My body paralyzed from head to toe, and there was only one thing that passed through my mind.

God, please wake me up from this nightmare.

"Hello, Amelia." Brandon's slurred and raspy voice whispered in my ear and reminded me that this wasn't a dream. It was a painful nightmare.

Brandon gripped my wrist tighter, twisting my arm as he pulled me out the door. The mop fell on the ground with a *thud,* heads briefly turned in our direction.

"Why are you so hard to find?" Brandon growled. He pushed me backwards, which made me almost trip on the brick paving.

I thought that was the whole point.

I hid away, so I never had to see his eyes again. I don't want to be reminded of my past mistakes.

"We aren't together, or are you too drunk to remember?" My voice harsh and thick with hidden emotions.

"I want you when I want you." He took a stride forward, which made me take one back.

His eyebrows and jaw tightened as he took another step forward. He rolled his hands into fists, ready to punch me.

After all this, was this always going to be my end?

After all the improvement that has happened, was this really how everything was going to end?

Brandon's voice sounded like a hundred lightning bolts at once, agony to my ears.

"You need me, and I want you. You need me for money and stability, and I want you for things you can do-" His fingers intertwined themselves in my hair.

My stomach tied in hundreds of knots, an uneasy feeling upon me. "I am doing better now than I ever did with you."

Any self-restraint that man had instantly snapped. In the blink of an eye, he had his hand wrapped around my neck. My lungs wheezed for air. And with his other hand, Brandon threw punches at my face.

The bones in my jaw cracked at the impact. *That's going to leave an enormous bruise later.*

"Women are merely objects for pleasure," His fingers tightened. "So stop acting like a fool and do what I tell you to."

His arm reeled back to give me another punch across the face, but then a powerful hand gripped his arm. The person pulled Brandon back with such force that my body was flung onto the floor.

A sharp and jarring shock flooded through me when my back hit against the concrete floor. Everything began to blur and fade away.

Focus, Amelia.

Brandon and the mystery man threw punches at one another. Their yells echoed off the walls. My head pounded, and the longer I fought against it, the more it hurt.

Then my body finally gave in. It gave into the pain and agony I was in. The darkness slowly crept into my vision. Whoever was fighting for me was going to remain a mystery, but I was forever grateful. The police sirens grew closer, signaling that the end was near.

Right before I was swept away into the dark, an arm

slipped itself underneath my head. His arms cradled me against his chest.

He smelled and felt familiar.

I didn't know if I was ever going to come back from this or how my life was going to move on from this moment. My mind couldn't fully process what had happened.

Yet the distant voice sounded like rushing waters. It was as soft as falling leaves in autumn.

"I am here, Sunshine. Stay with me."

Then the world went black. And I was glad that Mathias was the person who held me as darkness took hold of me.

"Sunshine, it's been three hours. Please come back to me. Let me take care of you."

"Amelia, you better come back before Mathias bounces off the walls. Miss you, bestie."

"Amelia, please come back. Lily and Mathias don't have enough strength to eat or drink, and I am starting to get worried. Miss your awful jokes."

"Hey sweetie, please come back. Mathias is driving me crazy, and as his momma, I need to be his cornerstone in this difficult moment. But I need you as well. Sweetie, you made a big difference in our lives, don't leave us again."

"Hey Amelia, it's Mr. Anderson. Just letting you know that we all miss you. Everyone is unsettled and worried, so please come back. My son misses you, and it hurts as a father to see his heart in such suffering. Also, do you prefer soup or a sandwich? Mrs. Anderson is already cooking for you when you wake up. Love you as if you were my daughter."

"Please wake up. We just fixed our relationship. I can't lose you."

"Hey, please wake up. I can't lose my daughter right after I had a heart attack. Do you want to give me another one?"

AMELIA

CHAPTER 35

My mind barely processed the things around me. The several blankets kept me locked in place. The aroma of beans, rice, and barbecue swirled in the air.

Every breath that I took, my lungs screamed in sharp pain. I couldn't recall exactly everything that happened, only flashing scenes of me falling on the floor crossed my mind.

Nothing was crisp or clear the moment I opened my eyes. With each blink, things slowly came into focus. First it was a table, then the bed, and lastly Lily, who was reading a magazine.

She hadn't noticed that I was awake yet, her attention solely focused on the words in front of her. My eyes gazed at things in the room. My mind tried to piece things together.

Where am I?

"You're in Mathias' room. He insisted that you slept here." Lily spoke softly, fully aware of the confusion written across my face.

My face, swollen and weary, cracked a tiny smile as I rasped, "What happened?"

She slowly closed the magazine and set it on the table beside her. Lily scooted her chair closer to me. "Your crazy ex, but now he's behind prison bars, thank the Lord."

My eyes burned, my head pounded to the sound of a hundred drums. "How?"

Lily cleared her throat. "Well, he came into the bakery and pulled you forcefully outside. I noticed you two yelling at each other and instantly called Mathias." She shifted in her chair, both feet tucked underneath her. "He came rushing and called the police. Mathias saved you, Amelia."

My throat, thick with overwhelming emotions. "Where is he?"

She smiled. "Jeremiah had to drag him away because he was going crazy. He didn't leave your side and kept making sure that you were breathing."

Something in my heart fluttered at those words. A small smile crept onto my face. Butterflies flew all around, making me happy despite the pain I was in.

"I just texted him."

A *hiss* left my lips. My hands instantly went up to cover my ears with another wave of jarring pain. Any sound was too loud, even the sound of typing on a phone.

Lily softly whispered, "I have to leave to go lock up the bakery, but I will come back to check on you."

She gave me a small wave as she left the room, the door quickly locked behind her. My face was the only thing I could move easily.

Thank you God. Even if I'm in pain, you kept me alive.

MINUTES FELT LIKE HOURS WHEN YOU WERE STUCK in bed doing nothing. Sheep hopping over the fence was the only sort of entertainment I had.

Then, a familiar scent flooded the room. A cologne I never got tired of. And I knew it belonged to the man I am deeply in love with.

"Mathias, I know you're there." I whispered into the silence, eyes glued shut.

Nothing.

My eyebrows furrowed together. "Mathias?"

My eyes slowly opened, and my eyes instantly saw him. Mathias was wearing jeans, a white shirt, his cowboy hat, and the boots I painted for him.

At first, I couldn't tell why he remained silent, but then I noticed how his skin was wet and swollen. Under his eyes were dark and heavy, his eyes were dimmer because of it.

His arms swayed side to side with each slow step he took. Mathias slowly reached for his hat and tossed it onto the chair beside the bed. There were no defined brown curls on his head. *He ran his fingers through his hair when he was nervous.*

"Aren't you going to say anything?" I struggled to speak. Speaking felt as tiring as running a marathon.

He finally reached the edge of my bed, not a single word left his sad lips. I began to lose hope that he was going to say something.

"I thought I was going to lose you." Mathias whispered into the dead silence.

His hands slowly crept closer and closer to mine, afraid it was too early. He didn't know that despite all the suffering I was in, I wanted his touch.

With a quick movement, his hand was in mine. Our

fingers intertwined with one another. The pad of this thumb rubbed against my hand.

"Sorry I wasn't here when you woke up. Jeremiah forced me to go eat something and get a breath of fresh air." He ran his other hand through his hair once more.

"Lily caught me up on what happened."

The silence was everything we needed. There were no words that needed to be spoken. Nothing needed to be explained. And deep down inside me, I knew how scared he was. Because this wasn't just almost losing the person he loved, this was reliving his past fears.

Time and time again, Mathias has shown me that he actually cared about me and it wasn't fake whatsoever. He showed me that he loved me, and that none of his words were in vain. Mathias displayed his affection towards me, not afraid to show me how he felt.

That phone call.

I was going to ask him earlier but ended up forgetting.

"I have a question."

His body swiftly turned in my direction, ready to listen to every word that I had to say.

The attention and sole focus he gave me made me squirm, but with a gentle squeeze on my hand, I knew it was okay to open up and ask.

"The day I gave you those cowboy boots," suddenly the room felt hot and small. "I heard you on the phone call with a woman."

His lips instantly pressed into a thin line, creases all over his forehead. The constant tapping of his foot stopped. Did I say the wrong thing? "And you said that you were in love with someone else. That you no longer were in love with her."

Mathias nodded, those words familiar to him. He remained quiet until I finished what I was saying. You could see the way he was trying to puzzle the words together. Explain everything with clarity and kindness.

I was prepared to know if it wasn't me.

"That was my ex." Mathias huffed, like a boulder rolled off his back. "She wanted to get back together, but I said no. Then she also wanted to meet up for coffee to explain herself, and I agreed only so that she would leave me alone."

His hands were no longer in mine, a cold and empty feeling replaced his soft touch.

"That day you wanted to meet and I said I couldn't was the day I met up with her. I promise," Mathias' body leaned closer to me. He whispered every word like it was something sacred to us. "I promise you that I shut everything down. I didn't give her any hints or make her think I was playing with her. How can I do that when my heart has been consumed by someone else?"

With the look he gave me, all my doubt was instantly gone.

Mathias leaned very close to me. Our breaths mingled together, he was only a kiss away. But Mathias was the definition of a gentleman, he respected the pain I was in.

Before I could reply to his sweet declaration of love, a shout of cheerful noise came from downstairs, "Amelia woke up!"

Elephant footsteps rushed up the stairs in our direction. And in that moment I knew that everything was going to be okay.

AMELIA
CHAPTER 36

As the days passed by, the better I got. My body grew stronger, the hope within my chest grew. It gave me hope of a swift recovery.

The doctors said the impact I had was enough to break my back, but by the grace of God I hadn't broken anything.

My life is a living testimony of God's grace.

Haven gave me a few days to rest and get better before I would go back to work. But I counted down the hours until I could work again.

Stuck in bed all day isn't any fun.

To my surprise, my mom and dad came over to see how I was. And before they left, they apologized to Mr and Mrs. Anderson. Mathias said that even my father got emotional.

My father has never shown a fraction of emotion since the day I was born. That man was a stone wall, but God was breaking his heart of stone.

Love Creek definitely had faith intertwined in everything. Everyone had a personal relationship with God. And you could tell by the way each person cared for one another.

This town was just an enormous family. Single mothers and widows always had the entire town to help them during hard times.

Maybe this accident helped me realize that I wasn't alone.

I am not forgotten.

I am not forsaken.

And yes, I have worth because I am made similar in the image of God.

I realized that there are people who love me. But that wasn't the best part.

The greatest feeling is knowing that there's a powerful God who loves me despite all my failures.

That was something that brought me comfort, even in the most difficult times.

LILY AND I HAD TO ROLL OURSELVES OUT OF THE bakery. The closer we got to the holidays, the more our legs and back begged for help.

When Friday finally arrived, we threw ourselves onto the sofa and let out a sigh. The sofa was warm and fluffy. It hugged us tight and didn't let us go.

Wine glasses in one hand and a snack in the other. We turned on the TV and zoned out. Our throats were exhausted from talking to hundreds of customers. Kids constantly screamed, adults kept changing their orders, and ovens that didn't want to work. I feel bad for Haven because she tried her best, but at the end of the day had a mental breakdown. She said she has been going through a lot, but is glad that she has both me and Lily by her side.

"Mathias?" she asked after an hour of our being .

"Haven't talked to him since the minor accident I had. Both of us have been too busy."

We weren't avoiding one another. Time just wasn't working in our favor.

We both took a long sip of the wine, a small moan left my lips. I had overcome my addiction, but had to be careful. Careful not to fall into the same trap I once lived in.

During the long ads, my body begged for a long hot shower. The lavender scented steam would wipe away all tension and worries. As I took a shower, Lily got up to make herself another batch of popcorn.

When I heard the movie play again, I rushed downstairs, skipping a step or two on the way down.

"Where is Jeremiah? I just noticed he isn't here to smother you in kisses." I commented.

She gave a weak laugh. Her eyes closed; *she is about to fall asleep any second now.* "He is out with Mathias, I think. Honestly, don't tell Jeremiah that I love him to pieces, but sometimes I just need a break."

My heart fluttered and skipped multiple beats. The mention of Mathias made me melt into a puddle of warm feelings. Before I could respond, I noticed she had fallen asleep. A light snore came from her lips; *she's knocked out cold.*

Minutes later, Jeremiah walked through the door. His face instantly melted when his eyes looked at Lily. He gently closed the door behind him and nodded in her direction. "What happened?"

"Let's just say today was a hard day and our bodies weren't able to keep up. The movie isn't even finished, and she's knocked out."

He threw his keys and phone onto the nearest sofa. Gently, Jeremiah took away the popcorn bowl from Lily's hands and picked each piece that fell in her lap.

Once he finished, he lifted her like a baby. Lily murmured against his chest, arms around his neck, "Baby, you're home."

"Hey baby, let me give you a long, hot shower. Then I'll give you one of my t-shirts, and then you can sleep in our fluffy bed. How does that sound?"

She snuggled even closer to him, even though there was no space left. "Sounds like heaven." Her whisper barely broke the dead silence.

My face burned with how big my smile was. It was so cute how Jeremiah treated her; the way he loved her.

"I'll be back." Jeremiah whispered before walking up the stairs.

I gave him a thumbs up and began cleaning our mess.

Thirty minutes later, Jeremiah quickly jogged down the steps. He went into the kitchen, grabbed himself a drink, and plopped himself onto the couch.

"She is in another universe." Jeremiah laughed to himself before he took a long sip.

"She worked so hard today. This week is taking every drop of strength we have."

Both of us were silent for a few minutes. Finally, the question I was dying to ask him slipped. "So how is Mathias?"

My attention focused on the hem of my shirt.

"Mathias is hanging in there. He had a tough week and

wanted to relax a bit." Jeremiah leaned his head back against the sofa, eyes shut closed.

"Did," I cleared my throat. "Did he ask about me or something?"

Jeremiah smirked, eyes closed. "He might or might not have talked about you."

A spark of hope made my chest flutter. "What did he say?"

He chuckled, "I already tell you too much. He would kill me if I ruin-"

"Ruin what?"

His eyes went wide like he just ruined something. Jeremiah pressed his lips into a thin line. He shifted his gaze to something else other than me.

He was keeping a secret.

"Jeremiah, ruin what?" I demanded to know, the anxiety already crept its way inside me.

"Nothing, I am just tired. I am going to head to bed," He pretended to yawn and dashed towards the staircase. "But I will tell you one thing. He needs you as much as you need him. Mathias is in the healing process, just like the rest of us."

AMELIA

CHAPTER 37

Today wasn't any different from the rest of my week. I woke up at the crack of dawn and prepared for the day to come. A hamster on a wheel described my daily life.

I hadn't painted in a few days, and my heart ached to do it again. It ached to be lost in the paint strokes against the white canvas. Yet time and life seemed to work against any desire I had.

My heart leaped outside my chest when my phone buzzed against my hand. My fingers gripped the phone tighter. I slowly brushed my finger across the screen to answer the phone call.

"Hey stranger." I responded with too much excitement. *Keep y0urself cool.*

"Good afternoon, Sunshine." Mathias' deep voice was soothing and calm. It made me miss his touch and the way he held me even more. I miss the smell of his cologne when he walked by. The way his smile blinded me; *I miss him.*

"We need to talk." we both spat out at the same time and chuckled.

"I will pick you up in two hours. Dress your best."

"Ok." were the only words that I managed to say.

I might have done a happy dance for a solid ten minutes. Lily burst into the room, gasping for air like she had run a marathon. "What's wrong?"

Hey eyes glanced me over and then the room, checking if something happened. The only thing that was out of place were my emotions. They bounced off the walls, excited for the night to come.

"He asked me out! I am finally going to see that amazing man." I squealed like a little girl.

"We need to get you ready. Hair, makeup, and a breath-taking dress."

She pulled me to her closet, filled with stunning dresses. The music was so loud that it rattled the glasses against the table.

I was going to make this man speechless.

BY THE TIME WE WERE DONE, I LOOKED incredible. Yes, it was a bit different from what I was used to, but I felt stunning. My hair was curled, and it cascaded down my back. I pinned back the front pieces to show off my neck and earrings. A delicate white bow held the strands of hair. My earrings glistened in the sun.

"This dress was made just for you." Lily happily spoke behind me.

The dress was a baby pink color, it hugged me in all the right places. Lily said it wasn't too much, but would still make Mathias swoon.

She lightly brushed on the final details of my makeup

and later handed me the lipstick, which I applied ever so carefully.

Her eyes glistened, fighting with herself not to cry. Her hands underneath her chin as she admired the full look.

"Don't cry! If you cry, then I am going to cry." I waved both my hands to dry any threatening tears.

"I just," her voice slightly wavered at the end. "It proves how God is faithful in everything. Look at where you were a few months ago and look at you now. You aren't using painkillers anymore, barely drinking, and finally living life again. God is good all the time and-"

That saying turned into a tattoo on my heart. "All the time, God is good."

We stood there and reminded ourselves of the goodness of God in our lives. Despite all my mistakes and failures, he constantly still loved me.

Ding, the doorbell sounded, my heart picking up the pace. From my bedroom, I could hear Jeremiah walking and opening the door. Light chatter flooded from downstairs.

Lily rushed into her room and came back gasping for air once again. "Lipstick, hairbrush, hair tie, phone, wallet, and setting powder. I think you're set." Lily handed me my bag and rushed down the steps.

You must have your moment to shine. Those were her last words before she ran away.

Slow, even breaths helped me keep myself grounded. A slight dizziness came over me from the amount of excitement that radiated off me.

I ambled down the stairs, careful not to trip over my white cowboy boots. I didn't want to fall unless it was into a certain cowboy's arms.

When I glanced at Lily, Jer hugged her from behind,

both their eyes filled with awe. They looked at me like proud parents.

I never thought that their approval would mean so much to me.

Then our eyes connected, and the entire world stopped. It was just the two of us. Mathias' jaw dropped, and by the time I reached him, Lily and Jeremiah had already sneaked out.

"Sunshine," his raspy deep voice sent shivers down my arms. His eyes took me as he admired every detail. Heat flooded my cheeks.

"You look ravishing. You look-" His hands slowly crept around my waist, and pulled me closer to him.

"You don't look bad yourself. In fact, you look perfect."

Mathias had a blue t-shirt and dark washed jeans. He wore the boots that I had given them. Those boots were now fused to his feet; *it's like he never took them off.*

"I look like nothing compared to you." His forehead gently leaned against mine.

"That's not true, you look amazing. You're my southern angel."

Mathias pressed a gentle kiss against my forehead before glancing at me once more. He grabbed my purse from my hands before pulling me out the door.

Mathias opened the car door for me and waited for me to slip myself inside. The moment he closed the door, I squealed.

I am living a fantasy.

Mathias slipped inside, the door shut behind him. His hand reached out for mine. Our fingers were once again intertwined, "Are you ready, Sunshine?"

I raised his hand up to my lips, my eyes never leaving his.

His eyelids slightly drooped when lips gently pressed against the back of his hand. "Take me away cowboy."

MATHIAS
CHAPTER 38

I had very little self restraint. Amelia made me want to scrap all the plans, throw them in the trash, and admit my love. I needed to tell her all my feelings because they were bursting at the seams.

Every detail was planned to perfection. From where we were going to spend the afternoon all the way to our sunset kiss.

And of course it was going to be at our secret spot.

"I am way overdressed for this." Amelia fumbled over her words. With each second that passed, it was harder to keep myself at a distance.

"No, you're not." I jogged to the other side of the car and extended my hand out to help her.

Amelia said she was much better after the fall she took a few days ago, but I wasn't going to risk anything.

Without question, her hand slipped into mine. Without letting her go, I kicked the door closed. Our bodies swayed in unison as we walked deeper into the garden.

Every few seconds I glanced at her, marveled at her

beauty. My mind couldn't comprehend how God completely transformed the both of us. How a prayer of ten years finally arrived, and it was far greater than anything I could ever imagine.

It was nothing short of a miracle.

Candles illuminated the dinner table. Small snowdrops made the ground look snow kissed. Warm yellow lights hung from trees, fireflies danced in the sky. I made sure everything looked exactly how Amelia liked it.

"How did you-" Her breath was completely taken away.

"A man never reveals his secrets." I pulled her closer to me, her hand instantly touched my chest. My fingers brushed up and down her soft skin. A dose of vanilla and cinnamon came over me every time her hair moved.

Amelia turned around, her beautiful back facing towards me. My hands slowly crept up to her shoulders to slip off her coat and reveal stunning golden skin.

The iron chair scraped against the stone pavement. Her brown eyes focused on me as I slipped my hand into my pocket, revealing a small cream colored envelope. I extended the note to her. Our fingers briefly brushed against each other; *I have fallen hard for this woman.*

Her eyes swept over the note that I had memorized by heart. I rewrote it until it was absolutely perfect, perfect for my perfect girl.

Amelia deserves my perfection.

Dear Amelia,

I wanted to write to you about a few things.
Things that I admire and love about you.
I love the way your cheeks get pink when you're

nervous or excited. I adore when you wear one of my hoodies and put your hair in a bun when you're painting. The way you can paint anything and make it breathtaking every time fascinates my mind.

Above all, I love who you are. I love that you allowed Christ to reign in your heart. How you allowed Him to heal the broken parts of you, and because of that you became the woman of my dreams.

That's enough compliments for now, but don't worry, I will shower you with more tonight.

Sincerely,

Your Cowboy.

P.S you look stunning tonight. You always know how to take my breath away.

Amelia's cheeks turned bright pink, the letter held close to her heart, she whispered, "You really know how to romanticize a girl, Mathias Anderson." Her fingers lightly brushed the wildflowers.

A small smile formed on my lips because of Amelia's reaction. I could tell she loved it by the color on her cheeks and the huge smile on her face. She was the only person who mattered to me.

She was the only person I wanted, that I desired.

WITH EACH WORD THAT AMELIA SPOKE, MADE ME fall even more in love with her. Each laugh she released was a dose of adrenaline in my body. Her laugh, her words, and presence filled that lonely space in my heart. That part that wanted to share life with someone. I was completely in love with Amelia, and there wasn't a greater feeling than finding *your* person.

The clock on my wrist reminded me that in thirty minutes I was going to tear open my heart to her. In one thousand and eight hundred seconds, I was going to find out if we were going to spend the rest of our lives together or not.

Amelia took my arm without question. Her head leaned against my arm, my mouth dry at her touch.

"Where are you taking me now, Cowboy?"

I chuckled because Amelia couldn't stand surprises.

"You'll see." I responded.

We walked further into the garden. Pastels slowly appeared in the light blue sky. The trees no longer blurred my vision. Before it vanished for the night, the stunning sun cast one final warm glow.

There were two garden chairs that faced the sunset, waiting for us. My head could not process anything; *How was I going to do this?*

I reached for her hands and pulled her closer. She was so close I could feel her breath against my skin.

I have to do this before it is too late.

"You are my sunshine, Sunshine. You are the sunrise I want to wake up to. You are the sunset I want to admire. You are my sun, and my heart revolves around you."

I shut my eyes to stop any tears from running down my face.

"I am hopelessly in love with you. I want you. I need you. Amelia you are what I think about when I wake up, what I think about when I go to sleep. You are what keeps me going when I am tired. You put a smile on my face when I want to break into a hundred pieces," my hand found its way around her waist to keep her close, "I, Mathias Anderson, am hopelessly in love with Amelia Johnson. Without you, there is no reason to keep on going."

Her soft, kind eyes glistened. Her breaths were slow and controlled. And mine were sharp and fast. My lungs gasped for air.

Both of my hands dropped to my side, my eyes searched of an answer. Knots and twists formed in my stomach.

Maybe she didn't feel this way for me? Maybe I had just made a spectacle of myself.

Amelia
Chapter 39

My tongue was completely tied. Not a single word slipped my lips as Mathias declared his love for me. His eyes burned with passion, love, and honesty. It wasn't too much, in fact it was perfect in every way.

He was perfect for me.

I took a step closer to him, our bodies brushed against each other. His perfect brown eyes searched for an answer, a piece of hope. I placed trembling cold hands on his steady chest.

If this is a dream please don't ever wake me up.

"So that was what today was for?" I muttered softly.

Mathias nodded his head which let me continue on, "So you love me?"

He nodded again.

"That is-"

He jerked slightly back, scared for my answer, "Romantic," I pressed a gentle kiss pressed against his left palm.

"Brave," another kiss to his right palm.

"Adorable," a kiss on his freshly shaven jaw. He began to hum to the responses, eyes closed and head leaned back.

"Heart warming," a kiss on the other one. "And my response to you is," a final kiss to the tip of his nose, "I am deeply," my fingers deep into his chestnut colored hair. His hand brushed against my skin, a trail of tingles followed his every move. "And crazy in love with you Mathias Anderson. I am hopelessly in love with you and I am honored that you chose me."

The world faded away, our kisses spoke what our hearts felt. We desired each other, wanted one another. His hands were in my hair, pulling me closer to him.

When we broke apart, our breaths were heavy with emotion and desire. His breath danced across my skin.

"I missed you. I missed your touch, your eyes, your lips." His breaths were slow, gaze focused on my lips.

Mathias brushed his finger across my cheek, brushing away the loose hair.

The baby blue sky was replaced by beautiful sunset hued colors.

And in that moment we were just Mathias and Amelia. No guards up, just two people hopelessly in love with one another. Two people who finally fell in love at the right time and with the right person.

We are destined for one another.

We wanted more of one another, my body melted into his embrace the longer he kissed me. Every worry and expectation faded away.

His hands held my cheeks like I was fragile glass.

This man is so precious.

Mathias Anderson treated me the way I always desired to be treated. He loved and cared for me constantly. A love that didn't depend on feelings. He loved me so much that he gave boundaries even if I didn't know that I needed them.

Every kiss tasted as sweet as a cup of hot coco on a stormy winter day. Calming like a cup of honey herbal tea. Invisible fireworks bursted in my heart the longer he kissed me. And he was never, not in a single moment, harsh or demanding.

Mathias was nothing like Brandon.

That single thought brought tears to my eyes.

"Why are you crying, my love?" Mathias whispered.

I pulled him closer and whispered into his ear. "You treat me with so much kindness. It melts every wall that I ever built up. I have always wished for this and it's finally here," his eyes softened as he brushed away my tears. "Sometimes I am scared this isn't real."

He chuckled and pressed a feather-like kiss on my forehead. "Don't worry, Sunshine. You ain't dreaming."

TODAY WAS FINALLY CHRISTMAS, AND MY HEART instantly filled with love and joy. Surrounded by people who loved and cared about me. My parents couldn't be here, so they called me. And my parents calling me to talk was the greatest blessing I ever received.

This was life.

An eruption of laughter filled the room when Jeremiah tried to sing like he was a part of the opera. Mrs and Mr. Anderson were wrapping up the final touches on dinner. Mr. Anderson kept sneaking spoonfuls of food into his mouth, pretending that his wife couldn't see it.

They are so cute.

Lily ran to the front to join Jeremiah in karaoke, the entire world disappeared to them. They sang their hearts out like no one was watching.

My legs were on top of Mathias' lap, his fingers caressed them. Stolen kisses every time no one was looking.

"I can't wait until everyone leaves." I whispered against his lips.

"I can kick out everyone right now." he joked, but I knew he would do that if I only asked.

You know I could just ask him to kick everyone out.

I kissed him softly, lost in his touch. "Just a few more hours."

I cuddled my face at the nape of his neck, eyes closed to soak in every moment. I wanted everything engraved into my mind so I could replay it for all the days of my life.

THE DINNER, MADE WITH SO MUCH LOVE, FILLED the air with a warm, inviting aroma. The old stories were retold, each word painted a vivid picture. Laughter erupted at every joke Mr. Anderson made.

And never once did Mathias let go of my hand underneath the table. We were fused together. Stolen glances like we couldn't believe that this was our life.

"Everyone, put your plates in the sink and head to the living room to open presents." Mrs. Anderson bounced up and down. She looked like she had eaten a bowl of sugar from how much excitement radiated off her body.

Before my hands even touched the white and golden plates, Mathias stopped me. "Let me get that for you, Sunshine."

I pressed a gentle kiss on his cheek. "Thank you."

I swayed side to side, waiting for Mathias. He lightly patted his hands on the dish towel before slipping his hand back into mine. We strolled into the living room and I noticed the way all the couples sat in their own corner.

Right as Mrs. Anderson opened her mouth, the door creaked open. Samantha poked her head into the living room, and everyone erupted in cheers. She gave a little wave to everyone before she sat beside me.

"Did I miss anything?" Her frigid cold hands squeezed mine.

I leaned my head against her shoulder. "No, you are just in time for the best part."

"Now we will open presents. I get to choose who will go first. And I chose someone who brought life and light back into all our lives, Amelia."

My heart did a backflip at the declaration. Mrs. Anderson waved her hands for me to come up as everyone clapped for me. I looked at all the presents under the tree and saw the ones with my name on them. Boxes of different sizes and shapes, but only one stood out to me. It was a small box, with recognizable handwriting.

I instantly picked it up and marveled over the details. It was a small, engraved wooden box. *M & A* was engraved on the top of the box. A loud gasp left my mouth when I opened it.

It was a ring, and not any ring, the *perfect* ring. It was gorgeous and when I turned around, Mathias knelt down right beside me. He was in tears; *see. Men can cry and that doesn't make them any less than a man of God.*

His face glistened, never afraid to show his emotions.

Gently, he took the box from my hands. "Amelia, I have been in love with you since we first met. I was with you through the thick and thin parts of life." He struggled to speak, his voice thick and deep with emotions. "When you left, a part of me left as well because you are the sunshine in my life."

Mathias smiled, "You are what I admire and what I love. You are the reason why my heart keeps beating hope. You are my answered prayer after ten years,"

Tears of joy blurred my vision, his words were sweet as honey. "I am in love with you, and I only fully realized that after everyone else did."

Jeremiah yelled, *"Preach Brother."* The entire room erupted in laughter before going quiet once again.

"I love everything about you. I love your hair, your eyes, your beautiful smile, and your stunning personality. I know we have only been dating for a week, but I want you to myself. I want to wake up beside you, sleep with you in my arms, and grow old with you,"

Mathias grinned brightly, both of his dimples shown at full force. "So, will you do me the honor and marry me?"

His eyes were full of hope and love. Not a single word came out, my mouth dry and empty. My stomach fluttered incessantly as the reality of it all began to sink in.

"And I asked your parents for their blessing and they said yes." he added on and that's when I officially knew he was the one.

His proclamation of love was far better than anything I could ever imagine. Happy tears expressed what words weren't sufficient to say. So I lowered myself, both hands on his cheeks. He softly leaned into my touch, our eyes welled up with tears.

The only words that I managed to say were what I wanted to proclaim for the rest of my life. "Of course I will marry you."

Everyone erupted in cheers and congratulated us.

Jeremiah yelled, "Finally, he finally admitted his love!"

Mrs. Anderon kept praising God over and over, thanking Him for the engagement. She praised God for his immense grace and love.

Mathias slid the ring onto my finger and kissed me with his heart's content. With his lungs burning, all the passion and fire he possessed was put into soft, honey-sweet kisses.

He was mine.

Mathias was going to be mine until the end of time. We no longer had to let each other go. I wanted to grow old with him. Know every failure and perfection that existed within him. Grow our own family together and tell our kids about the grace that God poured into our lives.

This wasn't an accident. It was God working everything in our favor. Despite the times I walked away and rejected His plan, He never failed or rejected me.

This was because of a prayer. Not just any prayer, but a faithful and consistent one. A prayer from a certain cowboy who wanted to love someone with his whole heart like Christ loved him.

Once Upon a Cowboy's Heart

I hope you enjoyed Once Upon a Cowboy's Heart!

If you loved the book, please leave a review for my book on any platform.

Thank you!

Book 2 will be about: Graham & Haven

Acknowledgments

First of all, I wanted to thank my God and my Saviour; Jesus Christ. This is for you and you only. No one deserves the glory or the honor except you. I am thankful you have chosen me for this mission and I hope I am making you proud.

I want to thank my parents for always being supportive and always helping me. I wouldn't have done this without your constant prayer and support. I love you so much and thank you for everything you do for me. Thank you to my siblings and cats, who are the best hype squad ever!

Thank you to Melody for creating this STUNNING cover! I appreciate your dedication and everything you poured into this cover. You have been with me since the beginning and I already consider you a friend.

Thank you to my church and for all the support you show me and all the prayers you pray for me. Thank you for believing me and for pouring words of life over my life. My church: Family in Christ, it is the best one out there. And each member has become my family. I love each and every one of you.

Thank you to Rosie, The author group chat, my readers and supporters. Thank you for believing in me and always helping me. I love you all and you definitely made a huge impact on my life. Every author needs a girly hype squad and you ladies are definitely the best of the best.

Thank you Sara. I know we play around about being twins but we are. We are sisters from another mother and I love you so much! You have so much wisdom. You always remind me of the true purpose and goal in life. Thank you for being with me and always having a listening ear. You are one of the greatest blessings in my life.

Thank you to Melissa for formatting this book. Your patience and understanding was worth so much to me and I pray that God compensates you greatly! You are such a sweetheart and a blessing in my life!

Thank you to everyone who took a chance on this book and on a newbie author. I appreciate you and I hope this book touched you as much as it did to me.

Christ reigns forever and ever.

His Hidden Jewel

(Esther Inspired Fade-to-black Adult Romantasy)

About the Author

Sarah Da Silva writes Closed Door and Fade-To-Black love stories that will make you laugh, cry, swoon, and kick your feet at 1am. Her books have sizzling chemistry with heart and a meaningful message while keeping the bedroom door closed.

Her mission is to write love stories that bring Love, Joy, and Peace to those who think there is none left. She hopes that these stories shine a light in the midst of the darkness and that you should never lose hope.

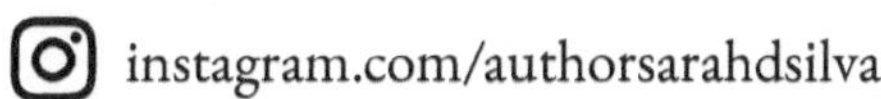 instagram.com/authorsarahdsilva